*Dedicated to Denise Howe: who has known a few mad hatters in
her time*

THE MAD HATTER MURDERS

BILLIE WILDE #BOOK THREE

MARRISSE WHITTAKER

To John + Carol –
Hoping that we are all
still crazy after all
these years

Seanna Whittaker X.

BLOODHOUND
— BOOKS —

www.bloodhoundbooks.com

Print ISBN 978-1-914614-68-2

ALSO BY MARRISSE WHITTAKER

1

TELL THE TRUTH

The murdered man was dressed in women's clothing. His long red wig skewed at a jaunty angle, winged diamante-trim spectacles having flown off, one lens shattered, perhaps as the first sod of wet earth had made weighty contact with Charles Carroll's head.

The crucifix at his neck and a little prayer book in his crocheted salmon-pink twinset pocket, showed the sad victim's devotion to a God who appeared to have been in a less than merciful mood at the time of his incarceration. Most bodies buried in graves having, at least, been confirmed as deceased beforehand. Definitely not the case with this particular devoted church volunteer.

A kitten-heel shoe, sized ten and extra wide-fitting, had been found next to a plaque on the inside of the church listing the former rectors there since 1200, along with a trail of blood and scattered flowers, which had shed petals in the same spot. Clearly he had tried to outsprint his killer, but constricted, as most women would immediately recognise, by three-inch heels and the limited speed and mobility afforded by the shackles of a pencil skirt in heavily-lined tweed, even one featuring a kick-pleat, Charles Carroll was going nowhere.

His final resting place had been in a shallow grave, on top of the corpse of an elderly woman nicknamed Hattie Mustard, who in life had few visitors, despite being housebound. A sojourn outside of her four walls being beyond her wildest dreams, she instead each year ordered a new hat from a mail order shopping catalogue, positioned it carefully on her head and looked out of the window. She claimed that the change did her good. Passers-by in a rush to get on with their oh-so busy lives, would occasionally wave and give her a quick thumbs up in recognition of her new attire.

Little could Hattie Mustard have imagined how many locals would later claim to have been a great friend, when her real name, Edith Mustard, and photo, made newspaper headlines after ending up with the cross-dressing victim of a shocking murder as a sleepover buddy. It was a shame that they hadn't met when they had both still been breathing. The now famous grave-mates could have been true bosom buddies, both being a dab hand with a crocheting hook.

Life was funny that way, Billie Wilde mused as she flicked through her case file in preparation for the trial that day, of the man named as the killer. Sometimes truth was stranger than fiction. Billie's truth today was that despite Will Cox having been spotted on CCTV hastily burying Charles Carroll in Hattie Mustard's grave and DNA confirming clearly that his spade had been used to cave in the side of the victim's head, she still had an uneasy underlying feeling that he hadn't actually committed the murder.

A kiss on the side of her neck and the intoxicating scent of lemony cologne, tugged her thoughts back to the present.

'Coffee and boiled eggs with toast soldiers.' Max Strong placed the tray of food on the coffee table in front of Billie. 'It's going to be a long day in court.' Max sat down opposite, smiling that crooked smile of his as she glanced up in thanks and reached for her mug. 'Did I tell you how sexy you look in your new specs?' He caught a drip of melting butter from his slice of toast, popped his finger in his mouth and slowly sucked the tip of his finger mischievously as he stared at Billie.

'Stop it, I'm trying to concentrate.' Billie rolled her eyes in mock disapproval. 'I only need reading specs due to the time I've spent going over these notes. I still can't shake off the feeling that Will didn't do this alone.'

She knew that it was just a gut feeling. The evidence was literally staring her in the face, with stills from the CCTV now revealed as she flicked from page to page. Will Cox had certainly dragged the unconscious body into the grave which had some depth of soil removed in readiness, and then covered it over again. Being a gravedigger by trade, it wouldn't have caused him the same level of unease as the action might have with most people, Billie conceded, but still, something felt wrong.

The Chief had insisted on forging ahead with the prosecution, determined to ensure that any major investigation loose ends were tied up by his teams as he wound down to his looming retirement.

'You are right. As far as Will's concerned, he didn't do it alone. As he's repeated at every one of our consultations, the voice told him to do it. He was having auditory hallucinations.' Max munched on his toast. 'We've already been through this, darling,' he added, though Billie was well aware of Max's point of view on this particular case. In the three months that they had been together, they had already shared so much, including a couple of court appearances in which Billie had apprehended a criminal and was giving evidence for the prosecution, whereas Max had been called as an expert psychologist for the defence. Just like today.

'Prosecutor should have listened to me in the first place and avoided all this waste of time and money in the courts,' Max continued. 'Yes, he is clearly guilty of the crime, but Will suffers from bouts of Insane Automatism. When carrying out the murder, he was acting in a state of physical involuntariness. So, where a witness may have seen him smashing the brains out of Charles Carroll's head with his shovel, all Will could see was this–' Max took the spoon on Billie's plate and smashed the top of one of her eggs. Yolk splattered out and oozed down the shell. 'Probably thought he was just sitting down to breakfast with his invisible friend.' Billie pushed her plate to one side.

'Thanks for that,' she answered, reaching for her coffee instead. 'But as I keep saying, there were no witnesses to the actual attack with the shovel. It's just that he genuinely didn't seem to have any problems with Charles Carroll. Billie thought of Jo Green, her former assisting officer. Her brother had also suffered from learning difficulties and had also been convicted of murder. It felt as though Jo Green was whispering in her ear this morning, telling Billie that just as in the case with her brother, Will Cox hadn't planned and executed this murder all alone.

'He may not have had a problem with Charles Carroll, but remember, on that day Charles was dressed as his alter ego, Alice.' Max raised an eyebrow.

'Will's mother was adamant that he didn't have a problem with that.' Billie hated going to court with a prosecution that she didn't feel in her heart was just, but Max didn't seem to have the same concerns that she had and perhaps it was time to bow down to his superior knowledge of what made people tick.

'Not consciously.' Max shrugged. 'But as I believe he has some internal cerebral deformity that we can't fully examine whilst he lolls on remand in the prison hospital wing, we can't know that for sure. Either way, when I convince the jury of my diagnosis, they are sure to reach a special verdict of not guilty by reason of insanity. Win-win for both of us.' Max smiled, dipping one of Billie's toast soldiers in the still oozing yolk. 'You refuse to believe he did it all by himself and don't like the thought of him being locked up in prison. I get to bring him to a specialist hospital where he can get help. When I visited him yesterday, he looked like he desperately needed it.'

'Just a different version of hell and he'll probably never be let out.' Billie thought of Will Cox's old mum left alone without her beloved son. The specialist hospital for the criminally insane was so far away that they might never see each other again.

'Which is a good thing, if he can't be cured. Don't you think?' Max reached out and grabbed Billie's hand. 'Come on. We can't have you getting all uptight. I have just the answer...' He pulled Billie towards him.

'I can't, I have to get in the shower...' Billie only half protested. She knew she would give in. She always did. It was just that this full-on, crazy, wonderful love affair took some getting used to after her relationship with David, her former fiancé, when passion definitely took a back seat to work – and in his case, other interests. As Max pulled her close to him, she could feel her stress falling away. He peeled first one sleeve of her dressing gown from her shoulders and then the other. She caught it around her, as his lips nuzzled her neck and his hands moved down the curves of her body. He tugged the gown away from her grasp. It slid to the floor.

'Just stand still and look at that beautiful view.' Through the wall-to-floor window, Billie could see down over the salt marsh of the stunning Alnmouth Estuary, at a point where waves rolled in from the open sea to join the river. 'Let me relax you...'

Billie started to feel her tensions ease. She had to admit that it wasn't a bad way to start the day after all, with the touch and smell of Max tantalising her senses and Mozart's stirring, unfinished 'Requiem' filling the room. It was one of Max's favourite pieces of music. He said that he loved the puzzle of the commission – that Mozart never found out the identity of the mysterious person who asked him to create the piece but came to think that he was writing the requiem for his own funeral. He died before he finished his swansong.

'Telephone call!' The door was flung open as Ash swung in, took in the view, and then shot backwards half closing the door. 'Shit. Sorry...' Billie grabbed her dressing gown from the floor and pulled it back around her. Max reached for the remote and switched off the music.

'Sorry. I did knock...' Ash sounded sheepish as he peeped around the door again.

'It's okay. Want some breakfast?' Billie ran her fingers through her hair, rolling her eyes at Ash, her best mate, colleague, and current lodger. She tried to hide a grin as she clocked the look of utter embarrassment on his face, though Max was clearly less than thrilled at the intrusion.

'No, sorry again. It's just that Boo couldn't get hold of you...'

Billie felt in her dressing-gown pocket for her phone. She must have left it by her bed. It was usually on twenty-four seven, but she and Max had agreed to turn off mobiles in the bedroom. All too easy to become the modern equivalent of the fictional Citizen Kane and his wife, engrossed in newspaper reading rather than each other, Max had observed. She had to agree. Through the years, her checking of phone messages seemed to have turned into a nervous twitch. But then something at work always seemed to be kicking off.

'I'll ring her now.' Billie started across the room.

'No, it's okay. I took the message.' Ash looked from Max to Billie. 'Actually, it affects both of you. Will Cox was found hanging in his prison cell, this morning.'

2

ROSEMARY FOR REMEMBRANCE

'I must send some flowers to his mother. Rosemary, that's for remembrance... and maybe white roses. Alice used to tell me that they represent innocence.' Charles Carroll's wife, Mary, handed Billie and Ash mugs of tea.

'Sorry to bring such bad news' – Ash took a swig from his tea – 'I'm sure that you were hoping for some closure on your husband's death today.'

'You think that Will was innocent, Mrs Carroll?' Billie couldn't help asking.

Billie and Ash followed Mary Carroll into her neat lounge. It was filled with photos of Charles Carroll in life – a balding, staid, portly and serious-looking retired college lecturer. Other snaps, in sparkly frames, featured his alter ego, Alice. In these photos Mary was alongside him, grinning in selfie photographs – two old girls out on the town, enjoying shopping trips and cocktails. An odd couple to be sure, but it appeared that they had been happy together.

'Well, you tell me that the CCTV shows he did it, but I can't believe someone didn't put him up to it. Bullied him even... Will was a good boy. Used to come to our house for tea and extra tuition from Charles when he was still at school. My husband liked to give back to the community. He didn't charge for his lessons out of college. Will was a bit slow on the uptake, but he was a nice lad. Loved the garden here. Charles liked vegetable growing, Alice preferred flowers, so when Alice came out more and more, Will would come around and help with the cabbage patch. It was Charles who put Will forward for the grave-digging job at the chapel in town, which is ironic, I suppose...' Mary trailed off.

Billie glanced at Ash. The Chief had already made a press announcement that they weren't looking for anyone else in connection with Charles Carroll's murder, but his wife seemed to be of a similar opinion to Billie. Here she was planning to send Will Cox's mum sympathy flowers.

'Can you think of anyone else who might have wanted to hurt your husband, Mrs Carroll?' She simply couldn't shake away the feeling that there was a miscarriage of justice here. Ash had quickly knocked back his drink, got up and washed his empty porcelain cup in the kitchen, probably in an attempt to signal it was time to go. The Chief's views on the matter had been hammered home to the team that morning before his announcement to the media. Billie took a biscuit from those offered on a pretty tea plate, instead of standing up.

'Well, there were times when Charles first retired that I could have happily throttled him, I will admit that. He just sat there in the chair like a giant jacket potato for a couple of years, with two little eyes blinking out, totally morose. Other times he would disappear into his shed for hours. Turned out he had Alice's wardrobe stashed in there. Told me later that he kept catching his tights as he squeezed past the blackberry bush for a stroll around the garden in the dead of night – in slingbacks as well...' Mary chuckled at the recollection.

'But you stuck by him?' Ash asked, no doubt reflecting on his own marriage that was currently coming to an end.

'Well, I was shocked at first, of course. I thought he didn't love me anymore, now that he was all togged up like a woman. Mind you, the state of him when he first dressed as Alice, he would have been hard pushed to pull a pit pony let alone a fit man.' She smiled at the memory. 'But I soon realised that cross-dressing doesn't necessarily equate to a sexual conflict. We hadn't exactly been swinging from the chandeliers anyway, in our dotage.

'Charles was obsessed with literature, writing, researching his favourite author, Lewis Carroll. That was his greatest love, if I'm being truthful. You'll note his choice of female name. So, he was just the same as he had always been in that respect. He'd simply been scared to show his true colours before. The only thing I had to fear was my own prejudices. Charles had always been a bit of a bore because he was hiding his real feelings, whereas Alice was a hoot.

'We would go shopping together and I made sure she dressed in good quality clothes, not the tat that she started out with, and toned down her make-up. Our social life perked up after years in the doldrums. If I'm truthful, it's Alice that I'm grieving for more than Charles. We had so much more in common. One of Charles's colleagues was a like-minded soul. He introduced us to a club where people like us could go and meet other couples in a similar situation. It's called Aunt Fanny's.' Mary chuckled. 'We went on a jolly charabanc holiday to Blackpool. All girls together...' She trailed off, reaching for a handkerchief in her pocket, embroidered with the initials AC, before dabbing her eyes with it. 'This was his. I only wish he'd shown his genuine personality earlier. Alice and I, we missed out on so much.'

Billie quickly took down the address for the club that Mary

had mentioned, catching Ash's eye as she did so. He raised his eyebrows, trying, Billie knew, to avoid the extra aggro coming her way if the Chief found out she was still on the case. Billie made a mental note to pay a visit when she was off duty. She knew that Max wouldn't approve either. She mentally rolled her eyes. She was getting as secretive as Charles Carroll here.

Her mobile suddenly rang loud and clear. She pulled it from her pocket. Max was about to go away for a few days on one of his secret missions abroad as a consultant with the army. Billie knew that she would be leaving the device on twenty-four seven until he returned, not least because she would be worried sick that he was in danger and out of reach.

'Where are you?' Boo asked. Billie could hear the background buzz of the busy Murder Investigation Room in the background. She got up and moved to the kitchen.

'Paying a courtesy call to Charles Carroll's wife, to tell her about the cock-up, rather than have her hear it via the morning telly news. What's up?'

'Oh that's good. You're just down the road.' Boo could be heard typing on her PC.

'From what?' Billie could see Ash behind her, engaging Mary Carroll in chat as they looked at photos of Charles in his Alice outfits. He might not always approve of her actions, but Billie knew he would always have her back.

'Call coming in that there's been a body found in woodland alongside the River Wear. Get this, the caller is from the film crew shooting that Hollywood movie that's rolled into town and the victim is one of the actors!'

Billie was well aware of some big-name stars heading into the area. It had been the leading story in the local newspaper and TV news bulletins earlier that week. She had been glad that it had taken some of the focus away from the impending trial of Will Cox.

'Okay. We'll get ready for our close-ups, Ms DeMille,' Billie quipped as she indicated for Ash to wind up his conversation. Billie sighed. She thought that the action of the day had already finished. But with lights, cameras and luvvies beckoning, was the big drama just about to begin?

3

HUMAN WALLPAPER

'In truth, it hasn't disrupted filming unduly, so far. Bit of a nuisance, but we left it there dead as a dodo, if you'll pardon the pun, with a runner standing by, to make sure that no one tripped over it. The individual was just an extra–' The small, wizened-faced man with bulbous eyes and over-dyed strands of hair spread carefully across his bald pate, flicked his wrist back, to where the corpse of a young woman lay amongst blood-red poppies growing beside the River Wear.

'Um, I think *support cast* is the PC term these days.' A female in a fleece jacket with a walkie-talkie attached whispered, pushing her round specs up her nose. She grimaced at Billie and Ash apologetically.

'*Human wallpaper* is my term, darling, simply background action. Will you be long with all of this fiddle-faddle, officers? We've had to put this scene back to later in the day and press on with the Walrus and the Carpenter, which is a bit of a bore...' He turned to his assistant, Delphine, Billie deduced, by squinting her eyes to read the lanyard hanging around her neck. She had turned away and pulled a tissue from her pocket to hastily wipe her nose. Her eyes were red-rimmed. Billie was relieved that at least someone was showing a hint of sorrow at the untimely death

'Has anyone set off to pick the Walrus up from the airport?' He glanced at his watch and sighed. 'Oh my God, those bloody Oysters again. The budgets being what they are nowadays, we're having to use local am-dram children–' He rolled his eyes dramatically. 'Impenetrable accents and I do find that poor people are so ugly. I never have this problem in Hollywood. The children there are word perfect at eighteen months and have their ears pinned back and teeth fixed before they even *attempt* a casting session.'

Billie and Ash exchanged glances as Josta appeared along the footpath behind, closely followed by Charlie Holden and his crime-scene investigators, already dressed in protective clothing.

'If you'll excuse us, Mr...?' Billie loomed over the little man with the big ego.

'Arden Roy. *The Killing of Eliza Jane*?' the repugnant Mr Roy replied, pausing as if to receive coos of astonishment.

'Two Baftas and an Emmy nomination,' he added, appearing to be waiting for a round of applause. Billie blanked him, instead directing her words to Delphine.

'This is a crime scene now, so we will be taping it off. We'll head up to your base camp in a while to take witness statements.' Delphine nodded and scribbled down notes on her clipboard.

'If you really must,' Arden Roy huffed. 'Over lunch break if you please and we need that costume back ASAP. She was lighting stand-in for the Red Queen. Have costume found another body in the same size yet?' Arden Roy marched off with Delphine following.

'Welcome to the wacky world of showbiz.' Ash shook his head in horror.

'Maybe everyone is mad, just like they say in the books –

including Alice herself,' Billie quipped, as they approached the body.

'That sounds dark. I thought they were stories for children?' Ash answered.

'You mean you've never read *Alice in Wonderland* and *Alice Through the Looking-Glass*?' Billie was amazed.

'Nope,' Ash answered. 'Have you read the *Punjabi Sakhis*?' he replied.

'The what?' Billie raised her eyebrows.

'Exactly. I'll swap my childhood bedtime stories for yours, tonight.'

'With an offer like that, how could I refuse,' Billie whispered as they approached the body, stony-faced. The joshing, so often in truth a way to shed the tension of preparing to face scenes that many people couldn't even imagine, stopped as they were handed protective overalls. It was almost like an actor getting into costume and into character.

'Morning, loves! Or is it afternoon already?' Josta gave a genial wave as she made her way to the body. She gave it a quick glance. 'Poor dear. She's not much more than a child...'

'What are your first thoughts – suspicious death?' Billie had now carefully moved close enough to view the body. Dressed in stylised Elizabethan costume of red silk covered with colourfully embroidered shapes, the corpse looked like a storybook character.

'Hmmm, difficult to say with all this gubbins on her–' Josta started. The young male runner, who had been guarding the pathway, cleared his throat nervously. Everyone turned.

'She's not in full costume. The Red Queen has a ruff and wears a bright-red curled wig, but when Costume were tightening her bodice, she said that she couldn't breathe and Make-Up said that she complained of feeling queasy, so they just put the pale base on her, planning to quickly do everything

14

else when she was called for the lighting walk-through. She told me she was going for a stroll down by the river and when she had her ten-minute call I came looking...'

'So, you found her...?' Billie raised her eyebrows.

'Tom. Yes. She was just there, exactly as she is now. She looks like she fainted and hit her head on that tree stump. I just ran up and got the unit nurse. She checked and then rang the emergency number,' the young man answered, scratching his head in distress as a call came over the radio strapped to his chest, demanding he bring herbal tea immediately for the director.

'Sorry, I've got to run. Fredi can tell you more. She knows everything that goes on around here, what with the actors spending so much time in her trailer getting ready.'

'Which trailer would that be?' Ash asked as the young man started to literally run off.

'Make-Up,' Tom answered. 'It's the place for all of the hot gossip on set,' he called back. Billie could already hear him being chastised over the walkie-talkie for not having responded to the director's demands quickly enough.

'She definitely got a nasty crack on the head.' Josta leaned over the corpse as she spoke. 'But look at the rest of her body.' Josta looked up to check that Billie and Ash could see. 'It's yellow.'

'Fake tan perhaps?' Billie had seen some pretty suspect shades of fake suntan amongst the many witnesses she'd encountered. She sometimes wondered what damage it might do, just as lead poisoning had been caused by the opposite urge, to appear with snow-white skin in Elizabethan times. Even then, it seemed, everyone wanted to twist the truth.

'Terrible case of jaundice I would say. Caused by the breakdown of dead red blood cells in the liver.' Josta pulled back an eyelid. A dead brown eye, pupils dilated, stared back. The whites were as yellow as an egg yolk.

'My immediate thoughts are that the smack to the head might have been the final straw, but she was already heading for a cardiac arrest due to acute liver failure. As she doesn't appear to present as an alcoholic, I'm postulating that the cause of death is poisoning. Until I get her back for a fuller examination, I can't say if foul play was the cause, or accidental ingestion of something nasty.'

'We'll leave you to it. Head up to the make-up trailer to see if we can find out more.'

'Think the make-up lady can do something with me to make me more handsome?' Ash quipped, as they peeled off their protective overalls and started to head up the track to the base camp for the film unit. 'I hear GG Mills is playing the lead in this thing. Wouldn't say no to him.' Ash winked jokily.

'You should be so lucky. I think he said she was a make-up artist, not a magician.' Billie elbowed Ash. 'Maybe a toupee for that little thin patch on top.' She slapped him on the head.

'One more word and you're dead.' Ash chuckled for a second, before looking back. 'Poor kid,' he muttered in acknowledgement of his true state of mind. Billie nodded in agreement. The young girl had just taken her first baby steps onto the adult stage, when the spotlight had been cruelly snuffed out, shattering her dreams of acting stardom.

'I feel like I'm in the middle of some crazy dream,' Ash commented as they emerged from the woodland path into a large clearing. Around the edges of the field, huge trailers had been parked, some with the names of actors that Billie recognised on the doors. In the far corner a long queue formed at the catering waggon where lunch was being served. Amongst the crew, dressed in a random collection of heavy-duty outdoor gear, an assortment of probably the most iconic characters in fiction stood waiting in line. Billie immediately spotted a Dodo, a Mouse, and a six-foot-tall Caterpillar, who had the trailing tail part of his costume slung jauntily over one arm.

'Even you must recognise some of this lot,' Billie answered, as an individual, unrecognisable as either male or female, ambled past in full Humpty Dumpty costume, carrying a tray of food from the catering waggon, heading for a double-decker bus which seemed to have been converted into a dining area. Humpty Dumpty glanced across at them.

'The steak and kidney pudding is particularly good today,' he said in a deep baritone voice, perfectly pronounced.

'Thanks. Mind you don't trip over,' Ash replied, nudging Billie as they continued across the field. 'We all know what happened to him.' Ash grinned.

'See, you're getting there at last. Something must have sunk in with your education.' She glanced over the field where all the King's horses were having nosebags put on by all the King's men, obviously specialist acting horses with their grooms.

'Everybody knows the nursery rhyme. Are you telling me that features in the Alice books?'

'Got it in one,' Billie answered. 'Got to love Lewis Carroll.' She called over to a threesome also walking past with trays piled with food, in costume as a Goat, a Beetle and a man dressed in white paper. He had a bib fastened over his costume, presumably in case of any destructive spills. All characters that Billie recognised from *Alice Through the Looking-Glass.* 'Can you point us to the make-up trailer please?'

'Over there, darling,' the woman dressed as the man in white paper answered with perfect voice projection, as though attempting to reach the back of an auditorium from the National

Theatre main stage. She nodded to a huge trailer parked under a tree in the corner of the field. Next to it was presumably the costume truck, as a woman could be seen trying to stitch a Unicorn's horn which was flopping droopily forward, back onto the horse-like headdress. Next to them a Lion sat on a grassy hill flicking through a newspaper.

Billie climbed up the metal steps leading to the door and knocked hard, before swinging the door open. A smell of make-up, hairspray, and acetone assaulted her nostrils. 'I'm looking for Fredi,' Billie announced, immediately recognising the face staring back at her through a large mirror surrounded by lights, situated above a countertop laid out with make-up and brushes. GG Mills, the latest Hollywood golden boy. He was dressed in Victorian costume, crisp white tie fastened at the neck of his high shirt, dark curls parted in the style of Charles Lutwidge Dodgson – better known as Lewis Carroll, author of the *Alice* books. Billie blinked for a moment. The fan mags didn't do the man justice. He was absolutely stunning.

'Fredi?' he answered. 'Everyone's always looking for Fredi. Where would we be without her?' He smiled, nodding along the trailer to a second make-up area, similarly laid out, where a pretty woman was putting the finishing touches to the make-up of a mature yet handsome actor, with inky hair long and wild, wearing a costume of dark leather with hearts placed in various spots.

'For God's sake, lay off the tarts. You've got jam all over your scar.' She winked at Billie. 'I'm dealing with the dregs here, dear,' she said to Billie over the actor's head as though she had known her for a lifetime.

'Oh, come on, I'm Method-trained. I simply had to steal one. Blame the caterers for putting tarts on the menu.' He pulled a pretend pout as Fredi playfully swatted him with the powder puff in her hand. The Knave of Hearts bowed in mock apology to Fredi as she shooed him from his seat.

'Off with your bloody head if you do it again,' Fredi called after him playfully as he winked at Billie and Ash, squeezing past them and out of the door.

'Wow, the caravan my mum and dad had when we were kids looked like a slum dwelling compared to this!' Ash nodded at the fittings of the swish interior, which had TV screen, sink and coffee-making facilities at one end and large specialist make-up chairs in front of the light-surrounded make-up mirrors. Around each of them were Polaroid photos of the actors in various stages of make-up on set, pulling silly faces – clearly not the polished and Photoshopped versions on show to the public.

'I used to love caravan holidays when I was a kid.' GG Mills spoke with a soft Geordie accent, which was curious, Billie thought. She had always seen him in American films, so assumed that was his real voice. 'Amble by the sea,' he added. 'Just an hour's drive from home, but it was always the location of our family summer getaway. Fish and chips, freezing cold swims and the sweet-and-treat shop where I bought a bucket and spade and bacon-and-egg-shaped rock every year to start the vacation. Great to be back here in the area and get a chance to explore my old home territory again.' His striking hazel eyes locked with Ash's for a second. Billie clocked it. She held up her identification to Fredi.

'DSI Wilde. Are any of these photos of the girl found this morning down by the river?' Billie nodded to the jolly photos plastered around the wall. Fredi's face fell in sorrow.

'No. These are all the top turns–' Fredi started. Billie noticed now that her eyes were red and a little puffed. Had she been crying?

'So complimentary,' GG Mills butted in. 'Fredi likes to keep those of us above the titles in our place, "turns" meaning local clubland acts around this area.' He pretended to look offended. 'I think I need more haemorrhoid cream under the eyes, babe,' he added, 'the bags are still fighting to be stars of the show.' He moved over to Fredi's make-up place and flopped down on her seat.

'Well, you will stay out all night like a tomcat on hot tiles,' she chastised. Billie felt like the show was going on inside of the trailer as well as out. All very entertaining, but she was determined to focus on the case.

'You might want to put some on yourself, darling.' GG looked up at Fredi through the mirror. 'Poor little thing, all those tears shed. I'll have to teach you to hide your true feelings, like us cold, hard thespians.' GG glanced through the mirror at Ash again, as Fredi stopped what she was doing to blow her nose on a tissue that she tore from a box on her make-up station.

'I'm just so shocked about the girl,' Fredi answered, dabbing her eyes which filled up with tears once more. 'I met her, you see, unlike *you*, GG.' Fredi looked at Billie. 'The extras get ready in the Portakabins over there, with one of my make-up trainees working on that side of things. Otherwise, they distract the main cast, asking for autographs and such like.' Fredi squeezed some haemorrhoid gel from the tube onto the back of her hand and using a small brush, deftly stroked the clear gel under GG Mills's eyes. 'My magic shrinking cream,' Fredi said in way of an explanation. Billie couldn't see any sign of puffiness anywhere on GG Mill's face. She wondered if he was playing for time for some reason.

'What Fredi really means is that the support cast are on their mobiles all of the time getting calls for jobs from their agents, arranging to zip around the world, a day on this film, a day on that, whereas we, so-called leading actors, spend half of our lives out of work waiting for the next big thing. Honestly. We get so full of rage and jealousy,' GG Mills joked theatrically, flicking his striking eyes up at them through the reflection of the mirror. Billie could have sworn he was flirting with Ash.

'I actually had to go over and see to the poor thing,' Fredi continued, sniffing. 'Pippa, I think her name was. Yes, Pippa Sykes. She had a weird yellow skin tone, and my assistant couldn't cover it herself, even with white camouflage cream. She said that she'd had a really upset stomach for a few days before, but then had felt a bit better and she didn't want to miss the chance of being a lighting stand-in for Luna Da Costa. Not on her first day. She thought it might lead to something bigger.'

Fredi seemed to be confirming Josta's suspicions of poisoning. But it sounded like she'd eaten something days earlier.

'Unfortunately, she was probably mistaken.' GG Mills looked reflective. 'As I learnt, you can't stay in the provinces and get your name up there in bright lights. Make no mistake, Arden chose to film in this area of the world because the locations are cheap and the people need the income, so they take the pittance paid to them. We may be in Sunderland, but the film depicts Oxford, whenever we cut from the *Alice* stories to Lewis Carroll's real life. The River Wear will become the Isis, which is the part of the River Thames running through Oxford. Sunderland simply won't exist on screen, which is a shame. But I'm afraid, that's showbiz. All smoke and mirrors.'

'Her room-mate, Maddie Taylor, is sitting over there.' Fredi nodded out of the trailer window to a pale-faced girl with long blonde hair and a white gown. 'She's lighting stand-in for the White Queen. Oh, and I saw Tweedledum, or was it Tweedledee, heading down towards the river behind her his morning when she went to get some fresh air. He may have been the last person to have spoken to her.' Billie's ears pricked up at the information.

'Okay, Ash would you take numbers please and then have a

word with Maddie Taylor. I'm just going to grab Tweedledum and Tweedledee over there.'

'On it, boss,' Ash answered as Billie headed for the door, her mind focusing on the job in hand, rather than the utter absurdity of the situation.

∿

'Hey, stop you two!' Billie called after the two characters, who, wearing strange fat suits, caps and large prosthetic heads, reminded her of overgrown schoolboys. Both had the words 'Tweedle' embroidered on the back of their collars. One of the men turned and looked Billie up and down.

'And you are, dear?' The man had the word 'Dee' embroidered on the front of his collar.

'DSI Billie Wilde.' Billie reached for her identification and held it up. The man held out his hand to shake. 'Thank God. I thought you were one of those deranged autograph hunters for a moment, hell-bent on a selfie at any cost.'

'I assume you are aware that a female named Pippa Sykes was found deceased by the river earlier?' Billie asked, one eye on the other man, presumably playing the part of Tweedledum, who had continued onwards at a pace, as though he didn't want to get into conversation.

'Indeed. The gossip has swept around the set like wildfire! Poor girl. I thought she looked a bit peaky earlier. These young actresses are always keeling over on set. Constantly on extreme diets to look perfect for their close-ups.'

'Did you see her walking towards the river, perhaps amble in that direction yourself?' Billie had never interviewed a storybook character before. It was totally bizarre. He had specialist prosthetics fitted to make his head almost football-shaped, with only eyes and mouth showing his true, albeit heavily made-up, features.

'The sun was shining,' he began, and for a crazy moment Billie thought he was going to start reciting his lines from the Walrus and the Carpenter poem. 'And my eyes started tearing up with all of this greasepaint on them.' He pointed to the make-up around his eyes. 'So I had to go back for a touch-up job. Then someone ran in and told us all about the girl. Terrible situation,' he added. 'Don't start me off blubbing again. It doesn't matter if the tears are caused by sun or sorrow, this stuff they slap on still stings like buggery.'

'Thanks.' Billie left Tweedledee and gathered speed as Tweedledum appeared to be moving fast, disappearing from view behind the branches of a large prop tree. She quickly made up the distance behind him and tapped him on the shoulder.

'I need to ask you a few questions,' she announced firmly, 'about your little walk down by the river this morning. You were seen heading that way.' Tweedledum finally turned towards her, looking quickly from left to right.

'Keep your voice down,' he whispered as Billie found herself speechless with shock for a second, in disbelief at her sudden recognition.

'You are *joking*!' She slapped her hand up to her mouth in an attempt not to burst out laughing. Ellis Darque blinked out of his prosthetic disguise.

'Shut it, I'm undercover. I'm on a job,' he hissed through gritted teeth. Billie couldn't help a giggle erupting even though her hand was still across her mouth. She tried to turn the sound into a cough. Ellis Darque, the expert undercover National Crime Agency advisor on her last drugs-related investigation, was one of the best in the business. He had even helped save her skin on an earlier enquiry. But he had decided to take a career turn, leave the police, and set up as a private investigator.

'New job going well then?' Billie started to ask, before having to slap her hand over her face again, tears starting to well up in her eyes with mirth. The former ace investigator looked so totally ludicrous in his make-up and costume.

'Yes actually.' He nodded. Billie looked up at him, gulped and then had to wipe another tear of laughter from her eye with the sleeve of her jacket.

'It pays well. Lay off, will you? I'm going to be sussed out in a minute.' However, he couldn't help his own chuckle at the sight of Billie overcome with amusement. 'Tell you what, it beats being undercover in some scummy drugs den or dank jail cell.'

'Yeah. Beats that grey tracksuit you had to wear in the nick too.' She recalled the first time she had met him, when he had given her vital information whilst undercover. She also had a picture of him in her mind's eye looking pretty fit, in full armour and dark protective riot gear when leading a raid on a drugs den, whilst advising her on her last job. 'Mind if I take a picture to show Boo?' Billie teased. Ellis was in a romantic relationship with Boo, Billie's dear friend and colleague on the Murder Investigation Squad, who kept the office in order.

'Very funny. My sides have just split,' he answered. 'Looking into that business with the young lighting stand-in, are you?' He sighed. 'Life can be a bitch.'

'Yeah. Appears you were the last person to see her alive.' Billie nudged him. 'Anything you want to admit to?'

'Only having a quick pee behind a bush at the top of the riverbank over there.' He nodded to some bushes at the edge of the clearing. 'It's not easy to get into the honeywagon in this get-up, I can tell you. You don't suspect anything dodgy though, do you?' he asked. Billie shrugged.

'Not sure until Josta does the autopsy this afternoon. She certainly has a wound in her skull, which may or may not have killed her, but Josta's thinking she's also been poisoned.' Billie leaned back against the prop tree trunk, inadvertently activating a motion sensor inside. It made a noise like fiddles playing as the branches started moving. She sprang forward.

'Prop for my big scene.' He grinned.

'This is like some mad drugs trip,' Billie answered.

'There are a lot of crazies hanging around film sets, I can tell you. Anything to get attention,' he added. 'I'm doing some background investigation to do with one of the principals. Just observing how everyone operates when they think no one's watching.'

'Not that odious little director?' Billie inquired, leaning back against the tree once more. It started playing music again. She shook a waving branch away from her face, moving aside as her mobile rang.

'Saved by the bell,' Ellis offered in answer. The caller was Sandy, the chief of police's personal assistant, sounding quite unlike her usual chirpy self.

'The Chief needs you back here right now,' she announced.

'Is it about the Will Cox trial?' Billie asked, reminding herself that she intended to go and have a chat with the members of Aunt Fanny's club that Mary Carroll had mentioned earlier that morning, even though the Chief had made it clear that he wanted the matter closed.

'No.' Sandy's voice dropped to a whisper. 'Miriam Nelson's here, marching around as if she's already the new chief, laying down the law. I think something serious is kicking off. Just giving you a heads-up that he might need some support.'

'On my way.' Billie finished the call.

'Trouble at mill?' Ellis asked as Billie got to her feet.

'Looks like Miriam Nelson's muscling in two months early.' Billie referred to the incoming police chief who was due to take over when Billie's godfather stepped down. Unfortunately, she didn't have a big fan base amongst the Murder Investigation Team.

'The Chief will knock her back though. It's still his patch until his retirement date.'

'Looks like the new broom is sweeping procedure away. I've got to get back. Keep an eye open for any dicey characters, will you?' Billie stood up.

'Cost you by the hour. I don't come cheap,' Tweedledum teased through a smile.

'Break a leg.' Billie quipped the theatrical good-luck term with a wink as Ellis waddled away. Ash was heading towards her.

'Got to run. Any useful intel?' she asked as they headed towards the parked police car.

'I'm guessing she's poisoned herself with a dicky mushroom or something, then fainted and fell, cracking her nut on the tree stump,' Ash began, reaching for the car keys in his pocket. 'Flatmate says she went out with some guy the other night and he took her home and cooked her mushroom risotto. Sounds like they didn't waste time with a pudding. Anyhow, she hasn't been right since.'

'Got the guy's details?' Billie asked.

'Nope. Friend has no idea. Just some tasty guy who she found on one of those apps. First date apparently.'

'And last.' Billie sighed.

'Managed to get her moby from the costume department.' Ash waved a clear plastic bag with a mobile phone inside. 'I'll get the info off it fast-tracked. Charlie's team have bagged up the rest of her stuff.'

'Good man.' Billie patted Ash on the arm as he jumped behind the wheel, and she slammed the car door shut.

'Mushroom poisoning. That's a bit suspect,' Billie thought out loud as Ash pulled into traffic.

'Apparently it's quite common. The kid was vegan, so blame it on an unhealthy diet,' he joshed.

'No, what I mean is that in the *Alice* books, *Alice in Wonderland* to be exact, she eats a mushroom that makes her grow tall and then another that makes her normal height again.'

'Jeez. Magic mushrooms, and you tell me this is a kid's book?' Ash answered.

'Maybe my imagination is running wild. Let's wait for the autopsy this afternoon.' Billie ran her fingers through her hair. The day had started with them focusing on a man with a first and second name that linked to Charles Dodgson, better known as Lewis Carroll. His cross-dressing name being Alice. She had just bumped into her former crack undercover colleague, in the disguise of Tweedledum and now a suspicious death looked like it could be attributed to dicey mushrooms. In the words of Alice in Wonderland herself, this day was seriously getting curiouser and curiouser.

4

DEATH CAP

A crash alerted Billie as she and Ash approached the Murder Investigation Suite. Boo loomed into view, having just shaved another few millimetres off the door frame of the accessible toilet along the corridor.

'Bloody bitch!' Boo, Billie's friend, indispensable office manager and sometimes undercover operative, appeared to be in such a fury that she shaved another millimetre or two off the skirting board with the metal protruding from her shiny silver wheelchair.

'Our new chief spreading her charms again?' Ash wasn't really asking. Boo was normally as cool as a cucumber, but the incoming chief, Miriam Nelson, tended to bring out the worst in everyone she encountered.

'Look at this!' Boo pulled paperwork from down the side of her wheelchair cushion and thrust it out for Billie and Ash to see. 'She's hit me with a bill to compensate for damaging police property! Door replacements, paintwork on skirting boards…'

Billie and Ash couldn't help glancing towards the scuffed and chewed doors and paintwork that Boo had collided with in her haste to get jobs done. Her nickname came from the warrior queen Boudicca after all, who had reputedly sported blades on her own fighting chariot.

'She can't do that.' Billie frowned. Technically Boo *was* guilty of trashing the woodwork of the office, but big deal. Having suffered life-changing injuries in the line of duty for the police force, she now ruled the roost as far as incoming evidence, and movement of the team was concerned, ensuring that everyone carried out Billie's instructions exactly as given. She had also saved Billie's life on the last investigation, bravely operating in an acutely dangerous location, acting as a volunteer undercover officer.

'Give me that.' Billie took the paperwork from Boo and swept up the corridor and into the Chief's huge office, with stunning views across the surrounding area. The Chief himself wasn't present, but several men in overalls were, emptying drawers and cabinets. Documents and personal belongings were piled on the floor or in the process of being bagged up.

Miriam Nelson, tall, broad, and formidable, a terrifyingly exacting dark bob haircut under her polished Deputy Police Chief cap, stood in the middle of the room, watching the procedure with her cold, hawk-like eyes. She switched her view to Billie, who was well aware of the rumours that the senior officer had already been holding her in her sights for some time. Hawks having binocular vision, allowing them to see their prey from far away before planning their attack.

'What's going on?' Billie demanded, not one to be intimidated by authority.

'*Ma'am.*' Miriam Nelson viewed Billie as though she were something that had just dropped from the bottom of her shoe. 'In future, address your superior in an appropriate manner, DSI Wilde. Let me remind you that you are no longer dropping in for a jolly get-together with your godfather for preferential briefings.' Billie ignored the dressing-down, waving Boo's bill for damages under Miriam Nelson's nose.

'This is a joke, right?' Billie demanded. 'DS Mensah is an outstanding member of the team, who, based on recent events, has been recommended for the highest bravery award. What she *doesn't* deserve is this bill for...' Billie read the amount printed on the paper, her eyes widening, resulting in her shaking the papers even more forcefully under Miriam Nelson's pig-like nose. 'Two thousand quid!' Billie shook her head in disbelief.

'I would advise you to step back, DSI Wilde, otherwise you will find yourself slapped with a police misconduct charge for unprofessional behaviour.' Billie moved a step forward.

'This' – Billie ripped the bill given to Boo up into tiny pieces and scattered it on the floor – 'is a total insult. It is also unlawful disability discrimination at work. Hell will freeze over before I let this go further.'

Miriam Nelson folded her arms, unmoved. She was like a huge rock of a woman, Billie noted. A formidable foe, but she wouldn't be beaten on this argument.

'Continue with that tone, young lady and you will be going the way of your darling god-daddy–'

Billie cut across the senior police officer's words. 'Where is the Chief? What's going on here?'

'Suspended, pending further enquiries. I am the acting chief until I take up my permanent role officially in exactly two months. I warn you, there are going to be some major changes around here, DSI Wilde.' She wrinkled her nose. 'No more nepotism in my force.' She shook her head disparagingly. It was an accusation that always riled Billie. Yes, her father *had* once been chief of this regional police force, a post her godfather currently held. But she had worked above and beyond any call of duty in order to speed up the ranks to her current position as

DSI heading up the Murder Investigation Team and it infuriated her when people insinuated otherwise.

'No more silver spoons, or easily won high ranks at a way too early age, caused by being in with the "in-crowd". I'll be watching you night and day, Wilde. That's if this current investigation into the Chief's misconduct doesn't drag you down too. Which...' – Miriam Nelson bent forward and stared into Billie's eyes – 'I have every confidence it will. Now get back to work, or I'll have you for wasting police time.' Miriam stepped back as a man in overalls started bagging up more stuff. He picked up a photograph in a frame on the Chief's desk.

'Here.' Miriam Nelson took it from him and held out the picture. It showed both Billie and the Chief in police uniform grinning at the camera. 'Anyone can see what's been going on. That era is over. Needless to say, I won't want this piece of tat adorning my desk.' She let the photo slip from her fingers. The glass shattered on the floor, a crazy paving of broken shards obliterating the faces of Billie and the Chief. Billie, almost overcome with anger, swept out of the room and into the main office. The shocked faces of her team all turned her way, desperate for answers.

'She said she's going to dismantle the team,' Rina Hoy, the squad's statement reader said, looking worried.

'Bring in her own people,' Jim Lloyd, Exhibits Officer added. 'Said we're all being deployed elsewhere or laid off as we haven't had any homicides in a couple of months.'

'Due to our sterling work to clear up the streets of low lives,' said Boo sweeping in, running over one of Ash's feet in the process. 'County lines would have been running amok without us,' she added.

'No one's going anywhere. Not while I'm still here,' Billie announced. 'Let's just keep our heads down for now. Get on with the job in hand. We have a possible suspicious death today on the film production that has been hitting the news recently. I'm off to the autopsy in a minute, but I want us to go through the Charles Carroll murder stuff again with a fine-tooth comb. Find out if there could be any links to anyone involved with the film or the girl who died this morning.'

'But, boss, the Chief said–' Ash started, reminding her yet again that they had all been told that the Charles Carroll murder inquiry was closed, regardless of the fact that Will Cox had hung himself without having been convicted of any crime.

'The Chief has been stood down, probably due to some jumped-up misconduct investigation.' Billie folded her arms as the others shared surprised looks. 'I'm guessing that it's all a pile of bollocks, but I'll find out more from him ASAP. The best thing we can do is forge ahead with the suspicious death and I'm already sensing some tenuous links to Charles Carroll, so opening that investigation again is now completely kosher, as I'll explain to the Chief when I see him. But the main thing is that we find out the absolute truth about both of the deceased. We owe it to them, and we owe it to their loved ones. The Wicked Witch of the West can stomp around getting power crazy, but we are just going to get on with the job.

'Ash, you follow up on Pippa Syke's mobile phone. See if it gives us a link to the romantic dinner engagement.' She checked her watch. 'I'm off on my own date – with death.'

The messaging service kicked in once again as Billie entered the mortuary. The Chief was proving tricky to contact. Josta beckoned Billie inside, where the body of Pippa Sykes already lay on the table, the examination underway.

'Welcome, my dear. I appreciate that you are as always, pressed for time, so I can confirm immediately that the young lady died of traumatic brain injury. There is evidence of irreversible tearing of nerves and fibres as the brain collided with her skull. However, she had already been mortally wounded by a mushroom and sadly had little time left. Put simply, if the hole in her head hadn't done for her, the mushroom poisoning definitely would have. As I pointed out at the scene of death, she was severely jaundiced – a sign of liver failure due to progressive deficient protein synthesis, causing cell death. This has also resulted in extremely damaged kidneys, brain oedema, lung congestion and signs of haemorrhage...' Josta added as she continued with her work and her assistant recorded her findings on his laptop. Billie recalled that Pippa had complained of difficulty breathing according to Fredi, and Josta's findings seemed to fit in with the comments of her room-mate about the date with the mushroom chef.

'Intensely yellow liver of creamy consistency and diffuse subcapsular haemorrhaging. Fatty infiltration and enlargement...' Josta looked up at Billie as her specs slid to the tip of her nose. 'Extremely dark-red kidneys and severe gastric erosions in stomach and intestines,' she continued. 'Heart shows coronary artery obstruction. We have already confirmed the toxin known as alpha-Amanitin in her blood and urine. This is due to ingestion of the Amanita phalloides mushroom species...'

'Crazy that a mushroom can wreak so much havoc.' Billie sighed, running her fingers through her hair.

'Death Cap is the common name. Grows all over our area, especially under trees. They are very hard to distinguish from your everyday shroom,' Josta replied. 'I do wish children could be educated about these things, especially as foraging and so forth is becoming all the rage these days. We taught Max to differentiate when he was a youngster. It only takes half of a Death Cap to kill an adult and I come across several cases of cessation of life via ill-identified fungus every year.'

'So no way of telling if a crime was committed?'

'We'll look further into what exactly caused the brain injury, though all signs currently point to the tree stump. But that is all I can say for certain at this time.' Josta turned to a line of bags on the countertop. 'I do hope this is a sad but accidental situation. Lola has been hammering the phone since dawn, harassing her agent and various casting directors, desperate to bag a part on the film. She loves the *Alice* books. Used to read them to Max in bed every night when he was a wee mite.'

Billie decided not to get into conversation about Max and bedtime. All she could say was that he had grown up a lot since then. She could tell a much jauntier story about the nocturnal activities of Josta and Lola's precious son these days. He was still cute, but definitely not so innocent. She forced herself to concentrate on the job in hand.

'Oh, there is one other thing that is probably nothing or something, possibly a film prop. But she had this in her pocket.'

Josta held up the clear bag. Inside it was a small cake. In currants on top a message read 'Eat Me'. Billie felt her body tense on high alert once more. In *Alice in Wonderland*, Alice had taken a bite out of a cake with those very words upon it as well as a mushroom. But why on earth would the lighting stand-in for the Red Queen have the cake in her possession? Billie was determined to find out.

5

LOVE LIES BLEEDING

B illie's mind was racing as she sped off from the mortuary. She had made a quick call back to base for an update. Word was that Pippa Syke's mobile phone wasn't showing any dating app at all or interaction with any obviously shady characters. She was a student and most of her calls had still been back home to a now devastated mum and dad, or texts to arrange call times for rehearsals and arrival on set with the film team.

Billie and Ash had tread very carefully on their earlier visit to the film set, not being able to pinpoint enough suspicions about the death to lay down the law on questioning. But now Billie felt they needed to act fast, if only to capture the still fresh recollections of witnesses to Pippa's last movements. She had instructed Ash to take the murder squad over to the filming location, even if it did stop the show going on. She would be joining the team very soon and after her run-in with Miriam Nelson, Billie was not in the mood to take no for an answer, even if it did annoy the hell out of director Arden Roy.

Fortunately, her route from mortuary to film set took her past the Chief's house. He still wasn't answering any of the messages that Billie had been leaving for him, so she intended to swing by and visit him in person. She felt nervous butterflies in her tummy, dreading the thought that he was in any real trouble. The Chief was the only person still standing from her childhood days. He'd been a dream godfather to her and a great boss, putting up with her fiery temper and often unorthodox ways of catching dangerous criminals. Was that nepotism, as Miriam Nelson had intimated?

Yes, in truth, few other officers could get away with refusing to take orders from the Chief in the way that Billie sometimes did. But wasn't that simply because of her record of getting things done, albeit in a sometimes unconventional manner? Or was she just pulling the wool over her own eyes?

Little quips about being the daughter of a former police chief and the god-daughter of the present incumbent, had followed her around like a bad smell throughout her police career. It had only made her more forceful in her determination to show that she was more than up to the job. Surely she had more than proven herself, so why wouldn't the chief of police back her all the way?

Billie swallowed hard as she swung the car off the main road and down a leafy side street where the Chief's smart Victorian villa stood. Police vehicles were parked outside on the road as well as on the drive. Billie was about to pull in and ask what the hell was kicking off here, but suddenly spotted Miriam Nelson in the doorway. Had the Chief actually been *arrested* for something? Billie, thinking quickly, sped onwards, engaging her car phone, and ringing the Chief's number again.

'It's Billie. I'm worried sick. There's a forensic team crawling all over your place and your office. Miriam Nelson is terrorising my unit. Please, Pacino' – she used her teasing nickname for her godfather – 'get in touch. Love you.' She meant it. Though she realised it was actually the first time she had ever uttered those words in his direction. Like most people, she had just taken for granted the older people around her, who made up a real or virtual family, the people who are always there to help. One thing was for certain, if the Chief needed help, she was willing to fight to the death to support him.

'I won't have this. We're making a film here!' Arden Roy was kicking off big time, as though making a film was obviously much more important than the ever more suspicious death of a young woman. Billie approached, clearly not in the mood to take any flak from the odious little man. Luckily for him, Delphine got to Billie before Billie got to him, ready to give her own not very complimentary direction.

'Um, DSI Wilde,' Delphine started, glancing nervously behind her, to where Arden Roy was shouting at a group of young children in costume, 'in order to avoid any further disruption to the filming schedule, I wonder if you would be happy to arrange interviews via our casting manager, Ken Chen?' Delphine nodded to a man with a clipboard, already appearing to be liaising with Ash. 'That way, we can give you access to the artistes who are simply waiting for their scene, rather than actually acting in one, at the time needed for questioning.'

Billie nodded. 'Okay. Unless we feel we need to speak to a particular member of the cast urgently,' Billie acquiesced, despite silently cheering on Ash who was refusing to be intimidated by any refuseniks.

'Absolutely,' Delphine answered, 'but Mr Roy is at pains to point out that the sad demise of the girl took place away from the film base, as she was walking on public ground by the river and before she had actually stepped onto the film set, so

technically, it's not an issue to do with the production...'
Delphine eyed Billie warily. It was clear that she wasn't the
organ grinder as far as this argument went.

'I'll be the judge of that,' Billie answered, mentally shaking
her head at the lack of sympathy being shown towards the
young actress. Clearly the low-paid extras were simply the
flotsam and jetsam of the film world and poor Pippa Sykes had
already been flushed from the septic tank that lay in place of
Arden Roy's heart.

'Make-up!' Arden Roy shouted across to a minibus where
Billie could see Fredi, the make-up artist, loading what seemed
like enough baggage for a two-week holiday. 'The Oysters need
some attention. The bloody police have upset them with all this
barging in. Costume! What the hell has happened to the
Carpenter's hat?' He waved his hand towards a Walrus and a
Carpenter who were climbing onto the minibus.

Fredi still appeared to be slightly out of sorts as she
responded to the director's temper tantrum, lifting a fishing box
full of make-up brushes and assorted paraphernalia off the bus
again. She carried it over to a group of sobbing children dressed
as oysters. Billie was certain that Arden Roy, rather than her
team, were the cause of the children's distress. None of her
squad would have interviewed children without strict measures
in place, even with their chaperone present.

'We're moving down to the beach location to shoot *The
Walrus and the Carpenter* scene,' Arden Roy called over to Billie,
having spotted her approach with his beady little eyes. 'I trust
we won't be dragged off to the gallows for that? After all, the key
artistes were on a plane from London when this cursed situation
happened and surely no one is accusing the Oysters–'

He was cut off in mid-sentence by Fredi, who was clearly well
used to the director's drama-queen tirades. She was looking past

him, where Billie could see Maya, the beautiful daughter of Ellis Darque, a brand-new trainee police officer, currently on attachment to her department. She had obviously clocked her dad in full Tweedledum costume, as she was currently in fits of laughter, lifting the poisonous atmosphere sitting like a cloud over the area as Arden Roy reacted against his total control being removed.

'She's a dead ringer for Luna Da Costa. Make a great lighting stand-in.' Fredi eyed up Maya, who did indeed have a similar fine bone structure and colouring to the actress playing the part of the Red Queen.

'Similar height and size. She'd fit the dress.' Joanne, the costume designer nodded in agreement.

'Well, don't just stand there, dolts, get it sorted!' Arden Roy headed for his chauffeur-driven car. Pippa Sykes was now officially history, simply a body for whom the cap no longer fit. As the Oysters had their make-up touched up and were quickly loaded onto the minibus, Billie noticed Ken Chen heading towards Maya and Ellis. She jogged behind him, catching his arm.

'Just a minute. I need a word with her first.' Ken Chen nodded, clearly thinking that Billie was off to interview a support artiste, not one of her own team in detective wear of jeans and T-shirt.

'Maya,' Billie called. Her voice fell on deaf ears, Maya still being in a fit of giggles over her father's disguise. Billie strode over to join them.

'God give me strength. This goes from bad to worse.' Ellis, still dressed as Tweedledum, groaned. 'Why not bring the whole squad around? We can have an undercover party,' he protested in mock annoyance.

'It's you I want a word with,' Billie said quietly and quickly to Maya. 'The crew haven't clocked that you're with us. They think that you are an extra. They want to cast you as a replacement for Pippa Sykes. Are you up for it?'

'No way! What if there's a lunatic targeting the Red Queen and they go after Maya?' Ellis reacted in a totally fatherly way, Billie noted. Protective as expected.

'But I really want to do it, Dad!' Maya replied. 'It'll be great training and you can teach me all the tricks about being undercover,' she added.

'Yeah, cos I'm doing such a fantastic job with that today,' he quipped. Billie grinned.

'Okay. It's a deal. Stay clear of the mushrooms if you're eating – that goes for the both of you. Just in case there is any connection to the film unit. Get any info you can on dodgy characters. This one for a start.' She slapped Ellis playfully on his Tweedledum head and nodded to Ken Chen that he was safe to approach Maya.

Billie had spotted Maddie Taylor, Pippa Sykes's room-mate, being removed from her White Queen costume for the day. She pulled off her wig and was sweeping a wet wipe over her face to remove her make-up as Billie reached her.

'Hi, Maddie? DSI Billie Wilde. I'm so sorry about Pippa. I believe that you shared a place together?'

'Yeah.' Maddie nodded. She looked absolutely forlorn. 'I can't believe what's happened. Really, I wanted to run off home and cry, but the director, Mr Roy, he said that the show must go on, so...' Billie patted Maddie's arm. She could see how the overbearing director would have intimidated the young acting student.

'Look, why don't I give you a lift back?' Billie offered. 'I can see that you're a bit shaken up and we can go over this date that Pippa had, where she may have eaten the mushrooms.'

'It's all right, I have a bus pass and I've already told the police everything I know, twice now...' She trailed off, looking like a frightened rabbit trapped in headlights.

'I need to look around your flat anyway,' Billie continued. In fact, she wasn't offering the young woman a lift home, she was telling her that she was taking her. It was important, Josta had said, to find out if there were any remaining mushrooms anywhere, not only for safety purposes, but for extra confirmation of the poison that killed the girl. Unlikely that she would dig anything up given the story about the app date, but Billie knew that sometimes going that extra mile brought results.

'Did I hear you say that you are going by the student flats?' Billie suddenly noticed the man getting out of his Tweedledee outfit at the back of a costume lorry. His prosthetic head had already been removed. 'I couldn't cadge a lift, could I? It's just that you can wait hours for a bus around here and I've got to get changed. I'm off out tonight.'

'Must be nice to have a social life,' Billie answered. She knew that Max was due to fly off on one of his jobs with the army any day now, as soon as he got the nod, and she wanted to spend as much time as possible with him before then. *Call me a little old romantic*, she silently joked to herself, but much as she was still utterly dedicated to her job she had learned, since her relationship with Max, the importance of committing to time with the ones you love and although she hadn't said those words yet, she was definitely falling hard for Max Strong.

'I'd look into that fellow playing Tweedledum,' the man added as he took a comb through his ginger hair. 'I haven't seen him at any am-dram events before and he's a shifty sort,' he added, causing Billie to smile. She would pass that info on to Ellis later. He was coming around to her house for dinner with Boo. Looked like it was going to be a late supper at this rate.

As Billie loaded Maddie and the man, who had introduced

himself as Dougie Meeks, into her car, she offered to drop him off first. She needed time alone to gently interrogate the girl. Being in a state about her friend and in the high anxiety location of the film set on a new job with Arden Roy at the helm, meant that she might have forgotten something vital.

'So kind, darling. I'm doing a show tonight at my club. Any excuse to dress up and sing. I have to pay the rent and film jobs are few and far between in this part of the world. We all need to think of our futures after all.' Billie noticed Maddie glance into the back-view mirror, towards Dougie. Her face was a picture of stress, but she appeared to be trying hard to make an attempt to join in the conversation.

'Pippa and I used to busk together, by the underpass at the hospital. All those sentimental songs would get the visitors slinging change at us,' she added reflectively. 'I'm not sure I'll be able to do it now by myself.' Billie made a mental note, as she pulled the car out into traffic, that perhaps Maddie wasn't quite as pure and innocent as she looked, clearly happy to play on the emotions of troubled souls.

'We all do what we have to, to survive, dear.' Dougie Meeks patted Maddie on the shoulder. 'I have a regular spot at Aunt Fanny's.' Billie's ears pricked up. Wasn't that the club that Charles Carroll's wife, Mary, had mentioned? Dougie Meeks cut over her thoughts. 'Ivor Fullcrotch, that's my drag act,' he added. 'I've got quite a following.'

'With a name like that, you'd be rather hard to forget.' Billie mentally pictured her demure adoptive mother turning over in her grave at the conversation and smiled at the thought. 'What time does the show start?' Billie asked as a sign saying 'bingo', flashed brightly in her mind's eye.

'In an hour. I've still got to iron my corset and sling some heated rollers in my wig,' Dougie Meeks answered, as Billie pulled into the roadside to let him leap out of the car. 'Thanks, officer. You are a sweetie. Bye, dear.' The soon-to-be Ivor Fullcrotch bent to wave at Maddie in the front passenger seat. 'Don't do anything I wouldn't do. Stay safe.' He winked. Maddie responded with a weak smile, though her eyes still registered heartbreak.

'I might just drop in,' Billie called after him, checking her watch. She had time to suss out Pippa Syke's living situation and also get more background on Charles Carroll. Was the day that had started so darkly, actually starting to brighten up after all?

It didn't take long to look around the tiny flat shared by Pippa Sykes and Maddie Taylor. They had been dossing down in the cheapest of student digs, despite their having walked in the shadows of Lewis Carroll's Red and White Queens. Maddie opened the door into a terraced lower, so-called 'Tyneside flat', built around 1900, similar to many others in the north-east area of England, including, ironically, in Wearside. A smell of damp immediately assaulted Billie's nostrils.

The flat consisted of two lacklustre bedrooms with carpets that may have started off another colour, but were currently brown, and a tiny lounge area, leading to an even smaller galley kitchen, decorated with tiles that were so out of date that they were in danger of coming back into fashion. Tacked on the end was a jerry-built dingy shower room and toilet where the outside privy may have once stood. The sad building was in a street of similar shoddy homes.

The tenant above them was playing an undistinguishable piece of music, save for the thump of a bass banging through the ceiling. Billie imagined it was hard to study in such an uninviting location, but then as she had been reminded already today, she had been born with a silver spoon in her mouth – or so Miriam Nelson thought. Few people still living actually knew the truth. Billie pushed the senior police officer from her mind, checking her mobile again as she followed Maddie around the rooms. The Chief still hadn't made contact.

'Can you tell us anything more about the person who took Pippa out for dinner, Maddie? It may well have just been a sad accident, but it appears that she ate poisonous mushrooms...'

'Oh my God!' Maddie put her hand over her mouth in horror. As the sleeve of her sweater rode up, Billie noticed cut marks around her wrist for the first time, perhaps having been covered by the costume she had been wearing earlier. Maddie was clearly a troubled soul at the best of times. Billie didn't want this incident to push her over the edge all alone in this dark dank place. 'I don't know.' Maddie chewed the edge of her jumper. 'It was just a casual hook-up thing, no strings attached. Most of them just have usernames anyway. Pippa wasn't looking for a long-term relationship...' She trailed off. Billie reflected that the modern dating scene, using apps for casual sex under assumed names, sadly didn't make her job any easier.

'So the guy she was seeing that night–' Billie started before Maddie cut her off.

'I don't even know if it was a guy. She'd just been breadcrumbing–'

'Sorry?' Billie suddenly felt her tummy rumble, realising that she hadn't eaten all day.

'Breadcrumbing – sending out flirty texts and stuff. But she never mentioned any kray bae–' Billie suddenly felt extremely old.

'Kray bae?' she asked, wondering if she'd been picked up by Martians. Indeed, Maddie was looking at her like she had just arrived from another planet.

'Crazy boyfriend or girlfriend. But then Maddie liked to do a bit of monkeying,' she added, looking pained. She glanced up and to Billie's relief, clarified without her having to ask, probably due to the blank look on her face. 'You know, she moved from one relationship to another, without any time between – like a monkey swings from tree to tree.' She spelled the situation out as though Billie were a particularly dense three-year-old. She wondered whether she should bring Maya with her in future whilst interviewing anyone under the age of twenty-five.

'So, what day exactly did she have this get-together?'

'Sorry, I feel like, sick...' Maddie rushed off to the back bathroom, where Billie could hear her throwing up. Waiting, she looked around at the squalid kitchen with dirty dishes piled up in a sink and black mould growing along the sealing tape where vintage tiles met worktop. Billie wondered whether she should double-check that it had definitely been mushrooms that had killed the girl rather than just the general poison surrounding her now.

Suddenly she spotted a small free-standing fridge, wedged between the kitchen cabinets. She bent down and pulled at the handle. The door swung open showing a half-eaten tin of baked beans, a pot of houmous and a family-sized packet of Haribo. Billie had to admit that it wasn't too different from the way her own fridge had looked before Ash had moved in as her lodger, transforming her eating options with his amazing culinary prowess. It was as Billie moved an opened box of custard, with caked residue around the slashed corner, that she spotted it. A bowl of mushroom risotto. She hauled the dish out at the same moment that Maddie unlocked the toilet door and stepped out. Her look of guilt said it all.

'Funny, they don't look dangerous.' Billie sniffed and looked into Maddie's wide eyes. They were now filling with tears.

'I didn't mean to hurt her...' Maddie's emotions erupted into a wave of seemingly heartfelt sobs as she watched Billie carefully whip out gloves and an evidence bag. She slid the bowl inside, secured it tightly and ripped the gloves off, dropping them in the bin which was already full to the top. Ripping off a square of kitchen roll standing on the countertop, Maddie blew her nose with shaking hands and still gulping for breath, managed to say, 'I love her.'

Billie left the poisonous bag on the countertop for a moment, took Maddie's arm and led her through to the tiny lounge.

'Okay. Let's go through this again.' She sat the young student down on an ancient-looking sofa.

'I've always had a crush on her… Pippa, right from when we started college together. She's so vibrant and fun and *everyone* loves her…' Maddie trailed off. Billie noted that the fact hadn't sunk in yet, that Pippa was now well and truly in the past. She decided to let it go. This wasn't the moment to ram home the truth. 'But she wasn't interested in me, well, not in that way anyway. I mentioned it to my counsellor at college and they said maybe if I cooked a special meal one night, she wouldn't be out dating other people and then I could tell her how I felt and, you know…'

Billie ran her fingers through her hair. At least the girl was seeing a counsellor already. That was good news. It looked like she was going to need some support moving forward.

'So, you made the risotto, Maddie? Did you eat any yourself?' Billie asked, puzzled. After what Josta had told her, Maddie shouldn't logically have been here to tell the tale either. Maddie gulped as tears started to flow down her face again. She shook her head.

'No, I hate the things. They like, give me the creeps. That's why I made it for Pippa. She used to joke about me having like a phobia against the things, so she would know how much I totally cared, by making it especially for her, with wild mushrooms and stuff.' She held the kitchen towel up to her lips as though she was about to throw up. Billie couldn't help reflecting that the youngster's mushroom phobia had just been fed big time. Billie was starting to feel a bit ambivalent about them herself.

'So, did you pick the mushrooms yourself?' Billie gently asked, her mind racing. This really did appear to be simply a case of accidental poisoning.

'No. I got them off a friend.' She started to wail, her head hanging forward, a trail of snot landing on her jeans.

'Can you ring your counsellor, Maddie?' Billie crouched down and rubbed the young woman's arms. She was clearly in a state, but they would have to take her in to make a full report and looking at the cuts on her arms, Billie felt that despite her being eighteen years old, an appropriate adult would need to be called to ensure her well-being.

'No. They've like, just left. So I haven't got anybody,' she sobbed. Billie swore under her breath. She stepped into the kitchen area and made a phone call to Boo to put arrangements in place for the full interview. Ash, luckily, was still on the film set so her plan was to hand Maddie and the offending mushrooms over to him to take the girl in whilst she headed for Aunt Fanny's.

'So you don't know anything at all about a small cake that was found in Pippa's costume pocket with the words "Eat Me" written on the top in currants. You didn't make that cake or give it to Pippa?' Billie wanted to be clear on the point.

'Oh yeah, I remember that. Just like in *Alice in Wonderland*. We were like, comparing costumes. Hers had a pocket. Mine didn't and she found that cake in hers. We had no idea what it was for, because in the book, it's Alice who finds the cake, not the Red Queen...' She trailed off, staring into space at the memory. 'But she didn't dare eat it, not because she was worried she would shrink or grow or anything mad like in the books.'

Maddie finally managed a wan smile. 'She just thought the director might kill her for eating the props...' The enormity of the situation seemed to sink in at that moment. 'But like, it turns out that she was already nearly dead anyway.'

Billie noted the look of utter horror crossing Maddie's pretty features as her mobile rang. She expected it to be Boo confirming that someone would be waiting to help ensure Maddie's mental health was compromised as little as possible as she helped them with their enquiries. Instead, Josta's distinct, booming, jolly voice cut through the air.

'Hello, dear heart. Hope I'm not interrupting anything important, but I thought you would like to know post-haste that the tests have just come in from the lab on the small cake found on the body of Pippa Sykes.' Billie could hear Josta flicking through notes as she spoke.

'It has tested positive for traces of Amanita phalloides. Probably not noticeable in the cake mix, so even a mushroom hater might have consumed it without realising.'

'Death Cap again?' Billie wanted to be sure she fully understood.

'Indeed,' Josta confirmed. 'It's not for me to postulate officially, but between two friends, be under no illusions. Someone was hell-bent on making sure that this young lady would wind up dead.'

Billie glanced at Maddie, still sniffing away tears as she reached for her battered biker jacket. Was she looking at the face of an innocent young student or in truth, a cold and calculating killer?

6

AUNT FANNY'S

Aunt Fanny's club was discreetly tucked down a side street, accessed via a staircase above a hairdressers and nail bar. Handy, Billie thought, as she arrived when the fun was already well underway. The room smelled of sweet perfume, lager and dirty fries. Dougie Meeks was rocking his alter ego, Ivor Fullcrotch, on a slightly raised stage at the end of the room, regaling the appreciative audience with songs and suggestive jokes.

Around the room, men were dressed as woman with varying levels of success, from stunningly polished and perfectly presented, in a way that Billie could only dream of as a natural-born female, to slightly comedic figures wearing ill-fitting frocks and wigs. Regardless of appearance, the group seemed to be a happy band of friends, a jolly mix of both male to female cross-dressers alone or with lady partners, mostly middle-aged and older women, wearing comfy slacks and colourful tops.

Billie could only imagine the soul-searching and pain that each of those present might have been through in order to reach the easy camaraderie they were sharing as they relaxed together projecting their true personalities tonight. Bingo cards were at the ready, drinks in hands and what looked like a pile of potato skins, dips and cheesy tacos being consumed along with the dirty fries, as they took in the show.

The totally accepting cheeriness lifted Billie's own spirits, especially after her less than effusive welcome return to the film set to advise Arden Roy that he would have to do without a White Queen lighting stand-in, at the very least for a day or two. Maddie offered the main pathway to answers about Pippa Syke's death and the oddities surrounding it and Billie sensed now that there was a lot more the young student could tell, with a little more encouragement.

Like a particularly irate Rumpelstiltskin figure, hopping up and down in fury, Arden Roy had threatened to make complaints to those at the top. Water off a duck's back as far as Billie was concerned, but something that Miriam Nelson would be onto like a dog with a particularly juicy bone, given half a chance.

She had left Maddie, still tearful, in the capable hands of Ash, assisted by Maya. Billie was keen to take advantage of the promising young police trainee's youth, in order to get to the facts regarding the poisoning of Pippa Sykes.

'Come over here, love. There's a spare seat,' a man perhaps in his sixties, wearing a sleek grey wig, blue twinset, and pearls, invited with a smile. The other people at the table nodded and waved towards Billie as she joined them – pushing the sharing platter her way. Billie took a potato skin and dipped it in the garlic sauce.

'Thanks.' She smiled, suddenly remembering her former housemate, Kate, and the number of girls' nights they had shared, stuffing their faces with similar fare. The memory hurt, a black cloud that she still struggled to deal with from time to time. She brushed it away, instead accepting a bingo card and pen that had also been slid across the table by her new friends.

'Take this, dearie.' A woman smiled across at Billie. 'I'm already playing six cards and Joe can't play so many with his false nails on.'

'Josephine here, love, remember,' her husband whispered. The woman rolled her eyes good-naturedly towards Billie.

'Josephine, I stand corrected.'

'Terrible business about the Alice Carroll killer topping himself before he could be convicted.' A baritone with a halo of dark curls, sequinned dress and kitten heels, sighed.

'Did you know him well?' Billie asked. She was scanning the room for any sign of Charles Carroll's wife, Mary, who might just be able to give her a vital link to a girl who had died of mushroom poisoning.

'Everyone knew Alice Carroll, dear,' the baritone piped up again, 'and we all loved her.'

'She was a real star.' Billie's bingo card donator added, as Dougie Meeks left the stage and the bingo machine was dragged on by two cross-dressers struggling in their slingbacks.

'A legend at our college,' the dark-haired baritone added. 'An expert on the works of Lewis Carroll. She even wrote a film script about the author's life. Got a letter saying that there was real interest in it.'

'Not the film that is being shot in the area right now?' Billie frowned. The dark-haired baritone shrugged.

'I doubt it, dear. Alice would have been shouting about that from the rooftops and we'd all be knocking back champers and caviar tonight rather than lukewarm lager and dirty fries.'

The lights suddenly flashed on and off as one of the men in slingbacks prepared to read out the numbers. The hall fell silent, just as Billie's phone rang out loudly. A communal groan of irritation filled the air and former friendly eyes stared at her askance. It was clear that bingo time was sacrosanct.

'Sorry, sorry.' Billie pulled an apologetic face and leapt up, heading for the door as the bingo caller reminded everyone sternly to switch off their phones and stop jangling their bracelets, or was it their chastity belts? he questioned, to a resounding chuckle as Billie heard the door bang behind her. It was the Chief's number flashing up. She took the call as she moved down the staircase, opening the outer door.

'Hi, are you okay?' she asked, hoping for confirmation that she had no reason to worry and that the situation at base was just some madness on the part of Miriam Nelson, which was going to see the woman getting a well-deserved bollocking. But instead, Billie heard the normally confident Chief sounding stressed to the point of panic-stricken.

'I need your help,' he said.

'Of course, anything,' Billie replied, racing across the pavement to her car. 'Where are you?'

'Ursula's place,' he answered. Billie's heart sank. There was no love lost between her and her former fiancé's mother. In fact, they detested one another. That location was absolutely the last place she would have chosen to be heading tonight.

'You need to come quickly. They've ransacked my house and it's only a matter of time before they come here for me,' he added. Billie was aware that he had been using David's mother as a glamorous plus one at events, but she didn't know, or want to, if it went any further. It wasn't a pretty thought.

'I'm on my way. Blues and twos.' Billie wasn't actually clipping her emergency lights on but she would be putting her foot down. She had never heard the Chief sound so distressed. It was the first time ever that her protector had begged for help. She had no intention of letting him down.

~

Billie made the journey in record time, pulling into the side road outside of David's mother's house. Her godfather, looking like a shrunken version of the polished, proud police chief that she knew so well, lurched out of the door, holding a large, rather battered-looking, black metal box in his arms.

'Here, don't stop. Take this and promise me you won't open it.' He lifted Billie's car boot ajar and slung the box inside, rubbing his head as though it hurt. He looked grey and tired, his breathing shallow.

'Okay. Are you feeling all right?' Billie caught his arm, alarmed at the distress etched across his face.

'Promise me, Billie. Promise!' he begged. 'And please, whatever happens, remember that I love you,' he added. It was so unlike the man that she knew that Billie was speechless for a moment, before finding her voice.

'Of course I promise, but what's going on?' she demanded once more, hearing her own feelings of stress rising. This was serious. As she spoke, three police cars turned into the long road which led their way.

'They're coming!' The Chief wiped his face as if preparing for battle.

'So I'll stay and find out what the hell is going on here!' Billie felt confused. After all, neither of them would normally be alarmed by a police presence. They *were* the police presence. Even allowing for the bitch antics of Miriam Nelson, Billie couldn't understand why this mad situation couldn't be sorted with a few well-placed phone calls to the top.

'No please, Billie. Take the box. Hide it well. I'll explain when the whole thing is done, but it's best you know nothing now. Go, quickly, or they'll ransack your place too,' he appealed.

'You've got your brief ready?' Billie asked, torn by the thought of leaving him to face whatever was coming his way, her natural inclination to kick into fight, rather than flight mode. The Chief nodded.

'Go and keep the box safe. Don't open it. That's the best thing you can do for me right now.' The Chief glanced up the road, stressed. It was no mistake, the police cars clearly had only one final destination in mind.

'All right, but I'm here, ready, the moment that you need me.' Billie felt helpless. 'Love you.' She gave her godfather a quick hug and then slipped into her car, quickly driving away, turning down a rat run known only to locals that avoided passing the police cars pulling up outside of David's mother's house. Billie at least thanked God that she had avoided the older woman. She guessed that as usual she would be putting on lipstick and powder whilst knocking back a glass of wine, lest the visitors catch her in dress-down gear.

Billie ran her fingers through her hair, turning her thoughts to the black box in her car boot that the Chief was so keen to have spirited away. It reminded her of another locked container that she had opened after her father's death and the Pandora's box of shocking dark family secrets she had found within it. By the sounds of it, this could be another bucket full of bombshells that, if found, would blow up in the Chief's face.

Billie shivered. She couldn't imagine anything coming to light that could cause such terror as that which she had witnessed in the eyes of her godfather tonight. Another disturbing thought suddenly hit her like a carefully aimed brick. Her own life from childhood to adulthood had been constantly entwined with that of her chief supporter, mentor and now boss. If he was hiding something that was about to tear his life apart, was it also going to bring Billie's own brief period of equilibrium crashing down around her ears?

7

KILLER SHARKS

'What time do you call this? Your dinner's in the dog,' Ash teased, from the comfort of one of Billie's sofas in the huge lounge/open-plan kitchen with spectacular views down over the River Aln estuary. Right now, the view was shrouded in inky darkness, save for a full moon peeping out occasionally from behind dark clouds. Ellis and Boo were sitting close together on another deep comfy sofa set at right angles, large glasses of wine in their hands, facing a TV.

Billie mentally relaxed for a moment, relieved to be in her comfort zone at last. She had carefully deposited the black box in the cellar at the bottom of the house, accessed from a curious door set at the side of the building, shaded by bushes, before she had entered through the front door. The basement was already jam-packed with both Billie's birth mother's belongings and Billie's own, from the move from her penthouse pad overlooking the River Tyne, shared with her former fiancé David. She felt that it was still too soon to rake through the physical debris of her life, although she had worked hard on her emotional responses to the massive upheaval in her world during the past year. Billie felt that the box couldn't be safer than in that location.

'Nice to see some people relaxing,' Billie joshed. 'Has the film star given you his autograph yet?' She nudged Ellis, the memory of him dressed in his Tweedledum outfit cheering her up, despite the various challenges of the day.

'Leave it out, will you?' Ellis chuckled. 'I'll have you know I once played Hamlet in a school play. I've got a much bigger range than just Tweedledum.' Billie had no doubt that he was telling the truth. That was probably what had made Ellis Darque such a brilliant undercover operative.

Ash joined Billie as she raided the fridge, taking out a bottle of spring water and pouring a large glass. She would avoid the wine. She needed a clear head to keep a grip of everything that was kicking off around her.

Ash took a dish of steaming lasagne out of the oven and popped a huge portion onto a plate, already loaded up with salad, next to a pretty folded napkin on a tray. He headed off over to the sofa and placed the tray on the huge driftwood coffee table at the centre of the seating arrangement.

'Madam, your dinner is served,' he announced in a mock French accent, with a bow worthy of a top waiter in a smart restaurant.

'Thanks.' Billie flopped next to him, lifting the tray onto her knee. 'I'm starving.' She tucked into her supper as she caught up with the gossip from the office and film set, keeping schtum about her recent meeting with the Chief and the mysterious black box.

'So did Maddie Taylor squeal any more info?' Billie asked Ash and Boo.

'A bit. We didn't want to push her too much tonight. I have to say Maya did a sterling job, getting stuff out of her that I would never even have understood,' Ash explained.

Billie commiserated, regaling the others with her own feelings of bewilderment when Maddie had been chatting about Pippa's dating habits. Ellis played the proud father, at every mention of Maya. He had been making up for lost time with the daughter that until a few months ago, he hadn't even known existed.

'Is everyone in the team up to speed on *Alice in Wonderland* and *Alice Through the Looking-Glass*?' Billie looked at Boo and Ash.

'Yeah, just about,' Boo started. Billie noticed Ash sliding a DVD under the edge of the sofa with his foot.

'You've read them?' Billie asked Ash before reaching down and pulling the animation versions of the film out on view. 'Or did you all just watch the cartoons?' She raised her eyebrows in mock annoyance.

'Oh come on, boss. I couldn't make head nor tale of them. At least I've got a bit of a handle with that,' Ash argued.

'Yeah, it was good.' Boo laughed. 'I mean, I think I read it as a kid, but maybe I just imagined that I did. It's one of those stories that everyone thinks they know...'

'These two are heathens.' Ellis rolled his eyes. 'We studied the books at school,' he added.

'Well, you went to a posh private school, mate.' Boo nudged him. 'Us heathens had to suffer stories of poor kids with druggie parents and mean neighbours or tales about living in brutal foster homes.'

'Okay.' Billie sighed. Having been privately educated herself, she accepted that she had probably accessed educational opportunities not necessarily open to all other schoolkids. The idea fell in line with the usual accusations about her speedy rise through the ranks, due to privilege and preferential treatment. 'I'll get someone to cobble together a synopsis and circulate it around the team first thing. I may be wrong about the Alice

57

connections to Pippa's death and Charles Carroll's murder. But it's something I'm not prepared to overlook.'

'Get your new friend Perry Gooch in to brief the team.' Boo appeared to be having a light-bulb moment. 'When she was still a newspaper hack, I remember she had a weekly nostalgia feature in the local rag. One of the stories was all about Lewis Carroll's links to the area. I hate to say it, but when she wasn't dishing the dirt on people, she knew her stuff.'

'Good thinking. Extra pudding for you.'

'I've already eaten it all.' Boo looked slightly sheepish. 'But I'll get on to her now.' Boo reached for her mobile and started texting.

At that moment, Max Strong entered the room. His stunning looks, fit body, dark hair flopping over brown eyes framed by the thickest eyelashes that Billie had ever seen, never failed to shake her equilibrium somewhat. He smiled that crooked smile of his in her direction, whilst also feigning surprise at the others gathered in the room.

'Did I miss the party invite?' he asked good-naturedly.

'No. Actually, it's an *Alice in Wonderland* convention,' Boo quipped. 'Still a drop of wine left, and the lasagne is in the oven,' she added, raising her glass to Max.

'But first you've got to cough up everything you know about the *Alice* books,' Ash called over.

'There's a rare neurological condition called Alice in Wonderland syndrome, which makes people perceive body parts and external objects incorrectly and also causes sufferers to get confused about time. I vaguely recall that sort of thing happens in the books.' Max shrugged as though he couldn't have cared less. *So much for all those story sessions Lola devoted to him at bedtime*, Billie thought, as she lifted her tray and joined him, hearing Ellis attempt to educate Ash and Boo on the intricacies of the *Alice* stories in the background. Billie kissed Max on the cheek, his wonderful lemony scent bewitching her as usual.

'Are you okay? You don't mind Ellis and Boo staying the night?'

'And Ash, as always...' Max added. He still had his own place that he retreated to when the noisiness of Ash's visiting children threatened to raise the roof, during his weekend child access. Billie loved the fun and noise, buckets and spades and endless sand in the house that Ash's sad separation from his wife had brought. Some small and very noisy glad tidings washing in, after the pain of the last year. She appreciated that Max, however, was an only child and needed his space. Even when not off alone, he was much happier with one-to-one relationships. As a top psychologist he had probably worked all that out for himself, Billie reflected.

'But you like Ash, don't you?' she whispered to Max, in reaction to the tone of his voice being quite unlike the normally softly spoken, calm counsellor that she had at first clashed with and then fallen for, even before her engagement had come to an abrupt ending. Max pulled Billie close, burying his face in her hair.

'Of course I do. I'm so sorry, sweetheart.' He pulled back, cupped her face in his hands and kissed her on the lips. Billie forgave his momentary brusque manner immediately. 'It's just been the devil of a day...' Max reached for the open bottle of wine and poured a glass. It was white, whereas he normally drank red, but he knocked it back in one long gulp, nevertheless. 'I needed that.' He smiled.

'Don't tell me, you've been counselling crazy police officers all day?' she teased, alluding to the fact that her first meeting with him had been set up by the Chief, in response to her earlier reaction to an investigation. Max had a contract with her force to help sort out the mental health of officers who were dealing with the various horrors of the job.

'Nope.' Max grabbed the bottle and poured out the rest of the wine. 'Those days are over. Seems your incoming chief, Miriam Nelson, is taking a new-broom-sweeps-clean view of her role. My contract was due to be renewed, but she's bringing in someone else.'

'No way! That blasted woman's creating all-round havoc.' Billie's thoughts turned to the Chief for a moment. She hoped he was all right.

'Indeed,' Max agreed, 'and my hospital contract is coming to an end, too, so sorry I'm not the most convivial of company tonight.' He rubbed his hand across his head. 'You don't fancy a walk along the beach, do you? Just the two of us. I could do with some fresh sea air to clear my mind,' he added. Billie felt a knot in her stomach. She had never seen Max looking so discombobulated before.

'Of course,' she agreed immediately, calling over to the others. 'Back in a bit.' They glanced towards her and nodded distractedly, already arguing over stories of Walrus and Carpenters, White Rabbits and hookah-smoking caterpillars, as Ellis attempted to summarise the *Alice* stories, whilst Boo and Ash, already both under the influence of a couple of large glasses of wine, jovially refused to take any of it seriously.

Billie smiled to herself as she slipped out of the French doors, despite her concern over Max appearing to be out of sorts. She felt thankful that she had such a tightly knit bunch of friends. They made her feel as though she could face anything, even the challenges that Miriam Nelson was now intent on bringing to her world.

She followed her sexy psychologist down through the terraced garden to the blue wooden gate at the lowest level, leading to the golden sandy beach. She smelled sweet peas as they passed through the vegetable patch that Ash had lovingly created, whilst he had been recovering from both his destroyed marriage and the injuries that he had suffered during their last investigation together. Though he was only a temporary lodger, the truth was that Billie would have been happy to have him share her house forever.

She took a breath of cool night air, tasting the salt on her lips. Even in the darkness she could sense the location of each clump of beautiful wildflowers defiantly growing in swathes on the sandy dunes, in daytime shades of purple, pink and yellow. Such was her familiarity with this shell-strewn pathway, that stretching her fingers out, she could immediately identify by touch a swathe of bird's-foot trefoil, tiny sunset-coloured slipper-like blooms, drifting into pink thrift, on her right, with small clumps of dune and marsh helleborine orchids to her left. The large magenta flowers of bloody crane's-bill, the county flower of Northumberland, were Billie's favourite and even though she couldn't see them at this moment, she was aware that they were all around her, like a much loved and very beautiful blanket.

In the time she had visited and then lived in Alnmouth, Billie had become well acquainted with the terrain, birds, bats, and sea creatures. They all now felt like dear neighbours. Tonight though, under some of the darkest skies in the world, when the moon slunk behind the clouds, all was velvet black. She could hear the sounds of the waves softly crashing onto the nearby shore and the masts of the small sailboats jangling in the breeze further along the beach. Billie felt an involuntary shiver run down her spine. Something in the air made her feel as though this was a moment hovering in time, a marker, when for evermore, all events would be viewed as before that night, or after.

Max caught Billie's hand and led her along the shoreline. They were silent for a moment.

'I have to go away, tonight,' Max finally said, his voice catching in the salty air as a large wave smashed across a nearby rock. Billie wanted his words to be swept away by the outgoing tide.

'Not tonight,' Billie finally answered. 'Please not tonight.' She wasn't a needy soul, though Max Strong had brought something out deep inside of her, that wanted calm and continuity, things just to stay the same. She had been through so much turmoil in recent times, but with Max spooned around her in the dead of night, the sudden panicked awakenings had finally been washed away.

'I'm sorry, sweetheart, but I'm afraid I'm going to have to take on more and more of these contracts, with my mainstream work drying up around here.' He sighed, lifting Billie's hand in his and planting a kiss on her tightly wrapped knuckles.

Billie's stomach tensed. As a former high-ranking soldier in the British Army, Josta had confided to Billie, Max was regularly called upon to use his criminal psychologist talents in treacherous and always secret locations around the world, often at a moment's notice.

'Not Columbia again? Surely you're a marked man there–' Max shook his head, pressing his finger to Billie's lips.

'A bit nearer home this time. The British Army are doing some work in West Africa at the moment. That's as much as I will say,' he added before Billie started interrogating him further about his imminent destination.

'But what about your work in the prisons and the high

security hospitals?' Billie asked. 'Surely there are enough insane people around here to keep you occupied for life?' she said through a smile, hoping that she wasn't sounding desperate.

'It's really not for me anymore, Billie. I need to be more engaged in the action of events. You should understand that.'

'But it's so dangerous,' Billie protested. Max pulled her to his side and hugged her, planting a kiss on her head.

'Think how I feel, every time you go all gung-ho, chasing after killers,' he answered. 'Don't you think I'm worried, especially after what happened to Nat?' He almost whispered his former wife's name, a paramedic killed in Afghanistan, having stepped on a landmine – as Max looked on. Billie desperately wished he would forgive himself for his wrongly placed guilt over the incident.

'It's not the same thing.' Billie hooked her arm around Max's waist, drank in his smell.

'Yes it is.' Max's voice was soft, hypnotising almost. 'We're two peas in a pod, Billie, you, and I. We're both excited by the same thing. Danger.'

'It isn't danger that drives me,' Billie argued, 'it's the search for the truth. With truth, comes justice and I want that for all of the victims that I'm fighting for,' she explained, as they reached the end of the beach, where a rocky outcrop lay. Billie loved to take Ash's girls fishing for crabs and tiny sea creatures at this spot, but right now the waves were crashing loudly against the jagged stones. It wasn't safe to go further.

Max pulled Billie down beside him as he reclined on a large rock, nestling her close against his shoulder. As the moon came out from behind a cloud, she could see the stunning profile of his face. She hoped to God that this wouldn't be her last memory of him and that he would come back from his latest travels safely and soon.

'You talk of truth, Billie, but I don't think there is such a thing.'

'What do you mean?' Billie said. 'I can list a number of truths and downright lies,' she argued.

'Can you really though?' Max softly continued. 'I mean truth is simply what one chooses to believe. For example, I know that you will have brought at least a few criminals to court who you know had *definitely* done the crime you have pinned on them. But a jury might listen to the facts and still find them not guilty. That is their truth and now the criminal is publicly deemed innocent of the crime. That is now the true fact.'

Billie had to begrudgingly admit to herself that he did have a point.

'It's the same watching a football game. One side claims a penalty that might win a major tournament. Fans of the other side genuinely believe that the penalty shouldn't have been given. The facts are disputed. The ref allows the penalty. It's now a truthful occurrence. Or try hearing, for example, about British rule in India from a different perspective than a British one. The truth is simply the belief that gets the most votes of agreement.'

'So I shouldn't be chasing the truth, is that what you're saying?' Billie ran her fingers through her hair. 'This is all getting a bit too deep for me, doc, after the day I've been through.' Max gently laughed. Then tipped her chin upwards.

'I'm saying that the truth is I love you.' Billie thought that she had misheard his words for a moment. It was the first time that Max had been so forthcoming about his feelings. 'I'm also saying that perhaps it's time for us to make changes – together. Maybe move away somewhere...'

The dark clouds covered the moon and Max's face again as Billie absorbed his words. She had her lovely new home, her job, her friends, Ash's kids and now Max telling her he loved her.

It was like winning the golden ticket. She actually didn't want anything to change.

'Move where?' Billie shivered again, pulling herself up straight. Max combed his fingers through her hair. He knew that the sensation soothed her at times of stress.

'Hmmm, dunno. Somewhere hot and with palm trees. Panama maybe? Great beaches and it's close to where many of my private contracts take me,' Max suggested. The thought of palm trees and golden beaches was tempting for a moment. Then she remembered where she was.

'But I love *this* beach and anyway,' Billie answered, trying to lighten the conversation, 'I'd probably land up bumping into half of those criminals you mentioned who the juries let off, but who are truthfully crazy mad. I hear that Panama is a good place for them to get away from it all.'

'There you go again, seeing things from the angle the UK newspapers take on the country, rather than the truth. It's also a fantastic spot for non-cons to launch new adventures,' Max answered, through a soft laugh. 'It's a beautiful place. I have friends there. You could make new ones. Some of them aren't killers on the run, but I'm sure I could root out a few if it would make you happier.'

'I'll tell you what would make me happy right now,' Billie answered, as the moon shone out from behind the clouds again and Billie could feel Max's dark eyes looking into hers. She started unbuttoning his shirt. 'This new adventure...' She pulled Max close and kissed him.

'You mean you've never done this on a beach before?' he teased, responding as he slipped his shirt off and slid his hand across her body, gliding his long smooth fingers under the hem of her top. The motion made Billie shiver. 'Probably because it's too cold here. I guarantee we could do this all of the time in Panama.' Max kissed Billie deeply, then suddenly pulled her over onto the soft sand. 'If the sharks don't get you first.' He laughed as the cloak of darkness once more fell upon them.

'I'm in paradise now, lover boy,' she teased as she pulled her top over her head and dropped it on the sand. 'And what's more, I don't have to keep looking over my shoulder here for killer sharks.'

8

DRINK ME

It was early when Billie woke, but Northumberland being so far north, first light usually arrived well before 5am. Not quite the land of the midnight sun, yet it didn't feel as though it lay that far off in summertime. However, it wasn't the bright light streaming through her bedroom curtains that had awoken Billie, but the fact that the pillow beside hers was ice cold, the sheets on Max's side of the bed turned back. Billie rubbed her eyes in order to focus on the note left on her bedside table.

I never did like long goodbyes. Love you forever. Max x

Billie immediately sat up, feeling a knot in her stomach. She had lost so many people dear to her in the past year that she didn't like any sort of goodbyes. Christ, she was beginning to act like a schoolgirl. They had both known the score as far as their jobs were concerned when they had finally linked up, so it was no good her bleating on now about him flying off every few weeks into dangerous situations, as he had reminded her the night before.

Billie smiled to herself as she slid her legs out of bed and threw on a dressing gown, recalling their late-night beach liaison. At least that conversation had resulted in a happy ending. No wonder she had fallen into a deep sleep and had been dead to the world when Max had slipped away earlier. She reached over for her mobile and realised that the battery was flat, other things having been on her mind when she and Max had returned home from the beach the night before, continuing where they had left off.

Heading downstairs in search of her phone charger, Billie met Boo, a steaming cup of coffee in her hands, munching a pain au chocolat in the kitchen lounge area.

'I was going to bring you breakfast, but no can do the stairs in the chair.' She nodded to her wheelchair. 'Well, that's my excuse and I'm sticking to it.' She grinned, taking another bite from her pain au chocolat. 'Can I get you something now?' she asked.

'Just searching for my mobile charger.' Billie started hunting through the room. 'Has Ellis gone off to find his spotlight already?'

Boo nodded. 'Yeah. He had to leave at three thirty am. Kept me awake until then, snoring.' She mock groaned. 'At least when he's asleep he's not trying to wrap me in cotton wool all of the time.' She was thoughtful for a moment. 'Sometimes I think you should be careful what you wish for.'

Billie's ears pricked up. Ellis and Boo had missed their chance for a romantic get together many years before, having been undercover operatives on an investigation that had taken a wrong turn, leaving Boo with life-changing injuries. It sounded like Ellis still hadn't stopped blaming himself for having taken his eye off the ball when it had happened. She hoped that the two would work it out. Boo deserved a bit of love in her life.

'I came through here to get a drink and spotted Max creeping out, must have been about three o'clock. It was still dark anyway. You two okay?' she asked as Billie finally found her charger and plugged her mobile in.

'Yeah. He was just a bit uptight last night. Looks like Miriam bloody Nelson is curtailing his contract as well, and he's going to have to take his secret squirrel jobs in far off locations more often. He wants me to move abroad with him.' Billie poured herself a coffee and sat down opposite Boo, pinching the other half of pain au chocolat from her plate.

'You'd better not!' Boo stopped mid-bite, spitting crumbs.

'The Chief was all for retiring somewhere exotic.' Billie realised that she was speaking her thoughts out loud. She desperately hoped that he was heading for a relaxed and happy retirement, but right now, it didn't look like his wind-down time was going to be all plain sailing. 'Nelson's after him for something. He was lifted last night,' Billie confided. Boo's eyebrows raised.

'You are *joking*? I know she was ransacking his office yesterday, but I thought she was just playing the Betty Big Baps. Throwing her weight around.' Boo shook her head in anger. Billie ran her fingers through her hair.

'I don't know. I think this might be something bigger.' Billie began to explain as her phone, now juiced up with a little battery life, started pinging messages. She reached over and scrolled through, stopping to read one in particular. 'It's him, the Chief. Looks like he's been released already so they can't have anything on him.' Billie perked up briefly before frowning as she read further. 'What time is it?' She looked up at the clock. It was six am. 'Damn, I've got to run!'

The Greek temple standing on the hill at Penshaw in Sunderland, dominates the skyline. Designed to be a copy of the

Temple of Hephaestus, in Athens, but to people of the north-east of England, it's simply the sign of home. Built in memory of John George Lambton, 1st Earl of Durham and standing at 136 metres above sea level, the much-loved monument can be seen for miles around, whether approaching the general area by air, rail, or automobile...

Billie had made the journey in record time, but she hoped that she wasn't too late. The message from the Chief had been to meet him here at 6.30am. She jumped out of her car at the base of the hill, breathing a sigh of relief as she checked her watch. She still had a couple of minutes to spare, and the Chief's car couldn't be seen.

She relaxed for a moment, still feeling her heart beating from the race to get there so speedily, cursing the fact that she no longer had her phone switched on and beside her bed at night. That would change, whether Max protested or not, Billie firmly decided as she climbed the grassy slope on this clear morning.

Her boots were wet with dew, the smell of green freshness filled the air, and the view was absolutely breathtaking. As Billie reached the summit, she could see across Tyneside, Wearside, and Durham. The panorama lifted her spirits, wiping away her anxiety throughout the journey there as to why the Chief would want her to drive fifty miles south to meet him, when she could have just popped in on him at his home. Did he think his house was bugged, or hers?

The thought alarmed Billie for a moment. The grounds for such intrusive surveillance were stringent and could only be authorised by the most senior police officer in the force, or Home Secretary, in the interests of national security or to prevent serious crime. Billie had certainly never made such a request herself and the idea that anyone, even the hideous Miriam Nelson, could make such an application in relation to the Chief, or her, was preposterous. Billie shook the thought away as she reached the base of the Penshaw Monument.

The eighteen, seventy-feet high, fluted columns held a rectangular structure on the top, without any roof. Billie walked slowly around the interior, scanning the surroundings to see if the Chief's car was approaching. As she reached the south-facing side, Billie realised that one column featured a door, which was presently open. She spotted that the lock was broken and peered inside, using the torch on her mobile. Noting that there were no new messages from the Chief on any delay, curiosity got the better of her. She decided to take a look.

Though Billie had been aware that a seventy-four-step spiral staircase did exist within the monument, this was the first time she'd had a chance to walk up the steps. Keeping her torch on, she stepped into the tight space and began to climb. Without the additional light, Billie realised that the interior of the column would have been raven black. A musty smell caught her breath as she carefully moved upwards, constantly progressing in a circular fashion. She considered that the journey would not be one for the faint-hearted, claustrophobic or weight-challenged, such was the tightness of the space inside.

It was with not a little relief that Billie turned her face up to a ray of sunlight as she made the final curve of the spiral. She took a deep breath of fresh air as she emerged onto a parapeted walkway which ran from east to west along the top of the column. From here she could see even further, across the River Wear and to the base camp for the film company. Already the crew could be seen milling about like busy worker ants. Whether Arden Roy liked it or not, her team would be continuing with their enquiries at that location today. Maya would be on set in her undercover role as lighting stand-in for the Red Queen, so hopefully in a position to get extra information not readily offered to police detectives.

Billie kept her hands on the walls to steady herself as the breeze, only apparent at this height, caught her red curls in a cloud around her shoulders. The stone barriers offered the only safety net to prevent one who might be dizzy from the ascent from tumbling to the ground way below. Billie guessed that they were no more than three feet high. She glanced away from the dark gritstone ashlar base in the inner part of the structure, feeling momentarily giddy, despite her own relative fitness compared to the average curious climber. It was then that she spotted the huddled figure at the end of the walkway.

Billie raced across to the body, desperately hoping that it was simply a sleeping drunk, though she knew the idea was utter nonsense. Her chest tightened as she reached the male, it was now clear to make out, even as a cloud passed the sun, plunging Billie's world into shadow. The face was turned away from her, the body huddled in a curl as she took a breath in and then felt for a neck pulse. There was none.

As the head fell back, Billie already knew that the body was stone cold and now clearly on view, as the sun tugged its way from behind the cloud, revealing shining brittle light on the scene. The Chief's dead eyes stared into Billie's own.

Billie heard an involuntary whimper, aware that she herself had made it. The Chief was clearly long past crying out for help. The movement also made his arm drop to the floor from its earlier position across his body. A bottle fell from within the folds of his jacket, smashing against the bricks of the walkway. Dregs of something strongly alcoholic trickled in a stream towards Billie. She didn't move. Instead, she was staring at a label stuck onto the front of the bottle. *Drink Me*, it read, referencing *Alice in Wonderland*.

Had the Chief just drunk himself to death? Billie didn't believe it for a moment as she hastily called in her team, trying desperately to hide the panic in her voice, whilst a silent scream of utter horror ricocheted around her brain.

'Josta has just called me. I'm about to leave. I don't know what to say, except that I'm so sorry, darling. Would you like me to come back?' Max's liquid chocolate voice was like a soothing balm.

In the background a child suddenly cried out. Billie guessed that it must be stressed by the strict procedures demanded these days at a busy airport. She'd imagined that Max would have been flying out from RAF Brize Norton, not a regular airport. A sudden picture skipped through her mind, of happy trips away with her godfather, the Chief, when she had been a child. Such innocent times. She forced away the most recent picture overwhelming her thoughts. The Chief's milky, dead staring eyes. What on earth had happened to make him take his last dying breath on the top of an iconic local memorial? Billie was determined that she would find out the truth if it killed her.

'Hello? Are you all right, sweetheart?' Max sounded worried, torn. Billie imagined the flight must be about to take off. The little boy was crying louder now. She hoped Max wouldn't end up sitting next to the poor distraught toddler.

'Yeah. I'm okay. Really,' she lied. 'Just come back safe and sound, that's all. Love you.' There, she'd finally said the words. She ended the call before Max had a chance to respond. She hoped that he would hold that thought close to his heart, ensuring that he headed back home soon and in one piece.

Of course, she would have preferred to have him with her, especially at this horrific moment, rather than about to fly off to some godforsaken lawless country on a dangerous mission, but that was his life and Billie knew that she had no right to change him.

Boo sped up and handed Billie a mug of coffee. Despite a couple of hours having passed since the harrowing retrieval of the Chief's body, Billie was still feeling shaky. Scaffolding had been required to get the corpse down from the top of the monument, as rigor mortis had started to commence by the time Josta and the team had arrived, making the descent down the spiral staircase entirely impossible. Boo and Ash were well aware of the full extent of Billie's heartbreak, despite her braving out the situation with the other members of her team.

'Perry Gooch is just finishing her briefing to the crew, if you want to come in and add anything.' Boo spun back around and headed for the meeting room, shaving more paintwork off the skirting boards. Billie wondered how much Miriam Nelson would bill her for that. She had been noticeable by her absence that morning, apparently away on a day's leave, despite the seriousness of the situation.

A news blackout was in place regarding the identity of the man found at Penshaw Monument and the jury amongst the team was still out as to whether the Chief had committed suicide or been murdered. Josta was due to conduct the autopsy in an hour or so, but Billie was already in no doubt. She had known the man almost all of her life, and though he had seemed under immense pressure the night before, when he had given her his box of personal items, he hadn't got the top job by being easily intimidated. Suicide just didn't suit his personality. Billie took a gulp of her coffee before moving forward, reminding herself that there was no room for self-indulgent emotions when in the pursuit of facts and she was determined to get to the truth.

As she entered the meeting room, Billie mused that her past year of life-changing upheavals had, on many occasions, turned her long-held views upside down. One thing she would never have imagined, even a few short months ago, was that one of her arch-enemies, Perry Gooch – a former hard-nosed journalist, who had been an endless thorn in Billie's side – would have been coming to her aid yet again today.

Perry and Billie had somehow forged an unlikely friendship during Billie's last investigation. Having lost her job in the process, Perry was now press spokesperson for the police in the region.

'Right then, so to summarise, Charles Dodgson, better known as Lewis Carroll, was an Oxford don, logician, mathematician and amateur inventor. On the one hand, your typical Victorian – dignified, conservative, highly religious. On the other hand, he was also a rebellious satirist and amongst family and friends, a fun-loving, witty and social animal, who adored art, literature and the theatre and was friends with the Pre-Raphaelites, very much the "in-crowd" of the time.'

'So what are the books meant to be about?' Ash enquired. 'Caterpillars smoking hookahs and offering magic mushrooms that make you grow small and tall – it sounds like one big drugs trip,' he added.

Billie reckoned that Ash was thinking about Maddie Taylor's statement re: the mushrooms. He had already told her that in his opinion, the 'friend' who had allegedly given Maddie the mushrooms was a fantasy figure that Maddie had created, to avoid fessing up that she had picked the fungus herself and then made both risotto and the small cake. Checks made with the film art director had confirmed that the prop needed for the scene where Alice in Wonderland actually eats a similar cake hadn't even been created yet.

'Some pop groups in the 1960s tried to put a drug-taking slant to the tales, as hippy culture was all the rage at the time,' Perry explained, 'but there is absolutely no evidence that the author ever took drugs. The stories feature nonsense events, similar to the funny clownish letters his own father had written to the author, playing with word logic. Made-up stories and mathematical games were a regular feature of the light-hearted entertainments created by his family, friends, and their children when they all got together, especially when visiting this area.'

'Is everyone clear on the basic stories?' Billie wanted to be sure that the clues that she had started seeing in the recent deaths wouldn't be overlooked by her team, possibly ignorant of the content in the books.

'Yep. *Alice in Wonderland*,' Boo started. 'Alice sits on a riverbank with her sister and is bored by the book her sis is reading as it contains no pictures... She notices a white rabbit with a pocket watch, who's complaining of being late. She follows it, falls down a rabbit hole and ends up in Wonderland, coming across some crazily eccentric characters, people and talking animals whilst trying to find her way home. She also finds a bottle marked "Drink Me" which she drinks and then she shrinks as a result and tries to enter a little door to a garden but can't reach the key required to open it, because it's on a high table. So, she bites a cake marked "Eat Me", which causes her to grow huge. Similarly, the hookah-smoking caterpillar sitting on a mushroom explains that one side will make her grow tall and eating a piece from the other side will cause her to shrink.'

'Hence my concerns re: the deaths of Pippa Sykes and now the Chief,' Billie said, suddenly remembering the little door leading to the top of Penshaw Monument, 'and I can't help wondering, yet again, about Charles Carroll, bearing in mind that Lewis Carroll's true name was Charles Dodgson,' Billie added 'and his cross-dressing name was Alice.'

'*Alice Underground*,' Perry suddenly announced. 'The original *Alice in Wonderland* was titled *Alice Underground*,' she continued. 'Wasn't Charles Carroll buried alive... underground...?' She raised her eyebrows.

'Yes. In St Nicholas's churchyard in Boldon,' Billie answered, startled at the thought.

'You *do* know that the Alice referred to in the books was Alice Liddell?' Perry asked. Billie nodded, shrugging in agreement.

'And that her father grew up in the rectory at Boldon, where, for a time, Alice Liddell's grandfather was rector of St Nicholas's church?' Billie slowly shook her head. 'You can see his name on the list of former rectors inside,' Perry explained. *Exactly where the axe made contact with Charles Carroll's head*, Billie recalled. She could see the spot in her mind's eye now.

'But surely Will Cox wasn't thinking of all that when he killed Charles Carroll?' Boo wrinkled her nose in disbelief. 'He didn't seem bright enough.' Billie totally agreed with Boo. She was sure now, more than ever that he hadn't been capable of the murder.

'William Cox?' Perry asked, 'I seem to remember that's what the press release said his full name was.'

'Yes, I filled in the charge sheet.' Ash nodded.

'Well, this is getting a bit creepy,' Perry announced, folding her arms. The hefty woman wasn't normally one to allow herself to be seriously spooked.

'William Wilcox, the collector of taxes at Sunderland Customs House, was Lewis Carroll's uncle. The author used to visit regularly when on breaks from Oxford. He finished his poem the *Jabberwocky*, from *Alice Through the Looking-Glass*, whilst staying with him. The story is thought to be based on the local myth of the Lambton Worm. Hedworth Williamson, the man married to Alice Liddell's cousin, introduced white rabbits onto his lawns when his sight started to fail. Apparently he liked shooting bunnies. Carroll was a regular visitor at their home too.'

'So Lewis Carroll clearly had big links to this area?' Billie asked. What on earth did it all mean?

'Yep. Carroll's favourite sister lived in Sunderland, cousins, close friends. In fact, at that time, the location was *the* fashionable place to be for actors, writers, artistes...'

'But I thought the whole Lewis Carroll and Alice thing was completely linked to Oxford?' Billie frowned. She'd never heard of such local links before.

'Well, Oxford would, of course, like that story to continue. But in reality, with almost half a year's worth of holidays from university, he got the hell out and spent much of it staying with the family and his many mates in the north-east of England.

'The truth is that the stories that he told Alice and her sisters whilst in a boat sailing down the Isis in Oxford, which eventually became *Alice in Wonderland* and *Alice Through the Looking-Glass,* were very likely to have been inspired by stories and events shared by him and his small friends at their numerous earlier get-togethers in Sunderland.'

'Looks like someone might be trying to bring that to our attention, albeit in a crazy, warped way...' Billie trailed off. The idea sounded like nonsense, but how else could she make sense of the recent events?

'Whoever it is, must be as mad as a Hatter,' Ash announced.

'He just can't help himself,' Boo replied, raising a smile from everyone. Despite her feelings of utter heartache, Billie realised that at times like these, the support of friends could be life-saving. Her way of dealing with immediate feelings of grief, she now understood, was to fiercely go into battle and then later, retreat to lick her wounds. She could only cling on to her sanity right now, with the help of the devoted crew around her, clearly trying to keep her spirits lifted.

'Wilde. In my office now.' Miriam Nelson had appeared at the exit door as Ash and Billie were heading towards it. Billie noted the words 'my office', despite the Chief not even being cold in his grave yet. Her hackles immediately rose. She threw a glance at Ash.

'I'll wait in the car,' he whispered. 'Keep calm,' he added, having clocked Billie's expression.

'Thought you were putting your feet up at home today, ma'am.' Billie used the term of respect grudgingly. She would certainly never call Miriam Nelson 'boss'. The senior officer sat down at her chair behind the huge desk that had once had Billie's photograph in pride of place on it.

'Indeed. But your dear departed chief put paid to that. He certainly liked to cock up people's lives, Wilde. Still, he's jabbed his last thorn in my side, thank God. His shenanigans would certainly have brought this force into disrepute, so the top dogs have ordered that the investigation is closed and sealed now he's snuffed it. Truth is, he deserved to be strung up rather than having drunk himself to death, but at least I don't have to deal with the fallout.'

Billie wanted to punch the woman in her smarmy face. She mentally marched her to the huge window, with spectacular views over the surrounding area and smashed her through it, enjoying the fantasy picture of her hurtling down at speed to a horrible death.

'I'm of the opinion he was killed. It wasn't suicide,' Billie started. Miriam Nelson raised an eyebrow. Billie gritted her teeth. 'Ma'am,' she finally mumbled.

'That's better, Wilde. You are not talking to your god-daddy now, wrapping him around your little finger. What are the grounds for your ridiculous claim?' She placed her hands behind her head and swung back on her chair, in a show of assertiveness.

'The bottle had a label saying, "Drink Me" stuck on it, for starters,' Billie began. 'It may link in with the other suspicious death on the *Alice* film set–'

'You mean the accidental mushroom poisoning that you are wasting far too much time and police energy on? I'm well aware that you like to be in the limelight, Wilde,' Miriam Nelson said, cutting across Billie's explanation, 'but my info from the custody suite is that they're hanging on to a frightened kid not long out of school who didn't pay full attention in cookery classes, hence her mate has snuffed it. A tragic accident. Let's hope she watches more Mary Berry on telly in future. But you're surely not trying to flag her up as a cold-blooded killer just to get your name in the headlines *yet* again?' She stared hard into Billie's eyes. The accusation stung, but Billie was determined to have her say.

'I think that Charles Carroll's murder could also be linked–' Billie couldn't finish her sentence before her new leader cut over her once again.

'Good God! I thought that job was well put to bed. You couldn't even convince *him* of that one.' Miriam thumbed across to the large photo of the former chief still on the wall, for a few last moments anyway. Billie's mind was racing. How did she know about her conversation with her godfather in this very office the morning before? Had the room been bugged? 'You've been allowed to get away with too many flights of fancy, Wilde. That's nepotism for you. Everyone is aware of the reason you've scaled to such heady heights in the force–'

'I've worked hard and done my job well.' Billie decided it was her turn to butt in. That accusation followed her around like a bad smell. She was adamant it was unjustified. Miriam Nelson sneered.

'You don't know the half of it, love. Well, let's hope so, because if I find out you were in on the corrupt practices of your dear old god-daddy then I'll have you strung up as well. I'm guessing that he didn't want to fill up your pretty little head with his dirty dealings. Did you a big favour topping himself. Think about that in the dead of night. He probably had you on his mind when he drank himself to death.' The new chief had a grim smile on her face.

'I don't need to listen to this.' Billie turned and headed for the door.

'Oh you do, my girl. From now on I bark, and you jump. Got that? I have no doubt you'll trip over your size sevens soon enough without me having to push. Then we'll get some proper coppers back in place. Now, get out there and mop up all of the dead ducks doing the rounds, without building them up to be bloody murders all the time. If you want the spotlight, my love, you should nip down to that film set and ask for a job as an extra. Plus, you'll finally have to shut that smart little mouth of yours and follow orders.'

Billie kicked the door with her boot and marched out. Give up on any murder investigation? It wasn't going to happen, not on her watch. *Over my dead body*, she screamed to herself, almost bumping into Perry Gooch.

'Pass the baton. My turn for the naughty step.' She winked at Billie as she headed in. Billie glanced over her shoulder. It was clear to see that Miriam Nelson was already eyeing up another scalp to add to her growing collection of battle trophies.

9

A PIG IN A BLANKET

The Chief's body had been 'canoed' in the slang police parlance, that neither Billie nor Ash were using today. Billie felt her body rocking on her feet slightly as Josta carefully conducted her extensive examination.

'I told you I would take care of this, boss,' Ash whispered, catching hold of Billie's arm, as she steadied herself against the back wall of the morgue. In the year since her horrific early childhood life had been revealed, during the Magpie investigation, Billie had learned to take control of the ever-decreasing incidents of post-traumatic stress that had plagued her throughout her lifetime. However, today, with the Chief's body more or less hollowed out of organs, disturbing memories had started to hopscotch through her mind once more. Billie silently but sharply gave herself a ticking off. She had to keep it together.

Josta glanced up at Billie through her specs which were, as usual, perched on the end of her nose, as she concentrated on the procedure. To her side, an assistant wrote up notes and carried out procedures as directed by Josta as she passed flesh, bone and organs across.

'Stomach contents are interesting...' she started.

Billie regained her focus. She'd been in the company of relatives who had not been allowed to view their loved ones following a disfiguring homicide and suffered terribly because of their not having felt able to say their last goodbyes. But what had always been clear to Billie and was the case not only now, but when the Chief had rolled over to face her on the top of the monument, was that the person had already left the building. That was how Josta had explained her ease around cadavers. They were just empty homes, that their former owners sometimes left in a mess. Billie brought that thought to the fore now.

'There wasn't much whisky left in the bottle,' Billie offered. It was the Chief's usual choice of spirit if he wasn't imbibing expensive wine.

'Not much evidence of any in his stomach either,' Josta replied. 'Alcohol, yes, but further tests will confirm that it is likely to have been mezcal, tequila's huskier, smokier cousin.'

'I've never seen him drink anything like that.' Billie frowned.

'How can you tell the difference?' Ash queried.

'Because of this–' Josta reached to one side and took a small dish from her assistant, waving it towards Billie and Ash. 'Tequila doesn't actually have a worm in the bottom of the bottle, whereas the theory goes that a strong bottle of pure mezcal can be spotted by the presence of an intact worm. There is also a myth that it can provoke hallucinations. Probably a marketing strategy rather than the truth.' Billie and Ash leaned forward, better to survey a fat maggoty creature.

'It's actually a moth larva, though people call it a worm, *gusano de maguey*, feeding off the maguey plant that the alcohol is produced from. This little fellow, had he not been drowned then digested, would have turned into a night butterfly called Mariposa.'

'But the Chief would never have eaten *that* whole.' Billie felt squeamish at the thought.

'In Mexico, these little grubs are extremely popular. Usually dried and ground into salt to take with the drink. They are also popular in tacos and similar dishes, simply as a protein source, much as we eat cows in the UK because they are handy. But my guess is that this might have been encased in an ice cube within the drink.' Josta lifted the dish back onto the counter.

'Why?' Ash shrugged.

'To send some sort of message?' Billie answered, her mind starting to work overtime.

'I'm afraid motivation is your bag, not mine.' Josta pushed her specs back into place. 'But what I will say is that the worm didn't kill him and it's unlikely that mezcal did either, though both were probably his last supper. His kidneys are shot to hell, he has high levels of urinary calcium oxalate crystals in his system and together with the sweet smell in the air, I'm guessing that the cause of death is ethylene glycol poisoning.'

'Who would have easy access to that?' Billie wondered.

'Most people. Antifreeze, to use its common name, is stored in most garages. Easy to mix in drinks because of its seductively sweet smell and it is colourless. I've dealt with it before, when a woman slipped it into a jelly and killed off her husband. At first it has similar effects to any booze overdose, for example slurring speech and stumbling or maybe just fatigue and headache...' Josta trailed off for a moment as she started to stitch up the body. Billie's mind turned to her approach to the top of Penshaw Monument.

'No way could the Chief have been drunk before he got up there,' she said, remembering the little door, the tight space to the top and the risk of tumbling over the low wall at the side of the walkway.

'The danger comes from the way in which the body

metabolises ethyl alcohol.' Josta completed a neat row of stitches, not unlike a master tailor tacking together a new suit. 'As enzymes break down, a cascading chemical reaction ensues, resulting in sharp crystals slicing the kidney's cells apart. Early reaction to such poisoning causes vomiting. Death doesn't usually occur until hours or even a few days later, when the kidneys become sufficiently damaged, should there be no medical intervention.'

'But he'd been in custody. Surely a doctor would have been called if he showed signs of illness?' Billie queried. She thought of his appearance when she had met with the Chief the night before. He had seemed tired and somewhat breathless and had been rubbing his head, but she had put that down to the stress of his imminent arrest. Had she missed an opportunity to save him?

'So, could someone have initially poisoned him with a big dose of antifreeze, then later, after he had been released from custody, helped him climb the staircase up to the top of Penshaw Monument before finishing him off with a large chaser of mezcal, complete with worm?' Ash asked Josta, clearly struggling with the scenario as much as Billie was.

'Possibly.' Josta shrugged. 'Or he could have drunk the antifreeze earlier himself. There are plenty of suicides with antifreeze. I understand your concerns re: the ability to access the scene of death whilst drugged and suffering the effects, but you would be surprised what some people are capable of when they have their minds set on suicide. I'm afraid where there is a real will, there is often a way found.' Billie still didn't believe it was possible. 'Another scenario could be that it was decanted into a soft drinks bottle, and he mistakenly drank it without realising.'

'I'm going to check what he had to eat in custody and if he needed any medical help there,' Billie announced.

'Also check the exact time that he was released,' Ash added helpfully.

Billie dug her hand in her pocket in search of her phone.

'Could this have been an inside job?' She frowned at Ash. It didn't seem possible but if the powers that ruled wanted some police misdemeanour covered up, was it such a wild idea? Billie suddenly thought of her father and his illegal police activities way back in time. The resulting truth had shattered many lives, yet, that desperately dark scandal had been well and truly buried. Billie felt a wash of shame. She had been complicit in the cover-up by not speaking out when she had discovered the shocking truth. It was a sobering thought, as was the realisation that the Chief's mobile hadn't been found by his body, yet Billie had received a text from it earlier in the night. Her own mobile suddenly rang in her hand.

'DSI Billie Wilde,' she answered, turning her gaze away from the harrowing scene in front of her.

'It's Mary. Mary Carroll,' the woman's voice clarified. 'I've bitten the bullet and made a start on clearing out Charles's belongings. I'm taking all of his Alice dresses down to Aunt Fanny's. His fem attire is far too big and bling for me. The girls down there will have a field day.'

'I'm sure,' Billie answered, before waiting for more. She doubted Mary had called to offer her a pair of her deceased husband's second-hand size-ten slingbacks.

'It's amazing what he had beavered away in that shed down at the bottom of the garden. His crochet stuff, handbag store, paperwork – he had a little office set up there too, for his writing and so forth.'

'I imagine it's all bagged up, if the police took it away as evidence.' Billie knew that there was zero chance that they would have unpacked it and put it away neatly again. She wondered where this conversation was going. Maybe Mary was simply feeling lonely and wanted someone to talk to.

'The police never went into the shed after Charles was killed. They said that there was no need. They had all the evidence required for convicting Will on the CCTV footage,' Mary answered. Billie's ears pricked up. She had been on enforced leave when Charles Carroll's murder had occurred, and the Chief had brought in a SIO from a neighbouring force. One of his golf buddies, Billie recalled. Had it been on her watch, the shed would have been stripped bare.

'So this is the first time the shed has been accessed since Charles passed away?' Billie still couldn't quite believe what she was hearing.

'Precisely.' Mary's voice changed slightly. Higher, a nervy edge to the word. Billie sensed that the reason for the call was about to be revealed. 'And as I was going through his handbags I found a mobile phone. In a pink cover, to match the bag. I've just charged it up, wondering if there were any photos on there from our girlie awaydays. One wants to cherish every memory...'

Mary trailed off, as a mortuary technician started to wheel the Chief's body away. His arm fell down as he passed by Billie, as though he was reaching his hand out. Billie longed to chase after the gurney and feel that reassuring touch one last time.

'But there weren't any photos,' Mary continued as the door slammed shut on Billie's last memory of the Chief. She hoped it was one that would fade in time. Billie tried to focus on the conversation. She hit the loudspeaker so that Ash could listen in too. 'Just text messages. Threats. Warnings for Charles to keep his mouth shut, or else and a shocking photo. It's made me feel quite faint.' Mary's voice wobbled. Billie and Ash exchanged glances. They had both started moving in unison towards the exit door.

'Do you know who they are from?' Billie asked, as they

entered the mortuary corridor and hurried out towards the car park. She glanced through an open door, spotting the Chief being slotted into a refrigerator cabinet. The scene was particularly ironic as Billie was well aware that he had been keen to retire to a place with different scenery. Somewhere he could chill out for the rest of his days.

'All the messages seem to have come from someone with the initials TMH. It's just the one name. I can go through the settings and–'

'No!' Billie heard the alarm in her own voice. Tempered it. 'Just put the mobile down in a safe place, Mary. We will deal with all of that. We're on our way now.'

'All right.' Mary sounded relieved. 'I'll put the kettle on. I think we need a cup of sweet tea for the shock.'

'You can say that again,' Ash answered, clicking on his car keys as they hurried out of the door and across the car park outside. Billie wanted to say that she wasn't shocked at all. A hidden truth had always felt to her like a splinter festering under the skin. Certain to aggravate its rotten way up to the surface and painfully emerge in the end.

'TMH?' Billie enquired as they stared at the photo. It was of a pig, throat slashed, bloodstains covering the baby-blue ribbon fastening the white frilled bonnet placed on its head. A crochet blanket lay open beneath the slaughtered animal revealing a large knife. Broken pieces of china scattered all around it. Underneath the photo was a text message. '*Don't squeal, pig, or you will be next.*'

'I really have no idea.' Mary's voice broke as she turned away with a pained expression on her face. 'He had lots of colleagues in the education world at various colleges before he retired and his Lewis Carroll appreciation group, so I didn't know all of his friends. But I've never heard of those initials before. I mean, why on earth would anyone threaten Charles?'

'It seems to stop him telling a secret,' Billie replied. 'Mary, think back to the time when Charles was still alive. Was there anyone at all that you can recall that he'd fallen out with? Maybe a friend who was suddenly no longer around?'

'Not really. We were a tight-knit team, especially Alice and I. Of course, I had my craft group and Charles his flower arranging at the church. But we always went to Aunt Fanny's together. Maybe that's it? Perhaps the texts were from someone who was afraid to show his true colours as a cross-dresser. Someone who didn't want Charles to spill to his wife, though it's most unlikely that he would. I often think now of those wasted nights when poor Charles felt he had to retreat down to his shed before he could transform into his Alice persona. It's sad the lengths that some people feel they need to go to hide such a harmless pursuit...'

Ash bagged up the mobile phone just in case the forensics team could find any deleted messages, as Billie poured tea into a porcelain cup laid out on a pretty, embroidered cloth covering the small garden table. She slung a couple of biscuits on the saucer and handed it to Mary. The older woman looked like she might be about to pass out any minute if she didn't get a quick injection of sugar. Billie poured out a couple of cups for herself and Ash too. They hadn't had time for the usual post-mortem cuppa and by God, she was desperate for one of those right now.

'It's so distressing. Charles had so much left to give.' Mary sipped her tea. 'He wrote a film script, you know, about Lewis Carroll's true inspiration for the *Alice* stories. He sent it to a top film producer. Eventually got a letter back turning it down. But I see from the TV news that they are filming something similar now in the area, so he was on the right track.

'Come to think of it, I do recall he was involved in some squabbling online with his Lewis Carroll group – they were either arguing that they deserved some credit for furnishing him with the details used in his script or alternatively, insisting that the stories had no connection to the north-east of England. But Charles wasn't unduly upset. He was very sure of his facts and proud of his work. Would you like to see a copy?'

'Absolutely.' Billie put her cup down and pulled out a pair of latex gloves from the pouch on her duty belt, following Mary towards the shed. A niggling memory was tugging at the edges of her brain, of a chapter within *Alice in Wonderland*, in which the protagonist nurses a crying baby that turns into a pig. In the Tenniel drawings which accompanied the original book, the pig was wearing a bonnet, identical to the one in the threatening photo. Whoever had targeted Charles was well aware of the *Alice* stories and Charles's interest in them.

'Here it is.' Mary lifted a printed script out of the top drawer of Charles Carroll's desk. It was richly bound, the hard cover printed in gold. Always a sign that the writer believed that their scribblings were precious and complete. An immediate signal to a professional in the film world that it had been sent by an amateur scribe. 'Charles always claimed that it was Alice, not he who had told the story. He shed a few tears when he got the final refusal. It was particularly disappointing, because a film bigwig had at first sent a very enthusiastic and positive letter. Then suddenly it came back in the post in a dog-eared envelope, from that same person, with a few terse words of rejection. Charles was so angry that he wrote back to say his copyright was protected and he would be trying elsewhere with his work.'

Billie took the script from Mary's hands and stepped back out of the shed. She was hoping the space was going to be a goldmine of unexplored material and she was at pains not to disrupt the area more than was absolutely essential right now.

'A lot of work had gone into this,' she mused. Clearly it had been a labour of love. Mary fished out the accompanying letter and joined Billie, placing it on top of the script.

'Clearly. That's why this was especially rude if you ask me,' Mary huffed. When Billie looked at the name of the sender, she realised why. Ash had come to peek over Billie's shoulder.

'It's from Arden Roy,' he exclaimed in disbelief.

'There's nothing wrong is there?' Tom whispered as he raced towards Billie from where he had been standing under a tree to her right. She was striding across some grass towards the film set at speed, with Ash close behind. By the layout of the table at the centre and the actors in costume, Billie could see that they were filming the Mad Hatter's Tea Party.

'Let's find out when I've had a word with your dear director.' Billie firmly moved Tom to one side as she continued in the direction of Arden Roy, sitting facing the action, on a black fold-out director's chair with his name printed on the back, lest any mere mortal with aching legs dared to rest in his hallowed space. He was staring at a monitor. Watching the scene directly from the film camera's feed.

'I'm sorry.' Delphine, holding a clipboard, came hurtling towards Billie from the left, also speaking in an urgent whisper. She held her hand up. 'We're filming a scene. You can't go over this line.' She pointed to a taped-off area that Billie was about to breach. The detective was momentarily reminded of a rugby match in which various players tried to tackle the ball carrier down. She dared any one of them to make contact with her. She reached Arden Roy, tapping him hard on the shoulder. He spun around in shock for a split second before recognition kicked in. The director tore his earphones off his head.

'I want a word,' Billie announced loudly. She noticed the Mad Hatter looking to his left and the Dormouse suddenly open his eyes wide, as the Mad March Hare trailed off in mid-speech. Alice had clearly decided that she was wasting time continuing the scene, as she stopped in mid-action, looking at Billie. Arden Roy's face had instantaneously turned puce with fury.

'How dare you. This is outrageous!' he bellowed. Billie waved Charles Carroll's script in the director's face.

'Yes it is. I believe this script, the one that you rejected from Charles Carroll, is the one that you are filming right now. The one that I believe you have been telling the world that you wrote yourself.'

'Cut,' the assistant director shouted. 'Let's take five,' he added. Though no one moved. All had eyes on Billie.

'How dare you. I shall make complaints at the highest level!' Arden Roy flung his earphones on the ground. Tom raced to pick them up and place them on the monitor unit before backing off.

'As I'm sure Charles Carroll would.' Billie held up the script again and pulled out the letter of rejection.

'Here's the letter you sent him saying you didn't want his work. I also have the copy of the earlier one you sent, claiming that you loved his script and were sure that you could get financial backing to make the film. He replied explaining why Sunderland would be a great location and hey, here we all are, as if by magic... or plagiarism.'

'Absolute rubbish. I receive hundreds of scripts from wannabee writers. Most of them are utter trash. My film is completely different. Box office gold.'

'I'm sure there's lots of money to be made from the film, so lots of reasons to shut the true writer up. Did you send this?' Billie flicked her mobile phone on, showing a copy of the threatening photo Charles Carroll had received. 'A baby that turns into a pig. The person who sent it certainly knew their *Alice in Wonderland*, and also how to scare someone into shutting up. Charles Carroll was dead two weeks after he received it. Bit of a coincidence, don't you think?' Arden Roy pulled his head back as Billie shoved her phone close to his face, then sprang up from his chair like a crazed leprechaun.

'Are you accusing me? Despicable lies! Haven't the police got anything better to do with their time? I'm trying to make a damn movie here. *My* damn movie. Do you hear?' he shouted, before storming off. 'You – bring me some herbal tea in my trailer.' Arden Roy flicked his fingers at Tom who jumped into action.

'That's code for strong drink,' a voice whispered in Billie's ear. It was Maya. 'I hear that Jack Daniels is his tipple of choice. It usually comes disguised in a coffee flask mid-afternoon. Ask our new caterer here.' Billie turned around to see Ellis standing next to Ash. He was wearing chef whites and a stripey blue apron.

'You certainly know how to make an entrance.' Ellis chuckled.

'Been demoted, Tweedledum?' Billie responded. She guessed that she was going to get it in the neck again from Miriam Nelson. Arden Roy would be pulling any high-level strings he could muster to shut her up and so far, though Ash was wavering, she was the only one totally convinced that Charles Carroll's murder was linked to that of Pippa Sykes and the Chief through the *Alice* symbols.

'Done all my acting stuff. Now my client wants me to hunker down with the catering staff. It's amazing what people will tell you for an extra helping of meat and two veg.' He winked.

'You get way more out of the make-up crew,' Maya said. 'The hot gossip there is that the lovely Arden Roy hasn't made a blockbuster film in years, and he would apparently sell his own mother to ensure it's a hit.'

'All the more reason to steal a script and take the credit.' Billie intended to get her hands on the actual script being used. She might yet be proven wrong, but she had a huge hunch that Arden Roy was hiding something big and she didn't have time to wheedle it out of him in a sweet courtly fashion.

'He's made a few enemies,' Ellis added, his eyes on the exceptionally beautiful up-and-coming actress Luna Da Costa, playing the Red Queen, as he spoke. 'Got a few secrets too, it seems. People might be threatening to spill some beans that would mess up his penthouse suite at the last-chance hotel.' Billie mentally high-fived herself, she knew that she had been right.

'Intriguing,' Billie answered. 'Is that what your current placement is about?' She nudged him. 'Is my main suspect already in someone else's sights? A MeToo type of claim, perhaps?' Like the rest of the world, Billie was aware of streams of actresses coming out of the woodwork to tell their casting couch stories. Some gave true heartbreaking accounts of abuse of power, others spun fairy tales, determined to step into the spotlight by any means. Discovering the truth was often a nightmare for investigators in those cases.

'Now, you know the rules. If I told you my secret, I would have to kill you.' Ellis gave a tight-lipped smile.

Billie suddenly spotted Perry Gooch wandering towards her.

'Didn't I just leave you hoofing it into the headmistress's office? Thought you would still be writing your hundred lines out and then staying late in detention,' Billie teased.

'Worse than that. Permanent suspension and a police guard from the premises,' Perry huffed.

'You are joking?' Billie exchanged glances of outrage with Ash.

'Nope. She gave me my marching orders last night, but I'd already agreed to talk to your troops by then, so I came in anyway. Hence saying my final goodbye to two hunky men in uniform. Got to look on the bright side. I upset her when I was a journo a couple of years back with a story I wrote in the paper, so we were never going to be bosom buddies. You know the feeling. Been there and got the T-shirt.' Perry winked at Billie. It was true, they had often been at loggerheads in the past when Billie had taken issue with what Perry had printed. Now she understood it had never been personal.

'Anyway, I've got a mortgage to pay at the end of the month, so I got straight on the blower and bagged this little job for the local freebie. On set with the stars. Upbeat vibe piece. I was just getting bored interviewing Luna Da Costa, who in my opinion has the acting capacity of a very attractive but empty bag of crisps, when you pop in to lighten up the day.'

Billie thought about the picture of the pig on her phone. She could be heading the same way as Perry if she went through with the idea suddenly forming in her mind. No doubt Miriam Nelson would go ballistic, but Billie thought of the Chief instead. He'd always taught her to trust her instincts and her instincts told her she had to work fast, or other people were going to be killed. She suddenly felt reckless with grief and anger.

'Look at this.' Billie held the picture of the slaughtered pig up for Perry to see. 'Any thoughts? You're our resident Lewis Carroll expert. Any of your contacts, when you did your research for your newspaper article about the subject, capable of sending this?'

Perry glanced at the picture, blowing air through her lips. She raised her eyebrows. 'Not another crazy to add to your long collection. This sent to you?'

'Nope. Charles Carroll, before he was hit over the head with a spade and then buried alive. I don't think that there's a chance in hell that Will Cox sent it. I need to catch this person before

they do any more damage. Can you print this in your paper?'
Perry appeared taken aback.

'Is that wise? Nelson will have your head–'

'She won't lose any sleep over the Chief, but he was my god–'
Billie stopped, alarmed that tears had sprung into her eyes. The
thought sank through Billie's brain that she should be used to
those by now, with her history. However, the waves of sorrow
coming from out of the blue never failed to startle. Perry put her
hand on Billie's arm.

'I know where you're coming from.' Perry nodded. 'He was a
good guy. Look, the little rag I'm doing this story for would be a
waste of time. But I've got a contact for *The Evening Post.* They
have a huge readership. Still got time to get it in tonight's edition
and on the web, of course. But can you take the flak? You know
that you are easy meat for newspapers, not exactly looking like
your average plod and you've never been flavour of the month in
the local press. They'll go to town with the package of you and
the pig. Put some unexpected spin on it.'

Billie heard what Perry was saying. But every instinct in her
body told her that there would be more suffering in store if she
didn't get the killer quickly. The photo would attract attention,
cause a lot of chatter, and hopefully bring in vital information.

'If it helps catch a killer, I don't give a damn what they say
about me.' Billie had bigger worries than getting pretty press
accolades...

'The pig in the bonnet has local links, by the way. The *Tithe
Pig* was a poem produced on the china made at the pottery just
up the road here, way before the *Alice* stories were written.'

'That's what the broken pottery in the photo must refer to.'
Billie looked at the photo again. Her money was on a killer with
local links, in that case. Few people would know the details that
Perry had just shared.

'Looks like it.' Perry nodded. 'It's the same sort of china. The rhyme follows a vicar trying to collect his tithes from a farmer and his wife. In order not to pay any duty on a newborn pig, the animal was wrapped up in a shawl and passed off as a child.'

'Just like the photo and the threat seems to imply a cover-up.' Billie felt her heart racing. She hoped that they were finally onto something important.

'Many locals think the poem inspired Lewis Carroll. He used to visit his sister who lived next door to the pottery. They also produced printed tea sets with a tea party design.' Perry shrugged. 'If you are certain you want to go for it. All the elements together will make it a front page in *The Evening Post*, for certain. Sure that you can live with that?'

Billie glanced across to Ash. Luckily he was deep in conversation with Maya and Ellis. She felt sure that he would counsel against her idea.

'Let's go for it.' Billie shared the photo and watched Perry rush off to sell the story. She swallowed hard. If Miriam Nelson didn't see the possibilities in her strategy, then her beloved Chief wouldn't be the only police officer marched out of the job and kicked in the gutter. Billie would also be police dead meat.

10

BILLIE NO FRIENDS

'Look away now, if you're feeling squeamish.' Boo tapped on her keyboard and brought up the online version of *The Evening Post's* news.

PIGS PORKY PIES?

Crime figures said to be sky high, but film production put in jeopardy whilst police try to root out pig killer. Top murder detective wallows in the spotlight once again. But is she about to get the chop?

The headline read in bold black lettering.

Underneath ran several columns of an interview with Arden Roy talking to a staff *Evening Post* reporter, in which he lamented the sad accidental loss of a much-loved cast member, having eaten a dicky mushroom. Yet he was determined to bravely continue on with the shoot. He vowed to bring the bacon home to the local people, who desperately needed the revenue brought in by the film, if only the police would stop harassing the production with their wild suspicions.

Two photos completed the front page. One was of Pippa

Sykes smiling prettily out of the picture, sadly never aware of her fleeting date with front-page fame. The other showed the slaughtered pig in babies' clothes, which had been sent to Charles Carroll. As far as Billie was concerned, it was a job well done. The police harassment insinuations were water off a duck's back.

'Well, that gives Miriam Nelson something to cut out and decorate her new wall with.' She smiled benignly at Boo.

'You know she's going to go ballistic?' Boo flicked the screenshot away. Billie shrugged.

'So what's new?' Billie answered. 'Seeing Ellis tonight? He's working on the catering truck now. Might be heading your way with a tasty morsel or two.'

'I'm not seeing him tonight.' Boo shrugged. 'Familiarity breeds contempt and all that...' she added.

'But I thought you'd gone all love's young dream, having been star-crossed lovers for so long?' Billie was surprised to hear Boo's lack of enthusiastic response. She and Ellis had just recently been reunited. They had harboured an underlying attraction as work partners years before and then been tragically separated. Billie had expected it now to be a story of living happily ever after.

'Yeah?' Boo sighed. 'Well, don't get me wrong, we still get along well, but the reality is that I have more of, I dunno, a sisterly love for him, you know?'

'Sounds like me and David.' Billie smiled sadly, thinking of her dashing former fiancé. David may have still been around now if they had been more truthful about the nature of their feelings for one another. 'Still, it's early days for you both... fancy a drink then?' Billie was hoping for a chance to go through any new leads with her key team members, in The Cop-Out pub around the corner, to delay facing the wrath of Miriam Nelson, newspaper in hand. If she was in the building, Billie had no doubt that the new chief would be heading her way in a murderous mood. Boo glanced at the clock on the wall.

'Sorry, got to shoot off. Got something on tonight.' She reached for her jacket. Billie had been aware of Boo's sparkling eyes and upbeat manner of late. She had put it down to having found her old flame Ellis, but now she wasn't so sure.

'Why the secret squirrel act?' Billie smiled. 'If I didn't know better, I would say you look like you're off on a date,' she teased.

'Always the detective,' Boo answered through a laugh. 'Me and men, it's like buses. Nothing comes my way for an age and then...'

'So you *are*!' Billie put on a show of shock.

'What?' Boo giggled. 'So I have more than one man interested in me. Why look so amazed? I am a pretty hot chick, you know. Who could resist these sexy wheels? Ellis and I haven't made any forever vows. I've lived too long by myself to put up with other people's quirks twenty-four seven.'

'And here was me expecting to have to rush out and buy a new hat any day now.' Billie pretended to be gutted.

'Yes, well maybe because you've actually found *your* Mr Darcy,' Boo joked.

'Ellis isn't bad-looking,' Billie argued. 'Quirky maybe, but quirky's good,' she added, as Ash entered, waving the evening newspaper with Billie's picture on the front. 'Right. That's me out of here, before Nelson returns on her high horse. Ash, are you coming to the pub to tell me how your afternoon interviews at our favourite film base panned out?' Billie grabbed her bag and stood up as Ash dropped his files on his desk.

'Sorry, boss. Nothing much new to tell and I've got to run. I promised one-to-one time with Indie,' Ash explained, reminding Boo of his intricate child-access arrangements. 'I'm bringing her round to ours for tea and then dropping her over to her friend's for a sleepover.'

'So we can hit the village pub later?' Billie raised her eyebrows hopefully.

'Sorry. I've got a date tonight.' His lovely smiley eyes crinkled as he grinned.

'What, you as well?' Billie pretended to be astonished. 'Okay that's me, Billie no friends,' she announced, following Ash and Boo out to the lift, thinking of Max. She suddenly desperately wanted him to be back with her tonight. As she waved her two closest friends off, Billie grabbed her car keys from her pocket. The visit to the pub had been aversion tactics in truth. She was well aware of the location she had to head to next and she was definitely not looking forward to it.

'You've got some nerve, to show your face here,' David's mother said as she answered the door, her eyes puffed and nose pink. 'Every time you come within the vicinity of this house, someone pays a terrible price.' She sniffed, blowing her nose with a delicate linen handkerchief. Billie wondered if the woman had ever paused to think of the losses that Billie herself had suffered in the past year. Her whole family, new and old members, wiped clean out and now her godfather, the Chief too.

Billie stepped in the hallway that she had once known so well, and shivered. It had always felt cold here. In the past, David's mother would have snapped at Billie to take her shoes off before entering, but today, as she picked up her glass of wine and turned towards the grand lounge, she was either too upset or too inebriated to remember.

'The Chief was here last night...' Billie started before David's mother cut across her.

'Before he was dragged away, and where were you?' she hissed. 'Where was his dear, beloved god-daughter when there was nothing in it for her?' She took a large swig of wine. Had the words come from anyone else, then they would have stung, but Billie was pretty much immune to the vicious pointed comments endlessly fired at her by the woman, arrows of wasted energy that largely failed to hit their mark. One thing that Billie had clocked throughout the tirade, was that the Chief hadn't told David's mum about his last-minute meeting with Billie just around the corner from this house, the night before, nor entrusted her with his box of secrets.

'Did he return here after being released?' Billie continued.

'No he didn't,' David's mother answered. 'More's the pity. But no doubt he hadn't wanted to upset me further after the terrible night I had to endure. The neighbour's curtains twitching, people coming out to urgently tend to their cars, ears flapping all the while. The shame of it all.' She took another large swig of wine, full of self-pity, Billie surmised, rather than grief.

'Did he eat anything whilst he was here that made him ill?' Billie continued. David's mother stopped drinking for a moment to turn her hard stare onto Billie. 'Or drink anything?' Billie nodded to the half-empty bottle of champagne standing on the table.

'Here? What are you trying to insinuate?' she demanded.

'I'm simply trying to be clear whether he ate or drank anything that may have contributed to his death and at what times any such intake may have occurred.' Billie ran her fingers through her hair. Talking of the Chief's death, in the vicinity where she had last encountered him alive, was starting to upset her somewhat.

'He didn't drink or eat anything at all whilst he was here. If I'd guessed what was about to happen, then I could have made him a special last supper.' David's mother finally flopped down onto one of the huge armchairs flanking the marble fireplace, suddenly thoughtful.

'I was known as a marvellous hostess, Philomena.' David's mother was the only person in the world who had ever used her full name. Thank God she had therefore rarely heard it. 'I did achieve some small measure of success myself,' she added. 'People always said that my vol-au-vents were to die for,' she whispered.

Like Billie's own adoptive mother, David's mum had been a trophy wife – well bred, well turned out and well versed in how to keep their men happy when at home – without asking too many questions about their murky dealings in the outside world. When her husband had died, David's mother's sense of survival had kicked in. She seemed to have avoided being swept away to the distant shores of has-beens, by clinging limpet-like to the chief of police, in the hope of leeching out any last vestige of reflected glory.

'The police were investigating some sort of corruption charge against him. Do you have any idea what that might have been about?' Billie asked. David's mother drained her glass and reached for the champagne bottle. Billie moved it out of reach. 'After all, you've kept a lot of secrets in the past,' Billie added, not being able to help herself. David's mother smirked.

'Think you know it all, don't you, young lady?' David's mother mocked. 'If I did know anything do you *really* think I would share it with you?' She leaned over and yanked the champagne bottle back, pouring her glass full to the brim.

'Maybe. If you are keen to get justice for the Chief. Clearly you've been mates shall we say, since, hmmm, I dunno, maybe a couple of minutes after David's dad snuffed it?'

Billie cursed herself for letting her emotions get the better of her. The Chief had been well aware, if not a little amused, at Billie's lack of enthusiasm for his liaisons with this irritating female. It was clear that he had a roving eye and David's mum, whatever she may have assumed, wasn't the only person that he courted. But this woman with the well-faded beauty and powdered, rose-tinted wrinkles, might be the only hope, Billie reflected, of shedding some truth on the Chief's demise.

'Maybe he couldn't face you digging about in his past,' David's mum snapped. 'We all saw how that ended up last time,' she added.

'I have no idea what the Chief was being investigated for, but I was ready to defend him, whatever the circumstances,' Billie answered firmly.

'Really? Surely you remember the threats that you hurled at my husband, just before his death?'

'I've kept schtum about the fact that you knew all about corruption amongst powerful men in this area and didn't intervene at the time. In fact, you benefitted,' Billie answered, swallowing hard as she remembered her former fiancé.

'Do you think that I had a say in anything that happened back then?' David's mother protested. 'You view the past through your present privileged position. When I married, I had to give up work. All women did. It reflected badly on their husband's ability to provide if his wife worked. End of story. I had my secretarial certificate, but I wasn't able to make use of that. I was given an allowance and expected to look pretty and *keep schtum*. Of course, when you knew my husband, he was older, more mellow, but in his younger days he didn't take kindly to anyone who tried to stand up against him...'

Billie suddenly had a picture in her mind's eye of David's father sitting as a judge in court. She had sometimes seen a cold dark glint in his eye, when addressing those in the dock. There was a beat of truth in his widow's words.

'Oh yes, the make-up course I took wasn't simply to while away the time, though God knows I needed something to fill my days, but it also helped me cover the black eyes, the bruises. I once had a broken arm. Had to present at hospital saying that I had stupidly stepped in front of my husband when he was taking a swing with his golf club. Nobody at all asked if I was on a golf course at the time. No, the esteemed judge's wife was cowering in the laundry cupboard paying the penalty because his shirt hadn't been ironed to his high standards. That was the truth of it.'

'I didn't know...' Billie started, absolutely shocked at the revelations. David's mum shook her head, a grim smile on her face.

'That's the trouble, you young women think you know it all today. Make judgements on other females who you don't think come up to scratch, based on your own easy rides. But you've known the truth about your own past for a year now and we don't hear about *that* in the news, amongst all of your front-page headlines proclaiming feats of derring-do. So, what's your excuse? Nobody's bearing down on you with their heaviest golf iron, pointing out that it gives more power on impact.'

Billie swallowed hard. The woman did have a point. With the killers unable to face a trial, the full background to the Magpie killings had never come to light. Billie had been desperate to protect her father's good name, despite the hideous truth.

'I'm sorry.' Billie rubbed her face, walking over to offer comfort to the woman. She suddenly looked crumpled and small.

'Don't you dare touch me.' She shied away as Billie reached out to touch her arm. 'It's too late. You're as bad as they were. Worse!'

'I'll do my best to find out who killed the Chief. Whatever people say, I don't believe that he took his own life,' Billie vowed.

'He would never have taken his own life. He had me.' David's mother wiped the tears trickling down from her eyes. 'And he'd just met his own child for the first time.' She sniffed. Billie wondered if she had heard right.

'The Chief didn't have any children.' She frowned. 'He would have told me–'

'Maybe he didn't like you as much as you think,' David's mother said through a vicious smile. 'Maybe you aren't the golden child after all. Don't expect to inherit all his worldly goods if that's what you were hoping–'

'I wasn't.' The thought hadn't even crossed Billie's mind. Her feelings swung from pity to disgust at the woman once again.

'Well, that's all right then. Because he was thrilled to discover that his bloodline would live on and my money's on his real kid getting the whole fandango.' She took a swig of her champagne, looking smug as Billie's phone buzzed. She glanced at the text message.

It's Josta. Urgent. Come around immediately. We have news.

Billie's heart hit the floor. Had something happened to Max? She turned around to face David's mother.

'This isn't over yet,' she said, still reeling from the new information.

'For me it is,' the older woman answered. 'Now do something useful for once in your life, close that door on your way out.'

Billie raced out to her car, leaving the door wide open. Praying to God that it wasn't over for Max too.

11

BEHIND CLOSED DOORS

B illie burst through Josta's door, her heart hammering against her chest, noting that she had been lucky not to have been pulled by a traffic cop on the way over. Max had said he was going to West Africa, but where exactly? Billie remembered the crying child close by, half drowning out their last conversation. She hadn't exactly been sitting watching twenty-four-hour news all day, so wasn't up to date on any new disasters that may have occurred around the world.

The hallway was silent, except for the loud ticking of the grandfather clock against one wall.

'Hello, Josta?' Billie called, moving along the hallway. She suddenly heard voices from the back of the house, where Josta and Lola's huge open-plan kitchen lay. Billie swallowed hard and marched towards the closed door, dreading what she might discover on opening it.

'Surprise!' Billie was faced by Josta, Lola and a bunch of smiling-faced people as she blinked in the bright light. She recognised Josta's old friend, Isabelle. The others milling around appeared to be friends of Lola, dressed in a mix of scruffy ripped denim and colourful, not-shy-to-show-off bohemian outfits.

'What's going on?' Billie approached Josta, who on seeing her had already started pouring from a bottle of her usual claret. She handed the large glassful to Billie, who shook her head in response, even as she took the glass being forcibly offered.

'We're celebrating some good news.' Josta smiled. 'I thought you could do with a celebratory drink after your traumas of today and, of course, you and I can also raise a toast to your dear departed godfather,' she added softly, chinking Billie's glass. Tears suddenly welled up in Billie's eyes, overcome by the emotion of the day. The horror of the Chief's demise, along with the panic that Josta's text had been related to Max's activities, had finally got to her.

'There, there, dear girl.' Josta patted Billie's shoulders as Lola approached in a colourful outfit.

'Has Josta told you my amazing news?' she asked, all eyes and teeth as befitted a lifelong actress. Billie looked from Lola to Josta, bewildered.

'No, I thought the text... I thought something had happened to Max.' She ran her fingers through her hair. Clearly she had misinterpreted the reason for the urgency of the message.

'My Teflon boy?' Josta chuckled. 'You'll have to stop worrying so about him, Billie dear. He thrives on getting out of tight scrapes. That's what makes him tick.' Josta's eyes twinkled at the mention of her beloved son.

'And we wanted you here, as you are soon to become family.' Lola, Max's other mother, stroked her fingers down Billie's cheek affectionately.

'Sorry, what?' Billie wondered if it might be an idea to go back out of the door, come in calmly and start all over again. Nothing seemed to be making any sense.

'I've just been told that I've landed the part of the Queen of Hearts in the *Alice* film shooting here.'

'So a star is reborn, my dear.' Josta wrapped her arm around

Lola's shoulders and planted a kiss on her cheek. 'Though she has always remained a star to me, even when she's been away treading the boards in some far-off godforsaken hellhole on the other side of the country, leaving me to make small talk with the dead.' Lola chuckled.

'You're still my number one, sweetheart,' she said, teasing Josta.

'First in line for your autograph, my dear.' Josta and Lola looked at one another like newlyweds.

'And you are to marry our darling boy' – Lola caught Billie's hand – 'so, of course I wanted you here tonight to share my good news, even though Max can't make it.' Billie wondered if they had been on the wine for some time, as she still wasn't making any sense of the conversation.

'Congratulations about the part,' Billie started, amusing herself briefly with the thought of Arden Roy taking on the direction of Lola, a character naturally slanted to doing things her own larger-than-life way. It would no doubt make for interesting entertainment.

'And to you also for bagging Max.' Josta clinked glasses with Billie again. 'He told me this morning that you are about to move in together, start plans to make it legal.' Josta winked. 'Though I always knew that you were made for one another.'

'He told you that?' Billie answered, her mind racing through the conversation that she and Max had shared the night before, about moving away together, after which he had told her that he loved her. He hadn't proposed though.

'He tells us everything, darling. We're his crazy devoted mothers after all.' Lola kissed Billie on the cheek, before one of her theatrical friends pulled her away into another group. Billie put down her glass.

'I think congratulations in my case are a bit premature,' she started to say to Josta.

'Forgive us, if we are getting overenthusiastic about the buying of hats.' Josta chuckled deeply. 'It's just after that business with Natalie, we didn't think that Max would ever settle again. Such a sensitive soul,' she added. 'You have certainly brought calm and contentment to his life since you came into it and, of course, because of our dear working friendship I am particularly delighted. Can I interest you in a sausage?' Josta reached over and lifted a plateful of sticky sausages from amongst an array of other nibbles. Each meaty tube had several deep knife marks in it.

'You didn't tell me that you're working a blade case?' Billie looked the plate over. Josta was notorious for testing out stabbing theories at home with her vast collection of knives and whatever cut of meat she could find cowering at the back of the fridge.

'Next door's patch, dear heart. I never kiss and tell.' She winked.

'Max did mention us travelling together a bit,' Billie said, trying to clarify the situation, whilst wondering if she had a sudden fit of amnesia. They definitely hadn't sat down and agreed to move in together, but was it such a bad idea? She was missing him like mad at the moment. Was it too soon after everything that had happened with David? It sounded like Max had finally put his heartache over the tragedy involving Natalie, his first wife, to bed. Would it be such a terrible plan?

'Hi.' Billie turned, taking a second to recognise the pretty, dark-haired young woman smiling at her. 'Fredi, the make-up artist from the film set, remember?'

'Oh, yes. Hi.' Billie was pleased to be able to turn her mind back to murder for a while. 'How's it going down there?'

'Bit stressy to be honest,' Fredi answered. 'And not just because of your lot coming from all directions asking questions. People on film sets have a lot to hide after all.' Fredi grinned.

'Really?' Billie's ears pricked up. 'Like what?'

'Well, like most things.' Fredi shrugged. 'After all, none of the actors look any different to the average guy or girl in the street until I've done my job along with costume and lighting, but the public never see them like that. And many of them have partners and families hidden away at home, though they play the part of being single and fancy-free, as far as their publicity is concerned. The PR teams insist on it. Fans want to fantasise about marrying them. They don't see the spots and styes in eyes that I have to cover up. Or the morning hangovers, with a sick bucket by my make-up place.' She shook her head in amusement at the assorted memories.

'Let's face it, lots of male fans would be heartbroken, if they knew the truth that our new star, Luna Da Costa has a husband and kid back home in some sad London suburb. Nobody recognises her hauling a pushchair on the bus without her make-up on, using her married name, or when she's working the till at the exotic pet shop she runs with her hubby when she's out of luck with acting jobs. They probably spend days cleaning out iguana and parrot poo.' Fredi laughed. 'Doesn't sound sexy, though, the truth about most actors' real lives, having to scrape a living between acting jobs.'

'I'm intrigued,' Billie admitted. Maya had been right, Fredi could offer a goldmine of behind-the-scenes information.

'We're away in a bubble for several weeks making every film, so a lot goes on behind closed doors. Sometimes it's safe for family to visit. But we have a saying in the business: "what goes on set, stays on set". It's a bit like a secret society.' Fredi grinned again. 'So this is nice. I just came along to measure up Lola for her wig, now she's been cast as Queen of Hearts. I hadn't realised that I was coming to a party.'

'Where Lola is concerned life is one long party.' Josta had overheard and shared her view of her beloved as she squeezed past, biting the head off a sausage. She had a plate of cookies in her other hand and placed it on the table next to Billie.

'Fredi brought these along. Baked by her own fair hands. I'll be putting my order in when Lola goes off to work,' Josta joked.

'I'm staying in one of those hotel serviced apartments. Cooking helps me chill out after work, so I had some of these spare. Something to snack on during the wig fitting.' She nodded to the cookies.

'Delicious, my dear.' Josta weaved her way through the crowd. Billie didn't think that she had ever seen her look so happy as she joined Lola, pulling her into a hug. Maybe this is what she had been missing – the devoted and uncomplicated love of a truly happy family? Perhaps it was now time to commit to Max? All she needed was for him to be here beside her.

As she watched Lola weave her sparkling way around her friends, Billie wondered whether she should have a quiet chat about staying safe on the increasingly creepy film set. She shook the thought away. With the shocking demise of her godfather, she had to check herself from getting too paranoid. She took a cookie from the plate and bit into it. It tasted heavenly. Perhaps, Billie reflected, at last, with Max having confided his feelings to his mothers, she could be strong enough to move onwards. What else could she do? Maybe, just maybe, it was time for her to put her past horrors to rest and look forward to her happy ever after.

It was late when Billie arrived home. The sky seemed to wrap around her like a black velvet cape, embroidered with tiny sparkling diamonds. The night air was deathly still, as though holding its breath, with not even a gentle breeze to tug Billie's hair or play the usual wind-chime symphony of halyards clanging against the masts of the yachts down in the sandy, salt-kissed harbour below her house.

She had found Fredi to be good company, regaling her with stories of famous faces and filming in strange places. It seemed that on this shoot, Luna Da Costa, the beautiful actress playing the Red Queen, was proving to be a real headache as far as Arden Roy was concerned, struggling with her lines, turning up late and generally acting in a less than professional manner.

Fredi had hinted that the director had his arm twisted to cast her in a major part in the first place, which had given Billie pause for thought. He didn't look the sort to be easily persuaded. Did the actress have something on him that she was using to get the part?

Billie breathed in the sea-salty air, as a wave of shock temporarily engulfed her with the truth that the Chief, her main protector and supporter within her career and wider life, had gone. She couldn't believe it, nor believe that she had spent the last couple of hours making small talk with a jolly crowd, when he was lying cold and dead in the mortuary. But in the past year she had learned that grief was different from depression, that it was somehow possible to function normally, laugh and joke, go about one's normal work and yet still have a fragment of utter devastation stabbing eternally within one's heart. Somehow, it was possible to carry such things around, without anyone else guessing the truth. Like a secret locked away in a box.

Billie suddenly thought of the box that the Chief had given her the night before. The one that he had made her promise never to open. Surely he had simply meant during his investigation, after which she would have handed it back intact? What now, though, when he was no longer around? Billie wondered if the contents might shed some light on the horrific events since he had handed it over for safekeeping? She suddenly saw a picture of the Chief in her mind's eye, begging her to keep her promise.

Billie made her decision. Promises were there to be broken and she needed answers. She looked up at the stars. Was he up there somewhere? She blew a kiss, just in case, though she'd never had much faith in these things. One fact she was sure of was that he had always loved her and been proud of her achievements and she definitely hadn't got this far by ignoring locked boxes that might just contain vital evidence. If unlocking it led her to the person responsible for the death of the man she had loved like a dear uncle, then it was a price well worth paying.

As she passed her front door and turned down the side pathway to the odd little outside door leading to the basement, Billie heard a noise in the darkness. She stopped. Was she imagining things? The lights were off inside the house, so Ash was either still out on his date, or had already turned in for the night. There it was again... a nocturnal creature, or footsteps? Billie shivered. It wasn't like her to be jumpy in the vicinity of her own home. The events of the day had clearly affected her more than she liked to admit, even to herself. It was at the moment that she started to push aside the bush in front of the door that a shadow loomed out of the darkness and caught Billie's arms.

'Jesus Christ!' she shouted, about to kick out as her arms were pinned back against the wall. 'Thank your lucky stars that I don't carry a Taser!'

'What a wonderful welcome back.' Max loomed over her, his intoxicating lemony smell teasing her senses. Billie didn't know whether to laugh or cry as he bent forward and kissed her deeply on the lips. She caught her breath as he let her arms drop free. She wrapped them around his neck and pulled him close again.

'What the hell are you doing lurking around the garden in the dead of night?' Billie had never felt so pleased to see anyone in her life.

'I was trying to find a way in. You've got this place like Fort Knox, and I don't exactly have a key, unlike all of your other friends.' He slid his hands down and cupped them around Billie's bottom, making her forgive him for almost giving her a heart attack.

'Only Ash. You can have a key, you never asked,' Billie said. 'I wasn't expecting you back so soon...' She pulled him close to her once more.

'You sound disappointed.' Max's liquid chocolate voice sounded even richer in the dark. Billie didn't think that she would ever tire of hearing it. 'We were boarding the plane when our operation was temporarily halted. I could have stayed over, as we've been rescheduled to fly out tomorrow, but I wanted to spend this night with you, after what happened to the Chief...' Max trailed off, combing his fingers softly through Billie's hair, knowing exactly how to soothe her. He kissed her on the top of her head. 'I wanted to be with you. Share your pain, if only for a few short hours tonight.' Max hugged her close. Billie felt tears welling up in her eyes. It felt good to be close to someone who knew her so well, someone she didn't have to put on an act of bravado for.

'I've been with Josta and Lola,' she explained. 'Lola got offered a big part in the film. Queen of Hearts,' Billie explained.

'Wow, great news. I haven't spoken to them this evening. I was so desperate to get back to you,' Max answered.

'Josta told me that you had discussed us moving in together?' Billie laid her head on Max's chest. She could hear his heart beating. It sounded good.

'If you want to, Billie. I would never push–' he started to answer before Billie put her finger to his lips.

'I think it would be a great idea,' Billie said softly, realising that she could think of nothing she would like better right now. She decided, love and support like this maybe only came along once in a lifetime.

'Well, I'm happy to come here' – Max kissed Billie again – 'get rid of my place, maybe buy a hideaway abroad for when I have to work far away, split our time...' he proposed. Billie hurled away any misgivings she may have had earlier about committing so soon in their relationship. They had already been through so much together. 'I think we both know that life is too short to waste time overthinking things,' Max added.

'So true. When you get back from this trip, let's make plans,' Billie whispered. It would perhaps end a period of monumental upheaval for her, a different happy ending to the one that she had mapped out for herself a year ago, but a much more truthful love. She shivered.

'So are you going to let me in tonight?' Max teased softly as they stood in the dark. 'This is a flying visit, and it would be such a shame if I didn't even make it to your bedroom.' He moved his hand along her body. Billie didn't need any further encouragement as she fumbled for her key in the dark.

'Or we could go back down on the beach again?' she joked as Max stood behind her, kissing her neck.

'Too far. I can't wait that long.' Max's answer was muffled. He wrapped his arms around her waist as the door finally opened. Billie caught his hand and led him quickly up the dark staircase. He stopped as they passed the bathroom.

'Just one moment,' he said, letting his hand slide away from Billie's bottom as he switched on the light. A totally naked man was suddenly illuminated like a rabbit caught in the headlights, his striking eyes wide open in shock. Billie recognised him immediately.

'Erm, Max, this is GG Mills.' Billie made the introduction as the famous actor reached to grab a towel to cover himself up. Billie had an urge to laugh, but one glance towards Max stopped her in her tracks.

'Right. So, this is why you weren't keen to let me in.' Max was deadly serious.

'Don't be so ridiculous,' Billie started as Max took one last look between GG Mills and Billie and then turned on his heel, heading back for the stairs.

'You've got it all wrong.' Billie raced after him, flicking on the hall light as he reached the bottom of the stairs.

'I suppose you're going to claim that you've never seen the man before? Please, Billie, don't patronise me.'

'Of course I have,' Billie argued. 'It's GG Mills. You've seen him on screen. He's an actor. I met him on the film set!'

'And you didn't expect me back,' Max snapped.

'Well, of course I didn't expect you back, but–'

Max cut over Billie's words angrily. 'Well, that's okay, Billie, because in truth, I was settling for second best. You were never a patch on Natalie.'

Billie was shocked to the core. His words had stung her like a hard and vicious slap to the face. This was a version of Max that she had never seen before.

'Well, I'm glad we've got that straight,' Billie answered icily cool, 'now get the hell out of my house and shut the door behind you.' She turned back, never thinking in a million years that she would find herself paraphrasing David's bloody mother. The faces of GG Mills and a similarly shocked and towel-wrapped Ash now rushing along the landing to join him at the top of the stairs, were staring back at her, like naughty schoolboys caught smoking behind the toilets.

12

MAD AS A MARCH HARE

'Stop. You're killing me!' Her face crumpled up in pain, tears running down her cheeks.

'You can't be in as much pain as me,' Billie replied, as she watched Boo bent double with laughter in reaction to Billie's tale of the night before.

'Don't, it hurts,' Boo pleaded. Billie couldn't hide a smile.

'I'm back to being Billie no friends again, whereas you lot seem to have hot men on tap.'

She hadn't told her all of it, of course, not the cruel words that Max had spat out about Billie in comparison to Natalie. She was still processing that, but through the long sleepless night, when she had tossed and turned in her bed, she had given herself a good talking to, got things into perspective. Her precious godfather had just lost his life. Her focus was to find out the truth about his, and the other murders, because she knew in her heart that's what had occurred. Natalie was another blameless person and Billie had no intention of feeling resentment towards a dead woman that she had never met.

She was furious, however, with Max, who had tried to bowl her over into making a commitment one minute then slung her aside in the next, with those oh-so hurtful words. She knew that he was under stress, but she had seen a side of Max that she had never known existed. As a top psychologist Max would have known the damage such a pronouncement would cause. As far as Billie was concerned right now, he had totally blown their relationship apart, but she wasn't in the mood to go crying on anyone's shoulder.

'Oh, here he is, the Hollywood groupie,' Billie announced loudly. 'Lock away all your film-star lovers,' she added, grinning, as Ash entered. Boo launched into peals of laughter once again.

'Can you get your hot boyfriend's autograph for me please? I can sell it for a fortune on eBay,' Boo teased. Ash couldn't hide a sheepish smile.

'Thanks for broadcasting, boss' – he pulled a face at Billie – 'and for the tray outside of the bedroom door with croissants and the red rose.' He shook his head in mock despair.

'Thought you would need a hearty breakfast after the workout you no doubt had with Superman,' Billie quipped. 'Don't worry, I had my earmuffs on for bed, because clearly *I* wasn't going to get any action.' She alluded to Max's reaction.

'I'm so sorry about that.' Ash took off his jacket as he reached his desk. 'I would have apologised to him if he had stuck around. I've left a message on his answering service just to set things straight.'

'Yeah, well he might listen to you and apologise for his big mistake, but maybe you did me a favour and stopped me making a bigger one.' Billie had always been worried that Max might never get over Nat's death. Now he had just made the fact crystal clear. She might have been living the life of a second-class lover for evermore if Max hadn't spilled the beans during his hissy fit.

'Sounds like the two of you in the buff sent him running away like a whippet with the squits.' Boo snorted, rubbing her eyes.

'Don't worry about it,' Billie joked. 'It was well worth the experience to see GG Mills with his kit off. That thought will keep me company through the long, cold nights ahead.'

'I'm sure when he lets me explain–' Ash started.

'Oh, no, no, no.' Billie wagged her finger. 'No explanation needed. My house, and my friends can do whatever they please in it. Max was only a guest and he's not welcome anymore. Now, let's get down to some work.' Billie flicked her screen open. An email appeared to have come to her work address from Maddie Taylor. Billie clicked on it and the accompanying attachment, before gasping loudly, making Boo and Ash turn her way.

'What's up, boss?' Boo asked, jesting repartee with Ash immediately dropped.

'It's Maddie Taylor.' Billie stepped back before grabbing her phone and calling the emergency services. 'Ambulance. Emergency...' She reeled off details of the girl's student address before adding her own details. 'On our way. Blues and twos.' Ash and Boo had joined her as she reached for her jacket.

'Oh my God.' Boo caught her breath as she stared at the screen.

'What time did she send the email?' Ash asked.

'Just before one am,' Billie whispered, berating herself for having turned her mobile off, straight after their row, lest Max ring her with apologies she wasn't in any mood to accept. She normally scrolled through any messages before turning in. 'That's where she lives.' Billie suddenly realised that the photo of Maddie, holding a knife covered in blood, slashes all over her arms and chest as she faced the camera, was actually a video recording. She clicked on it.

'I'm so, so sorry...' Tears rolled down her face, as she slashed dangerously near her jugular vein, between gulping sobs. Blood started to speedily trickle down her neck, mixing with the trails of gore from other cuts and jabs. Her white vest top was soaked through with it. 'I didn't mean to kill her. But... but... Now it's killing me. I'm going to tell *everything*.' She held up the bloody knife again to her throat as the picture cut off.

They almost knocked noses, the police car driven at high speed by Ash and the ambulance, lights flashing, tearing down the street and to an emergency halt in the centre of the road outside of the terraced flat where Maddie Taylor lived. Billie had already opened the car door and had started to leap out, even before Ash could come to a halt. She hurtled up the pathway and hammered on the door.

'Maddie?' She kicked hard, breaking through the flimsy door frame, and then reached through to open the lock, before racing into the hallway. A quick scan of both bedrooms showed them to be empty. As Billie continued onwards to the small back living room she came to an abrupt halt, immediately realising that as far as preservation of life was concerned, time was no longer of the essence. Maddie appeared to have been long gone, having bled out onto the brown carpet where her blood had merged with the general grime of the floor in the small lounge where Billie had interviewed her earlier.

The large knife that Billie recognised from the video sent to her was lying by her side, her long hair spread out like a halo. Near her shoulders and feet lay four individual pottery figurines, all depicting females. At their feet were square plaques each with the name of a season inscribed on it. Maddie's hands were holding a book open, smudged with blood. As Billie leaned forward, she realised that she was staring at a page of *Alice Through the Looking-Glass*. It was Humpty Dumpty's recitation of the poem '*In winter, when the fields are white*,' in which each of the seasons, winter, spring, summer and autumn, were mentioned.

'Looks like Sunderland pottery. My mum collects it.' The female paramedic had bent down to check Maddie's pulse and shook her head. Knowing she could do nothing at all for the poor girl, her attention was now firmly on the figurines. She stepped back as Ash moved forward.

'What do you think?' Billie asked. She closed her eyes tightly just for a moment as moving images of Maddie in the video slashed through her mind. Could she have saved her had she opened the email when it had been sent? Had she missed another opportunity, just as she had with the Chief who had almost certainly already been poisoned by the time of their last meeting, when she had taken the box from him? Was this heartbreaking scenario all her fault?

'It looks like a set-up job.' Ash's blunt reply brought Billie back from her stab of self-condemnation. 'You know I had my doubts about your theories as far as Will Cox was concerned and also Pippa Sykes. Even the Chief maybe had his reasons for wanting to get out, but I spent time with this girl...'

'She was vulnerable. I saw the cuts on her arms...' Billie said.

'She was also left-handed,' Ash answered. 'Before we started interviewing her, Maya got her a cheeseburger and fries. I remember her picking up her cola and fries with her left hand, not her right, as well as signing her statement with that hand. Think back to the video,' Ash continued. Billie braced herself to go there again and it was true, Maddie had been holding the knife with her left hand.

'See the deep cut to the throat.' Ash pointed. It wasn't a question. The major cut on Maddie's body put all of the others into the shade. It ran from below her left ear, then obliquely downward, then straight across the midline of her neck, ending almost at her right shoulder blade. 'And it's a single blade knife,' he added.

'You're right.' Billie followed through the line of the deep gaping wound. 'It's been inflicted from behind, by a right-handed person, with some force. No way could she have done that herself.' She rubbed her face thoughtfully as a clatter could suddenly be heard in the doorway. Josta stood there, all overalled up and ready for action.

'Well done. Go to the top of the class both and collect your Brownie points. And here was me thinking you were just glazing over, minds drifting off to sex and drugs and rock and roll during most of our mortuary get-togethers,' Josta quipped, as Billie and Ash stepped back. 'Furthermore, I've often found suicidal cut throats to be accompanied by cadaveric spasms, with the knife found firmly clenched in the deceased's hand, whereas the knife here' – she nodded across to the large weapon lying a couple of feet away, parallel to the body – 'has been placed pointing to that looking-glass there.'

Billie and Ash's heads turned in unison to a mirror propped up against the leg of a chair. It was a small compact type, the sort carried in handbags, that clipped open and shut. The lid section held a picture of Lewis Carroll's Alice. Was it just a coincidence in a student house that wasn't the tidiest spot in town? Billie tried to reason logically, having been criticised for her so-called flights of fantasy recently.

'This is definitely a murder, boss. I'm with you one hundred per cent now.' Ash finally said what Billie had been trying to scream out to everybody since day one. 'Stuff Miriam Nelson and her threats. I'll back you up all the way. This is one sicko son of a bitch. We've got to crack on and hunt them down, or I fear this won't be the last.'

'My thoughts exactly,' Billie answered. 'Can you see her

mobile?' Billie scanned the room as Charlie Holden moved carefully forward placing markers around the floor.

'I'll keep an eye open,' Charlie answered. Billie remembered that the Chief's mobile hadn't turned up next to his body despite him having sent her a text in the early hours asking her to meet him at Penshaw Monument at 6.30am the morning before. She had checked with the custody officer, and he had been released at 3.30am. She guessed that his brief had taken him home, as David's mother had insisted that he hadn't returned there.

'Any word on the Chief's movements yet, Charlie?' Billie had asked for any tracking evidence on the number available from forensics.

'Yep. Came in just before we set off here.' Charlie's pink cheeks, dark eyes and jolly face reminded Billie of a Toby jug that had stood on the Chief's mantelpiece when she had visited as a child. She had been so entranced by it, that he had joked he would leave it to her in his will. If indeed it had been, she would cherish it all of her life.

'Bit of an odd one actually. The phone was off whilst he was in the custody suite, then there was a ping from the local transmitter at about the time he left. Same position for about ten minutes before it suddenly went off again.' Charlie was scouring the crime scene as he spoke.

Billie wondered if the Chief had been dropped off at home, then had decided to go to bed for a couple of hours. Was that when he had texted her? She reached for her own phone and scrolled through the timings. The message had been sent to her at 4.30am, so that put paid to the couple of hours of kip idea.

'Then it came on again briefly at four thirty am, at Penshaw Monument,' Charlie continued, 'before going off again. Suddenly popped up ten minutes later, in the vicinity of the film set, just for a minute or so, before going totally dead.'

Billie swallowed hard as she took in the new information.

Had the Chief *really* sent that last message, or was he already dead at that point? She had thought it a strange request at the time. Perhaps the killer wanted Billie, in particular, to be the one to discover her dear godfather's body. Was that the sort of extreme sicko that she was hunting?

'This is absurd!' Arden Roy was almost puce with fury. 'No doubt your endless harassment was the death of the girl! She could simply take no more. I feel her pain,' he bellowed, though according to Maya, it was well known that his treatment of the supporting artistes was woefully lacking. Par for the course on film sets the world over, she was told. None of the main cast mixed with the extras and would hardly notice if any keeled over, during the long hours and often testing conditions they were forced to endure on location.

Ellis had already mentioned that as far as catering was concerned, the main cast and crew ate like kings, whereas the extras were fed cheap food and were allowed only one biscuit with their tea from the communal urn at breaks, the sort of beige, joyless square which invariably dissolved and floated on top of the paper cup, should anyone be brave enough to go for a dunk. Billie recalled GG Mill's take on the subject when they had first met.

'Keep your hair on, sir,' Ash warned in a serious fashion whilst glancing towards Billie. Maya had already regaled them on how the director spent an age in the make-up trailer before the actors arrived each morning, having his few heavily dyed strands carefully swathed and glued over his bald pate. He was hypersensitive about it.

'If you'll just answer the question,' Billie interjected. 'Was there a night shoot underway in the early hours of yesterday morning and if not, then who would be here in the middle of the night?'

'There was no night shoot. Really, what has this to do with the death of a nobody?' Billie had to hold herself back from grabbing the man by his throat and pinning him up against the wall.

'Maddie Taylor was her name. Get it? Maddie Taylor. She wasn't a nobody, she was a young girl with her whole life ahead of her and for some reason, whilst she was working on your scrap of nonsense, she was killed. Now, we're going to find out why it happened and who did it and if that knocks you off your sodding red carpet, then it's just too bad. Got it?' Billie leant close. He smelled of mints, trying to cover halitosis due to the endless detritus spilling out of his mouth, Billie mused. Not that she expected anyone else to get any nearer to the man, if they could possibly avoid it.

'First, yesterday's shocking behaviour, when we are trying to work and now this. Thank God the press got wind of your bullying behaviour! I'll make a formal complaint to the very top,' he hissed, stepping back a little as he peered up at Billie.

'Knock yourself out,' she answered, beckoning over a man in a security guard's outfit.

'Were you on duty night before last?' Billie questioned, noticing Arden Roy scuttling off at speed. He could run all he liked but she wasn't necessarily finished with him yet.

'No, I do the dayshift.' He shrugged. 'Sid usually does nights.'

'Night before last?' Ash asked, as a person dressed as a Dodo sauntered past carrying a plastic cup of coffee.

'Dunno.' The security guard shrugged again. 'You're the detectives. I'm just paid to see no one nicks the trailers.' The six-foot-tall Dodo bent towards Billie conspiratorially.

'Go and ask the March Hare over there, darling. Steph's her name.' The Dodo stage-whispered as though he were reciting

Shakespeare. 'She can't resist a uniform. Gossip going around like wildfire that she and the night watch have been at it like rabbits.' The Dodo winked and walked on.

'Got a needle to sew up my sides?' Billie quipped, as the Dodo turned and made a small bow, before continuing.

'I feel like I'm in some mad dream.' Ash shook his head as they walked towards someone dressed as a March Hare, as depicted by illustrator John Tenniel in Lewis Carroll's *Alice in Wonderland*. The actor was drinking what looked like a milkshake through a straw.

'Steph? Sorry but we need to interrupt your lunch.' Billie flashed her ID card. It wasn't March so she was hoping for a less than raving mad conversation.

'If you can call it that.' The March Hare smiled. 'I really wanted the fish and chips like him, but it's impossible to eat real food with these prosthetics.' She wiped a drop of milk from her whiskers. Billie glanced to what looked like a giant sleeping Dormouse, gently snoring, stretched out on the grass next to an empty plate with only a couple of chips and a dollop of ketchup left on it, that matched the smear on his nose.

'Were you here early yesterday morning?' Billie asked.

'Yeah, my make-up call was for six am and then it took two hours to fit all of this stuff on.' She indicated her special effects silicone pieces.

'Before that?' Billie pressed, trying to fling away her urge to laugh at the sight of a Mad March Hare, eyebrows raising up and down manically, eyes shifting back and forth, trying to wriggle out of the truth.

'Word has it you have a fondness for men in uniforms,' Ash said, cutting to the chase, 'particularly with the name of Sid. So, were you tucked up in a bed somewhere else at half past four yesterday morning, or bunny-hopping right here?' The Dormouse stirred and yawned.

'You might just as well say...' Billie thought she heard the Dormouse mumble before it then dozed off again. Was he talking in his sleep, running through his lines, or giving the Mad March Hare a nudge to spill?

'All right. I was here. They work him such long hours that he has to sleep through the day and I'm here, so sometimes I stop over. It's the only way we ever get to see each other...'

'I'm not interested in your love life,' Billie tried to reassure Steph, who sounded young and scared about having made her confession. 'We simply want to know if you noticed anything unusual around this base camp between four thirty and four forty-five am?'

'Maybe Sid might have. I mean, he's the security guard.' Billie sensed Steph was holding back lest her lover got into trouble.

'Might have been otherwise engaged.' Ash folded his arms, looking quite intimidating. Billie suddenly saw a picture of him in her mind's eye from the night before, in a towel, when the same could have been said about him. She smiled. The girl finally relented.

'Sid had heard a noise outside, around the back somewhere and had gone to take a look, but I suddenly spotted a light on in the other direction, over in the director's trailer. I did see something, but if I tell, will I lose this job? I need the money...' Billie thought that she looked, well, like a rabbit trapped in the headlights.

'At first, I thought I was imagining things... two women, well that's what I believed at first, but...' Billie and Ash exchanged glances as the girl described the scene that she had witnessed.

'And this was at four forty-five yesterday morning?' Billie asked the March Hare as she finished speaking.

'I think so, but I can't be sure... My watch was broken... I'm sorry, I don't want to waste your time. It's just that I couldn't believe my eyes.' Steph went on to spill her observations.

On hearing Steph's account, Billie was out of the trailer and across the grass in a matter of seconds, Arden Roy back in her sights once again. She cut across him before he reached his luxurious-looking Winnebago.

'Witness saw you here before dawn yesterday morning.' Billie blocked his way forward.

'That's showbiz. We work all hours. I don't expect the plod to understand.' Arden Roy tried to move around Billie. 'Now if you'll excuse me.' He managed to reach the door handle.

'Who was with you?' Billie persisted, pushing the door shut before he could get into it. 'The witness saw two people.'

'Well, your so-called witness might have double vision, because I was totally alone.'

'That's not what was reported,' Billie continued.

'Prove it then.' Arden Roy was defiant.

'The mobile phone signal of a murdered man was last picked up in this vicinity – after his death. Did you kill him?'

'Are you out of your tiny mind?' Arden Roy looked suitably shocked. 'I was checking over the double costume for the Red Queen, ascertaining if we had anyone else available to use the dress should you collar yet another of the artistes.'

Billie guessed that wasn't the whole truth and she had a good idea who else might have been with him that morning. She turned to Ash who had followed her across the grass.

'I want a fingertip search of this whole area. We're looking for the Chief's phone. Start in this trailer.' She nodded to Arden Roy's caravan. 'And speak to Sid on security. I want to make sure he didn't make any early morning treks up to Penshaw Monument, despite what the Mad March Hare is claiming. The place is full of actors, their livelihood depends on them being expert liars.'

13

ANGELS & DEVILS

'B illie, it's Max.' The voice caught Billie by surprise.

'I'm busy.' Billie's voice was clipped. She was already in a temper, not helped by the fact that director Arden Roy, incandescent with rage, had been straight on the phone to complain about Billie's disruption to his precious film shoot, for the second time in two days. However, the real reason for her anger was that she had taken a late afternoon detour on the way back to base via the Chief's house, only to find that all of the locks had been changed. Her own personal key was useless, so any hopes of finding something inside that might point her in the direction of his killer had been scuppered.

What's more, when she had peered through his lounge window, she had found that the precious Toby jug, the object that she had loved for as long as she could remember, was missing. Tears smarted the back of her eyes. It really did now feel like the end of an era. She didn't need Max at this bloody moment to put the final seal on that opinion.

'Always busy,' Max answered ruefully. 'Sorry to interrupt, but I've just landed, and I'm desperate to apologise for my behaviour last night. It was a terrible, terrible thing to say.'

'You said it,' Billie agreed. Right now, she wasn't in a forgiving mood. She fired up her PC, keen to read through the report on the Chief's mobile activity, which had been forwarded directly to her by Charlie.

'You sound like you're having a bad day,' Max continued softly. Billie could hear some exotic bird squawking in the background. She was aware that the British Army UN Force was currently in Mali, engaging with violent extremists. Her guess was that Max was calling from that location, but experience told her that he'd keep tight-lipped on the subject. *Shame he hadn't remained tight-lipped last night*, Billie mused, still hurt.

'I was having a hell of a day too, yesterday.' Billie did feel there was some genuine regret in his voice.

'GG Mills was Ash's guest, not mine.' Billie made it clear though arguing silently that she didn't actually owe any explanation. It was Max who had jumped to the wrong conclusion after all.

'Yeah, I didn't think. It's just, I wanted us to be alone and Ash is always there.'

'So you could have invited me to yours,' Billie argued.

'As I said, I didn't think, I just rushed to be with you. I only had a few hours free before having to shoot away again and I wanted to comfort you after what happened to the Chief...' Max trailed off. Billie felt a pang of guilt. He clearly had meant well, but such cruel words... Max cut into her thoughts.

'You see, yesterday was also the anniversary of Nat's death.' Billie felt her stomach tense. 'So I could guess how devastated you must be feeling about your godfather, and I admit I was a bit emotional about the date – I thought that I'd come all the way to be with you, only to discover that no sooner had I vacated your bed, then you were seeing someone else, a big-shot film star, no less. I know that's no real excuse...'

Billie blew out a sigh. Perhaps she *had* been too hasty in

throwing him out? She had vowed to be understanding about his first wife, Natalie, who was killed by a landmine whilst out on patrol in a war zone with Max, during his army days. She knew that he was still struggling hard not to blame himself, especially when he had learned only three months ago that she may have been pregnant when she had died. Max had continued to wake in the early hours, having had nightmares about the incident. Maya suddenly popped her head around the door.

'Chief wants you in her office now,' she called. Billie inwardly groaned.

'Look, I've got to go,' Billie said to Max, imagining him standing under a blazing hot sun. A tropical location filled with exotic birds sounded like a good option right at this moment, dangerous or not. Especially when Billie was being summoned to face a cold British bulldog, just along the corridor, waiting to bare her teeth.

'This is a lightning mission. I should be back in a couple of days.' Billie could hear the yearning in his voice. 'Please say you'll give us another go. I know we've got something special, Billie and in this job, I'm acutely aware that life is too short to waste on silly misunderstandings.' Billie rubbed her hand over her face. Things had been going so well between them before this. She desperately hoped he wasn't going to walk into terrible danger because his mind was on their situation.

'Chief is shouting for you,' Boo said, sweeping in. 'Don't get another bill like me.' She waved another invoice in her hand. 'Probably charges by the second for delay in reporting for action.' Billie walked over and whipped the new invoice out of Boo's hand.

'Okay.' She finally gave in to Max's pleas. 'We'll talk when you get back. Don't go doing anything silly,' she whispered.

'Promise. Love you,' Max replied.

'Wilde, my office, pronto!' Miriam Nelson could now be seen stepping out of her office as Billie switched off her mobile and marched out of her room and along the corridor.

'I've already explained. *This* is discrimination!' Billie slammed Boo's second bill down on the desk, determined not to give way on this issue. Miriam Nelson looked at it.

'So that's what you were ripping up first time when you had the strop? I totally agree. It didn't come via me. Must have been the new maintenance manager.' Miriam crumpled the bill up and threw it in the wastepaper bin. 'I'll tell him to wipe his arse with it.' Her answer took the wind out of Billie's sails somewhat.

'Feelings are running high, Wilde, about your high-handed tactics on the film set. Especially after last night's newspaper headlines.' The new chief folded her arms under her ample bosom and looked hard at Billie.

'Doing my job to the best of my ability, ma'am. Josta King will confirm we are dealing with murder in regard to the death of Maddie Taylor this morning, and as you are already aware, I maintain that the Chief was also killed. The last known whereabouts of his phone was in the vicinity of the film location base, after the signal had left Penshaw Monument, where he was found. Hence my request for an immediate search.

'As regards the newspaper, the finding of the slaughtered pig and the threat made to Charles Carroll alongside that photo, also confirms my earlier suspicions that Will Cox was not responsible for his death. If this had been investigated more thoroughly at the time, then more murders could have been avoided.' She tilted her chin ready for an argument, not least because she just couldn't use the name 'the Chief' in relation to anyone else but her dear deceased godfather and she was expecting to be reprimanded for it.

'You've got some spunk, madam, I'll give you that.' Miriam Nelson began to circle the desk. 'I've now had time to review the reports on the deceased, including the footage sent to you by Maddie Taylor and all of the forensics currently available. Credit where credit is due. I'm now reviewing my opinion that you are an airhead who's been given the golden slipper up the greasy pole. In addition, I can't find any evidence of you having aided and abetted the criminal activities of your godfather and believe me, I've looked.'

'I'd like to see that evidence against him, ma'am. I feel sure I can clear his name,' Billie answered.

'Don't push it, Wilde. It's not going to happen. I've told you; those files are sealed. However, due to the latest developments, I'm cutting you some slack. If you feel that the deaths are linked, I'll let you do further exploration. Do a good job of it and make this force hit the headlines for the right reasons, then I might even let your ragtag bunch of miscreants jog on in their jobs. Fail to wind this up quickly, however, and I'm jumping straight back on my original game plan of moving you all on, and bringing in a fresh, cutting-edge team, with no bad apples lurking in the pile.'

Billie remained tight-lipped. It was a struggle, but she had the welfare of her team to consider. Miriam Nelson seemed to be deep in thought for a moment, before tapping a framed photo of a young woman, which had replaced the earlier one of Billie and the deceased Chief on the desktop.

'Lost my own daughter to a mad murderer a few years back when she was at Middleton college. Never did find the culprit. Probably her drugs dealer. Strangled her when she couldn't pay up. She was such a good girl until she left home. No trouble. Had her sights set on being a high-flying copper, speeding up the ranks, just like you...' She paused for a moment. 'Wasn't to be, but I don't want yet more poor mothers ending up sad, bitter and grumpy old bitches like me.'

She gave a resigned smile for a moment. Billie realised that it was pain rather than spite that she had glimpsed in those steely eyes. Just went to prove, she reflected, that truth was often stranger and more poignant than wrongly placed assessments.

'I'm sorry to hear that, ma'am.' Billie wondered how many other misjudgements she might have made about people? Yet here she was giving Max a bad time about his mistake.

'Don't think that I am not aware of the personal grief you are feeling for your godfather, Wilde. But try to accept that just as I had no idea that my daughter was a junkie, you do not know the full story about him.'

Billie thought about the black box in her cellar once more. She would jemmy it open tonight, that was for sure. She needed facts and she hoped the secrets that he was keen to keep from those coming to arrest him would assist her in clearing his name, whatever the charge.

'Well, don't waste time. Crack on. I've ordered extra bodies out at the film location. That little squirt of a director might have to find something else to amuse his creative juices for the rest of the day.' She gave a hearty chuckle. 'If he doesn't have a heart attack first.'

'Thanks, ma'am.' Billie paused on her journey towards the door and gave a small smile, her view of the woman having changed somewhat.

'And don't forget that it isn't always the boys that are the bad guys. In the case of my dear Olivia, the only person who could be seen approaching her student let on CCTV that night was another girl. As I said, it was probably her heroin supplier. Never identified her, but long gone are the days when all females are angels and men devils.' Billie nodded; she knew that much from her own past. She headed back towards her team at speed.

'Maya, can you get a hold of any CCTV from Maddie Taylor's street for the hours before and after one am?'

'Yep.' Maya immediately jumped into action. 'I'm happy to work late. Dad was taking me for tea, but he's got to go and see his solicitor. His uncle has died and sounds like he's left him some money.' She reached for a phone to make calls. 'Don't ask me who. I don't know any of the wider fam, having only known him for five minutes.'

'Lucky him,' Boo said. 'I wish some long-forgotten relative would pop up and leave me a pile of money.' Billie suddenly noticed that Boo looked stressed.

'You're not in any trouble, are you? I can lend you–' Billie started. Boo cut her off.

'No, just me whining on. Ignore me.' Billie knew how independent Boo was determined to be.

'Best stick with Ellis unless the secret lover is a millionaire,' Billie bent down and whispered jokily.

'Yeah, well money isn't everything.' Boo switched off her screen quickly. Billie felt concerned having just caught sight of an advert for a loan company on screen with huge interest rates.

'I'm here if you need me,' Billie whispered again before remembering she had to make a call to a lawyer herself. The Chief's legal brief. Her call was put straight through, Billie having met the man several times in the past.

'Ms Wilde. You caught me just as I was leaving for the day.' He sounded cool, formal and polite as usual.

'Hi. The locks have been changed at my godfather's place, so do you have a key?'

'I'm afraid his next of kin insisted that the house should remain locked until probate is complete.' Billie suddenly remembered David's mother's words. She hadn't taken them seriously, deciding that the older woman had probably been so drunk that she hadn't realised what she was saying, or had merely been trying to antagonise her.

'As far as I'm aware, I am his next of kin.' Billie blinked hard. She hadn't even thought of any inheritance, she had simply been thinking of accessing the house to see if there were any clues to his death.

'I'm afraid that is incorrect.' The lawyer's voice was controlled. 'There is a claim on the estate from a close blood relative. An adult child as named in the will, who wishes to remain anonymous at present.' Billie swallowed hard. Maybe David's mum had been telling the truth.

'The Chief never mentioned it,' she stated, 'but if that is the case then I need the name in order to arrange access in connection with the investigation into his untimely death.'

'My instructions are that absolutely no one should enter the premises without a search warrant. The police have already left the home in a dreadful mess.'

'Then I will arrange one,' Billie replied. 'Did you take my godfather home when he was released from custody?' Billie presumed that's how he was aware of the breakages in the Chief's house.

'No. Alas not. His release at such an unusual hour was entirely unexpected. I can ask the next of kin whether they picked him up if that would help?'

Billie put the phone down thoughtfully. She turned to Maya, wondering if she was jumping to the wrong conclusion yet again.

'Did your dad say who the solicitor is that he's going to see today?'

Maya shrugged. 'Dunno but I can tell you where he's going to be later tonight if you want to catch up with him.' Maya suddenly connected with her call to request CCTV. Billie turned to Boo instead.

'Are you going too?' she asked. Boo shook her head.

'We do have lives of our own, you know,' she answered, slightly irritably. *And big secrets too*, Billie thought, but didn't answer out loud. She was beginning to question all of her close relationships. Maybe she really was Billie no friends after all.

14

A TWIST IN THE TALE

Entertainment at the Aunt Fanny's club was in full swing as Billie entered. She recognised a jolly rock and roll track from her childhood days, by pop group Jive Bunny, blasting out. Suddenly, memories of a family wedding, being swung around to this upbeat tune by her godfather, danced through her mind. That had been in the days when her only concerns had been whether Poppy, her pony, had been fit to enter the local gymkhana. The Chief had bought that, too, and her first pair of grown-up dancing shoes with actual heels.

Now the Toby jug had gone, Billie didn't care about inheritances and so forth. She had already benefitted materially from the demise of the closest people in her world in the last year or so, though she would hand all of it back in a heartbeat to have those people alive and breathing once again, even if some had to face less than endearing truths about their pasts. All she was focused on was getting justice for Charles Carroll, Pippa Sykes, Maddie Taylor, and the Chief. In his case, an unknown beneficiary to his will had a motive to ensure that life was deceased and until Billie could interview them, then they had to be on her list of suspects.

The main lights were switched off, but the mirrored glitterball hanging from the centre of the room and strobe lighting coming from a DJ's desk on stage, picked out flashing patterned effects on the faces of the dancers, their movement making their actions intermittent and jerking. Definite dad dancing, yet all of the disco queens were either matronly-looking women or men dressed in their female finery, able to relax and let their hair down in this private space. It lifted Billie's spirits a little, reminding her of more innocent times when people didn't have to fit into a certain mould, wear the right designer gear or appear perfect, to be acceptable. Here, people were just being true to themselves, reflected in their smiling faces and high spirits.

One or two people recognised her from her last visit and waved in greeting. Dougie Meeks in sequinned shift dress, peroxide wig and vertiginous heels was going for the full John Travolta 'I Want To Dance' routine from *Pulp Fiction*, opposite a petite individual with black bobbed wig recreating the Uma Thurman twist contest moves with some panache. Wearing an elegant, black-velvet knee-length dress and pumps, Billie had no idea if his partner was male or female, but they could certainly move on the dance floor. A cocktail of sweet feminine perfume like a huge bouquet of flowers, mixed with the musky smell of male sweat, enveloped Billie in a cloud as she made her way through the dancers.

It was when the DJ spoke that Billie whipped her head around, having located the individual she wanted to speak to.

'Okay ladies, we're gonna take a little break now, so swap to your slippers for a while if you've brought them. The pies and peas are about to be served, so form an orderly queue by the hatch at the back of the room. For anyone still following social distancing regulations even today, remember, you need to keep one cow between you and the next person. Now enjoy a little slice of muzak...' Ellis Darque removed his headphones and stepped away from the ancient double turntable DJ kit that appeared to have been found in the back of a cupboard.

'Got a minute?' Billie stopped him as he moved to the side of the stage.

'Got all night. The real DJ is starting after the break. I just offered to do the warm-up. I actually came over with the pie-and-pea suppers. Tweedledee over there' – he nodded towards Dougie Meeks who was kicking off his high heels and sinking into a pair of pink fluffy slippers – 'did a deal with the film caterers to redirect the night-shoot food over here, as someone not too far away stopped play there today.' He grinned.

'Didn't have you down as a pop picker,' Billie retaliated. 'Thought you were having to take on extra work. Maybe the new job isn't paying, like the old one.'

'I've certainly got a few extra outgoings with Maya on the scene. I'm determined to make up for all that time I missed out on her growing up, so the kid deserves a few treats. Still got my little one and the ex-wife to support as well, of course,' he added, referring to the breakdown of his marriage due to his dedication to undercover policing.

It was at that moment that the person who had been dancing with Dougie Meeks earlier came into Billie's view as she looked over Ellis's shoulder. He was carrying a plate with an individual pie and a mound of luridly green peas. His knife, fork and serviette were clutched in his pink manicured nails, the black skirt of his dress swishing as he deftly flitted around tables and chairs. Billie wondered if she was dreaming for a minute. She even shook her head slightly, but the image didn't change. Arden Roy had been the nifty performer channelling his inner Uma Thurman on the dance floor. As she watched, he sat down, flicked his dark bobbed wig behind pearl-stud-adorned ears and tucked his napkin down the front of his outfit, in order to avoid spills. It was clear he wasn't a newcomer to the cross-dressing stage.

Billie pushed past Ellis and made for the table, sitting down opposite the director. He reacted with shock, dropping a forkful of pie, which bypassed his napkin and landed on his skirt. Billie handed over a wad of paper serviettes that had been stuffed into a beer glass in the centre of the table.

'Did you a favour mucking up your night shoot it seems. Here you are at party central,' Billie said as she watched the flustered director wipe at his dress.

'I'm beginning to think you have some vendetta against me, Constable Wilde.'

'Superintendent,' Billie corrected. 'I'm simply trying to help solve the suspicious deaths of a few people, two of whom worked on your production. Is it too much to ask for the truth about who you were with, in your trailer at four forty-five am yesterday morning? I know that you weren't alone, whatever you claim.'

'Can you blame me?' Arden Roy pushed his plate away, losing a false nail in the process, a sugar-pink island in a sea of mushy peas. 'For all the talk in the media of diversity, people like us are still targeted as figures of derision. Especially by creatures wearing uniforms, funnily enough.' He rubbed at his dress again. The stain stubbornly refused to go away.

'So give me a positive identification on the person you were with before dawn yesterday morning and I'll give you some space,' Billie persisted. Arden Roy dumped his crumpled napkin onto the table, giving up the fight against the immovable stain.

'It was just a friend, helping me try on some outfits.' He looked bereft, his bright red lipstick seeping into the creases around his lips. 'It helps me relax before a long day fraught with demands. I'm not a murderer, officer, though the way some people view anyone who chooses to ignore the genetic dress code, you would think we were killers, rather than simply expressing the feminine side of our personalities. I don't see anyone here complaining about your jeans and hulking big boots after all,' he added.

'I'm not interested in how you choose to dress,' Billie argued sincerely. 'I'm simply trying to identify anyone in the vicinity at that time in order to be able to eliminate them from our enquiries.' Arden Roy remained tight-lipped.

'I don't want any other innocent people hounded,' were his only words.

A thump on the back of Billie's chair alerted her to another person dragging a seat out next to her and forcefully sitting down, dumping a plate of pie and peas on the table.

'It was *me*, all right?' Dougie Meeks hissed in Billie's ear. 'So give him a bloody break, will you? I have to get on site before dawn if I'm doing Tweedle blinking dee, it takes so long in make-up.' He started forking his food in his mouth as though he was a starving man.

'If I recall, you were acting as a playing card yesterday,' Billie argued, making a note that this was one of the most bizarre interview scenarios she had ever found herself in.

'Later, yes. First scene was a pick-up. Ask *him*, he's in charge.' Dougie Meeks nodded over to the director.

'Tweedledum messed up a line. We had to reshoot,' Arden Roy agreed. 'There's a printed call sheet to prove it.'

At the mention of Tweedledum, Billie glanced up to see Ellis striding across the room. She shot off her chair and blocked his path.

'Were you at the film base location at four forty-five yesterday morning?' she demanded.

'Woah.' Ellis chuckled. 'This sounds like a police interview. I'm still getting used to me not being the one doing them,' he added.

'So were you?' Billie persisted.

'Probably. But if this is going to be a full-on interrogation, let's head across the road to the pub. I'm gasping for a pint and if you play your cards right, I might even treat you to a pie-and-pea supper.'

~

'Blackmail?' Billie stopped mid-bite. A fish finger fell out from between the two chunky white bread slices that she was tucking into. She caught it before it hit the table.

'Sextortion. All the rage these days. Seems your favourite director likes dressing up in feminine outfits and getting frisky with certain online contacts. Only this time, one of them has recorded the footage and is threatening to release it to the media. Some of the things that they've said has led him to believe that it might be an individual involved in this film, hence me being on the job. Good catch, by the way. I didn't have you down as a fish finger type.' Ellis nodded cheerfully at Billie's pub supper as he tucked into his steak.

'So? I don't know much about your real personality either.' Billie shoved the stray fish finger back between the bread and took another bite. 'UCOs should have their own acting Oscars. Anyway, I didn't want to wipe you out, by choosing something top of the range. You said you were strapped for cash, so I'll pay.'

One of the gastropub waiters arrived with two glasses and a bottle of Château Batailley, a Bordeaux that had been the Chief's favourite tipple. Billie wasn't a big drinker by a long stretch, but she had bought a very similar bottle for the Chief's birthday. She knew that there wouldn't be much change out of a hundred quid for this 2005 vintage, and then some. 'Can you forget what I just said there?' She turned the label to face Ellis. He chuckled.

'Don't worry. I said this was my shout. Anyway, we need to

toast your old god-daddy with his favourite tipple. You put on a mean brave face, Billie Wilde, but don't tell me what's happened isn't tearing your heart to shreds.' He poured the rich dark wine into their glasses.

'How do you know his favourite wine?' Billie needled.

'Took me out to dinner, to persuade me to come and help with your last case.' Ellis chinked glasses with Billie. 'Best thing that ever happened to me. Found Boo and my long-lost girl. Laid a lot of ghosts to rest and made me put things into perspective.' He took a sip of his wine.

'Did you know the Chief before?' Billie had to ask. Ellis had been at a solicitor's a couple of hours earlier, after all.

'Nope. My reputation goes before me.' He winked mischievously. It was true that Ellis had been known as one of the best undercover operatives in the business. Well, that's what the Chief had told her anyway, but had there been more to the relationship?

'And now you've found a long-lost uncle in the area too.' Billie looked straight into Ellis's eyes. He stopped drinking for only a split second before putting his glass down and grinning at Billie.

'Don't get to be a super when you're still so young and good-looking without being a crack investigative detective. Congratulations, you are spot on with your inside knowledge.'

Billie feigned exasperation at his words.

'Maya mentioned. Your daughter *is* assigned to my team, remember?' She took a sip of her wine, hoping that her comment had been offhand enough. Could he be the Chief's child?

Billie remembered the black box in her cellar. As soon as she got home tonight, she would open it and find out what the Chief was so desperate to hide from the coppers coming to arrest him. Ellis was watching her carefully, silent for a moment. She hoped to God she was wrong about this and anyway, just because he might end up having a motive for killing the Chief, it didn't mean that he *did* harm him. Billie's mind was racing as she thought of Boo, Maya, and the resulting fallout if her crazy imaginings turned out to be true.

'You're right,' Ellis finally answered. 'He's left us his house.' Billie's stomach tightened into a knot. 'So I can move out of the room above here in this pub and give my daughter a proper home whilst she's doing her degree. Have her little sis up to stay sometimes too. But tell you the truth, I would give all that up just to have had a relationship with my old unc. Got a case full of photos out of his house when I went to look. He seemed like a nice guy. Got a haircut like me. It must run in the family.' Ellis grinned and touched his bald head. 'But seriously, I don't have to tell you how being in the force fucks up family relationships,' he added. 'Anyway, onwards, and upwards. Come on, drink up. Toast to the Chief!' He held up his glass once more. Billie raised her own, hiding a big sigh of relief. The Chief had had a full head of hair. On the other hand, Ellis was clever, he could be playing games.

'So back to blackmail.' She took a drink from her glass and picked a rapidly cooling fish finger from the sandwich now lying on her plate. The conversation had dimmed her appetite for a moment. 'Why would anyone want to blackmail Arden Roy?' Billie asked.

'Good question, you should join me as a private dick to find out.' Ellis started tucking back into his steak.

'So you know, but aren't telling?' Billie pushed. 'It might be important to my investigation. Two of his actors have died in suspect circumstances and I now have four murder investigations on the go all tied up with *Alice in Wonderland* content.' Billie pinched a chip from his plate.

'He thinks it's because of the cross-dressing thing.' Ellis

slapped Billie's hand away playfully as she went in for another chip before grabbing a handful and dropping them onto her plate.

'I don't buy it.' Billie reached for the gastro ketchup, sitting in a small bowl. She tipped half of it onto her chips.

'Take my bleeding eyes and come back for the sockets, why don't you?' Ellis teased, taking his ketchup back and tipping the remainder onto his plate.

'It could be spot on...' Ellis dipped a chip in the sauce while he pondered. 'After all, how many cross-dressed film directors have you seen stepping up to receive an Oscar? He thinks his career will be over if word gets out, hence his early morning costume calls... maybe someone got wind of it and thinks they can make an ongoing income out of the knowledge. Starts knocking off the actors when he won't cough up...' Ellis's brow wrinkled.

'You don't really believe that, though, do you?' Billie answered. 'It doesn't explain the other deaths, which are related to the *Alice* stories but not directly to Arden Roy.'

'Well, I don't know enough about the other murders, do I?' Ellis pulled a face at Billie. 'Not now I'm just a lowly PI, not a cop and you've drilled my lovely daughter well, because Maya's refused to spill any beans, no matter how much I try to bribe her.'

Billie sat back and laughed, giving a silent round of applause for her new apprentice, training on the job, as part of her degree in policing. She came to a decision. One that could get her jailed if her character assessment of Ellis turned out to be wrong, but rules were sometimes meant to be broken.

'I can give *some* details. All highly confidential, of course,' she offered carefully. Ellis pretended to think about it for a moment before giving a mischievous grin. He leant back on his chair and caught the attention of the waiter, before asking for another bottle of wine as he emptied the bottle they were drinking.

'Okay. Tell you what, you show me yours and I'll show you mine,' he offered. It was a proposition that Billie simply couldn't refuse.

15

NOTHING HAPPENED?

It was the snoring that woke her. It was thunderous enough to put the Royal Corps of Army Music marching band, complete with wind and fanfare trumpets, to shame. Billie shot out of bed, almost rolling onto the floor in her haste, before realising that this wasn't her bed – or her floor. She squinted around and then swore out loud, yanking the corner of the sheet to cover her naked body. Ellis Darque lay similarly unclothed, on the other side of the bed.

'Whassup?' He screwed up his eyes, turning his body towards her. 'Who's making the noise?' Billie swore again, backing away, dragging the sheet with her. Ellis jumped out of bed and spun around to face her. 'What the...?' His eyes suddenly shot wide open in astonishment.

'What are you doing here?' Billie hissed, trying to get her still wine-addled brain to kick into gear.

'It's my bed.' Ellis looked down, appearing to be making sure that it was, in fact, the case. He grabbed his T-shirt from the floor in an attempt to cover some of his body.

'Jesus Christ!' Billie spotted her clothes strewn on the carpet and rushed to grab them. 'This didn't happen, please tell me this didn't happen!' She dropped the sheet and stepped into her pants, feeling her face flare pink in alarm. Finding her jeans, she managed to get one leg in before tripping onto the bed. 'Nothing happened, right?' she called over her shoulder, sitting on the bed with her back now to Ellis, scrabbling for her top from the floor. He was speedily throwing on his own clothes.

'No. Nothing happened...' He hopped on one foot, pulling on a sock. 'Did it?' They both managed to look at each other at last. 'I can't remember...' He trailed off sheepishly.

Billie, horror-stricken, scoured her memory. It was a blank. She'd never drunk so much in her life before that she had lost her memory. A couple of glasses of white wine usually got her tipsy, but she preferred to be in control at all times.

'You *must* remember,' Billie pleaded, still trying to kick her brain into gear.

'So *you* tell me what happened?' Ellis counter-argued.

'We drank the second bottle, then... I have no idea...' Billie closed her eyes tight in revulsion and pain, as a headache began playing a drumbeat on the back of her head.

'So, you couldn't drive and just decided to doss down here,' Ellis reasoned. It was a totally plausible argument, Billie agreed to herself, but didn't explain the lack of clothing and the fact that Ellis's arm had been wrapped around her body when she had flung herself out of the bed.

'I feel sick,' she mumbled, heading for the bathroom. She caught her reflection in the mirror as she splashed water over her face. She looked ill... or guilty... or both.

'So that's all it was,' Ellis started in full flow as Billie emerged back into the bedroom. 'Let's just forget anything happened because nothing did,' he reiterated.

'Right,' Billie answered. Nothing they could remember, she quietly agreed, but she already had a history of post-traumatic stress episodes and in her experience, memory blanks didn't stay buried for long.

'I love Beddy,' Ellis announced, using his pet name for Boo. 'I don't want it all to go wrong a second time.' He rubbed his face in distress. 'You won't tell her, will you?'

'She's one of my best friends!' Billie announced, her voice full of stress and remorse. How on earth could she do this to Boo of all people? Billie started striding back and forth across the room.

'So neither of us want to hurt her, Billie, or Max either. It looks like you've got something good going with him...' Billie didn't want to even go there at the moment. But it would be the final nail in the coffin for sure, should he get wind of this little episode. Ellis started to straighten the sheets, trying no doubt to make the bed look like less of a crime scene.

'Let's just put this thing to bed–'

'Christ!' Billie cut in. She didn't want to hear that word right now. She felt sick again. Her mobile suddenly started to ring, from somewhere amongst the bedding. Billie started hurling pillows off and tearing back the sheets again, undoing Ellis's feeble work. She finally found the mobile under the bed. On Ellis's side.

'Hi, it's me.' Billie heard Ash's voice. 'Where are you?'

'I was just working late over at the film base, so I grabbed a hotel room for the night.' Billie closed her eyes as Ellis came into view searching for his lost sock. She wanted the floor to open up and swallow her.

'I stayed over at GG's hotel,' Ash confided, 'so I've just nipped back to ours for a change of clothing. Sorry to be the bearer of bad tidings, but you've been burgled.' He let his words sink in for a moment before adding, 'Place is a bit of a mess.'

'You're joking?' Billie felt her stomach lurch again.

'No. Sorry. Place has been turned over. Even the basement

door has been jemmied and ransacked. Best come over before heading into work,' he advised.

'What time is it?' Billie scoured the room. She finally spotted her watch on the floor.

'Six thirty,' Ash replied. 'You okay?' he added.

'Yeah. Never felt better. I'm on my way.' She ended the call and rushed to the bathroom to be sick, almost knocking heads with Ellis, who already had his head down the pan. They finished, and both stood up, pink-faced and wiping their mouths on strips of toilet paper.

'Well, look on the bright side. The day can only get better,' Ellis offered, as Billie turned on her heel and raced for the exit door.

It was the Japanese bowl which upset Billie the most, though much of her lovely new home had been turned over. But the indigo-blue bowl, with a crazy paving of gold decoration had been gifted to her by her birth mother, who had so admired kintsugi, the art of putting broken pottery pieces back together with gold. It had stood on the table in the hallway, exactly where it had been when she had first been reunited with her mum in this house.

The kintsugi skill had been built on the idea that in embracing flaws and imperfections a stronger, more beautiful, and resilient piece can be created. It had been Billie's guiding light through the year of loss and restoration of her own life. Now here it lay in pieces once more.

The bowl had been the only item broken, though drawers and cupboards had been pulled out throughout the entire house, as well as several bottles of red wine emptied with some energy as the red trails splattered up walls, across floors and the pale ivory sofas in Billie's lounge.

'Only the Château Batailley.' Ash collected the empty bottles strewn across the floor. 'Somebody's got expensive tastes. They left all the cheap plonk.' He nodded to the otherwise well-stocked wine rack. Billie had got the case of special wine in for the Chief's visits. She suddenly remembered the night before once again and felt her stomach turn.

'It's a mess, but nothing appears to have been nicked.' Billie walked around the rooms, noting that the usual expensive and portable electrical items remained in situ. Her home office had documents scattered all over the floor, but she rarely kept case files in her house, if that's what anyone had been searching for.

'You'll have to check out the basement. I have no idea if anything has gone from there. It's such a vast space and half of the stuff was your mum's or from your last place.' Billie suddenly remembered the Chief's black box. She sprinted out and around the side of the house, followed by Ash. The key to the door was on her keyring, but it wasn't needed as the door was jammed wide open, so that Billie and Ash had to squeeze around the bush immediately outside to enter.

'Must have been someone who knew this was here.' Ash stood in the doorway as Billie flicked the light on. 'How else could they have targeted a door practically in a giant shrub?'

Billie was pushing boxes and chests out of the way, already knowing in her heart that the black box was missing. She cursed herself for not having opened it immediately, asking herself silently but forcefully whether she was losing her touch. But if she was being honest, she knew the answer. Despite her protestations of the Chief's innocence, she was terrified that she had been deluding herself, that more earth-shattering secrets might have emerged from inside. Just as they had when she had opened a box belonging to her dad after his death.

She hastily climbed over all the material objects that had made up her life history. Much of it she hadn't been able to yet face exhuming. An old clockwork white rabbit suddenly rolled across the floor, sparking a long-forgotten childhood memory to hopscotch through her mind's eye. At least it was a happy one. It had obviously been a cherished toy of hers as a child, kept for so many years by her mother. Billie sighed loudly. When this investigation was over she really did need to brace herself for the job of sifting through everything or get a house removal firm to simply come in and ship the lot out.

'Missing something?' Ash asked.

'Maybe.' Billie sighed, running her fingers through her hair. Her head had started throbbing again as her mobile rang. It was Boo. She felt as though she was going to throw up.

'Hi, I came in early.' Boo sounded downbeat. Billie felt even worse about the night spent in bed with Boo's partner. 'Thought I should remind you that Miriam Nelson has arranged for a criminal psychologist to come in first thing to run through a profile, now that she's agreed that we really do have a serial killer on our hands.'

'Right, thanks.' Billie ended the call quickly as a wave of guilt washed over her. She turned to Ash. 'I'll check later. We've got to get a move on. Seems like the new chief has booked in Max's replacement to give us all a pep talk on what a serial killer is meant to look like.'

'God give me strength.' Ash sighed. 'I'm not doing a downer on Max or anything, but most criminal psychologists that I meet seem to spew out stuff that a toddler could have worked out and it's always intel after the event, never anything that actually helps us catch a killer.' Billie wasn't sure that she agreed, Max had given her one or two useful pointers in the past, that on reflection had turned out to be spot on.

'He was just having a bad day, when he kicked off the other

night,' Billie started to explain as they headed for the car, wondering why she was covering up for Max's bad behaviour. 'It wasn't anything against you personally.' She couldn't resist a chuckle at the memory of Ash and GG Mills at the top of the staircase looking like naughty boys as Max had ranted at her.

'All the same,' Ash answered, 'I think it's time I moved out.'

'No!' Billie grabbed his wrist. She had gotten used to Ash's sunny presence, his kids, his wonderful cooking, even if Max had hinted about wanting her all to himself. 'I'll die of starvation if you move out. You'll find me deceased in the garden, with foxes tearing at the last vestiges of flesh from my bones,' Billie protested. Ash laughed.

'Not when there's a chip shop within a five-mile radius,' he teased. 'You're more likely to die from furred-up arteries,' he added, as he reached for his car keys. 'GG's going to be doing his next film in the area, so I'm hopeful he'll be around a lot more, get to know my girls. I'm ready to start building my own little family nest.'

'So tell him he's welcome to stay,' Billie countered. 'God, I'll be the envy of every woman in the world, with a film star lolling around in the attic.'

'You'd be the envy of lots of guys too,' Ash reminded Billie. 'But it's early days for us yet and let's face it, he spends most of his life jet-setting around the world. This is partly about me feeling that I can move forward independently, establish an alternative forever home for the girls. They need that stability. Anyway, turns out he's got a little cottage that he's doing up for when he next stays. Belonged to an ancient aunt. It's in Boldon.'

Billie's ears pricked up. Could GG's family have had any local connections with Charles Carroll, who was killed in St Nicholas's churchyard in the same village? The delectable GG Mills was hovering very close to an investigating officer. Was there more to it than instant attraction? All this publicity about the film would certainly be keeping him in the spotlight, Billie mused, before deciding that it was a mad idea. The only killer part of GG Mills was his looks.

She hated herself for being so eternally suspicious and not only that, but her heart sank at the thought of seeing Ash's adorable children less regularly. She loved the time they spent at her house, playing on the beach, fishing for crabs, eating endless ice creams. It reminded Billie of the best bits of her own childhood. She had a sudden idea.

'So what about the basement?' Billie perked up for the first time that morning. 'It's huge. Way big enough to be converted into a flat, with bedrooms for all of the girls and access straight to the garden and the beach. You could have your own front door, completely separate from me, divide it all legally...' Billie gripped Ash's arm. It seemed an ideal solution and from the look on his face the idea appealed to him too.

'Are you serious?' he asked, his warm dark eyes crinkling at the corners in a wide smile.

'Absolutely!' Billie high-fived Ash. 'You'll have to help me clear out the place first though,' she added. There would no doubt be a few tears along the way and there might still be an outside chance that the black box had just tumbled into a dark corner somewhere inside. Billie silently rebuked herself about that once more. How could she constantly hammer home her core values of the pursuit of truth to her team of detectives, when she had avoided the chance to discover a hidden secret about one so close, herself?

'We promote them, elect them and many people feel more comfortable with leaders who are technically psychopaths.'

As the small, mousey, bespectacled criminal psychologist,

Doctor Zelda Mead droned on, Billie checked her watch and stifled a yawn. Ash was right. The new shrink on the block hadn't told them anything so far that they didn't know already about serial killers.

'The title is a colloquial one, the technical diagnosis officially is "antisocial personality disorder",' she continued as Miriam Nelson slipped into the back of the room attempting and failing to do so discreetly, judging by the way everyone started to sit up straighter in their seats. 'Usually psychopaths are cunning, have an inflated sense of self-worth, callousness, and lack of empathy.'

A few heads turned, eyeing up Miriam Nelson. Ash nudged Billie and swivelled his eyes in the new chief's direction. Billie's team had been fidgeting like kids in class who've had to sit still too long. She was expecting chewing gum to be flicked at the lecturer from someone at the back of the classroom any minute, so felt that she had better intervene.

'So from the evidence we have shared with you today, Dr Mead, can you throw any light on the type of personality that we should be on the lookout for?'

The small woman turned and eyed Billie like a slightly disapproving owl. Billie guessed that she'd been tipped the wink about Billie's friendship with her predecessor.

'Pippa Sykes was slowly poisoned before she was pushed, or fell, as was your former chief. Maddie Taylor was made to suffer the pain of being coerced into becoming the killer of her friend, before her own murder. This leads me to conclude that you are dealing with what we call a process-focused perpetrator. Such personalities gain intense pleasure from prolonging their victim's agony and watching their suffering. They gain their kicks from killing slowly.

'This sort of torment can take many forms and can continue over several months or years before the victim's final demise, with the offender carefully planning their wounding acts. They will often keep diaries documenting details of the various hurts inflicted so that they can relive the excitement of the anguish suffered without forgetting any detail.' She paused to take a sip of water before continuing.

'With process-focused serial killers, we have two main subcategories – hedonistic thrill seekers and power killers. My educated guess is that you are dealing with the latter – a highly organised individual motivated by a need to control.'

'Without any previous convictions on record, there's no way we can use those details before we've already arrested him though.' Ash folded his arms, appearing less than impressed. 'There are no obvious patterns of behaviour,' he added.

'He appears to have a fixation with the *Alice* books and has some in-depth knowledge of their possible connection to the area,' Dr Mead replied. 'As DSI Wilde has already perceived.' She gave a tight smile in Billie's direction, leading Billie to decide that she had misjudged the doctor's seemingly disapproving look earlier. 'I would also add that your killer will have superficial charm, will blend into a crowd and will be manipulative and intelligent. He or she will most certainly have links to the area and will possibly have experienced a dysfunctional family situation.'

'Haven't we all?' Billie whispered to Ash.

'So, how does that help us work out where he's going to strike next?' Ash piped up again, clearly less than impressed with the psychologist's briefing.

'Why is a raven like a writing desk, officer?' Dr Mead folded her arms and gave her peculiar little smile.

'What?' Ash replied, bewildered at the question.

'It's a line from *Alice in Wonderland*,' Billie explained. 'The Mad Hatter puts the conundrum to Alice.'

'Precisely.' Dr Mead nodded at Billie. 'It's a riddle, like most murder enquiries. My job is simply to furnish you with some clues that may lead you to the culprit. Your job is to decipher them, in order to find an answer.'

'So what was the answer?' Ash continued. 'Why is a raven like a writing desk?' Everyone shrugged.

'Nobody knows,' Billie replied.

'Jeez!' Ash rolled his eyes. 'I think we could do something better with our time than wasting it in asking riddles without answers.'

'That's more or less the answer that Alice gave the Mad Hatter.' Billie chuckled at Ash's exasperation as Miriam Nelson approached the front of the room and thanked Dr Mead with a smile. The woman was clearly her own pet criminal shrink.

The team moved back to their desks to crack on with their work, Billie weaving through them on the way to her office.

'It could be a woman rather than a man,' Maya piped up from behind her PC, as Billie approached her desk. 'Look at this CCTV footage, from outside Maddie Taylor's flat on the night that she died...'

Ash, overhearing, shot over to join Billie, leaning over Maya's workspace, where she had obviously been surreptitiously scrolling through CCTV footage during the talk. From the viewpoint of an outside camera positioned high up in the street where Maddie Taylor lived, they watched a person stepping into shot. From the back view, Billie could see that the individual was female. Tall. Long legs encased in leggings, tucked into light-coloured cowboy boots, and wearing a short denim jacket, like many students. It was the hair that caught Billie's attention, long and blonde, with what appeared to be a streak down one side that caught the light.

'Any way of ramping up the colour on that?' Billie leaned over Maya's shoulder, staring at the screen as the police trainee reran the footage showing the female walking up to the gateway of Maddie Taylor's student flat before disappearing out of shot.

'Charlie might be able to work a miracle, but I'm guessing not,' Ash muttered. 'Time code is saying it's 1am so the CCTV will be operating on infra-red LEDs which can't differentiate on colour.'

'Here's the same street, only at the bottom end from a different source.' Maya clicked up another stream of footage. 'The person either went into Maddie's place, or one of the other houses between Maddie's and the end of the road...' She started to explain.

'There are only three of them,' Billie answered, 'so she would have appeared on this camera within less than a minute if she had been heading out of the street. Okay. Ash, will you nip down and check the movements of all the neighbours between these two points. See if they clocked any visitors within that time. Maya, get this over to Charlie to see if forensics can enhance it. Good work.' She patted Maya on the back. 'Your dad would be proud of you.'

'He said he is already.' Maya giggled at the memory. 'Mind you it was at two am this morning when he told me exactly that and he did look as though he was under the influence of heavy drink,' she explained.

'This morning?' Billie frowned. 'Where?' She had been under the impression that both she and Ellis had been clapped out in birthday suits in the same bed, at that time.

'Outside that pub he's been staying in. I was on my way back to the halls of residence, with some of my uni pals when I spotted him. Thought he must have been working. We'd been on the half-price drinks, mind, so I wasn't interrogating.'

'Was he wearing any clothes?' Billie suddenly realised by the looks on the faces of both Maya and Ash, that she had verbalised what she had intended to be an inner thought.

'Of course he was.' Maya pulled a surprised face.

'What? Are you going to reveal that he's an undercover nudist or something?' Ash nudged Billie, chuckling. She responded with a grin that wasn't registering within.

'Sorry. I'm not making any sense. I'm not with it this morning,' Billie said, managing to wriggle out of the conversation, *because I thought I had been in bed with your dad all night*, were the words that were ricocheting about in her head.

Had Ellis gotten out of bed in the middle of the night and dressed then slipped outside? If so, then for how long and why? Even worse, had he come back, stripped off and got back into the bed, knowing that she was in there and also as naked as the day that she had been born? If so, what else might have happened? She rubbed her head, feeling sick with the thought.

'You look how I feel.' Boo rammed the back of Billie's leg with the footrest of her wheelchair, transferring the immediate feelings of pain from head and stomach to her lower leg. 'I'll stand you a couple of headache pills if you buy the coffees,' she offered, already wheeling her way out. Billie sighed and followed, suddenly feeling like a lamb to the slaughter.

'It's dead anyway.' Boo shrugged as Billie's heart sank even further. Personally, she didn't have the stomach for food, but Boo was tucking into a full English breakfast in the police canteen, like a starving woman. Anyone would have thought that she hadn't eaten for days.

'I'm so sorry…' Billie trailed off.

'Stop saying you're sorry. You've done me a favour.' Boo dipped her sausage into her egg yolk. Billie blew out a sigh. She had come clean to Boo about the night before, not being able to bear keeping such a secret from one of her best mates. Ellis wasn't going to thank her for it, but Ellis hadn't come completely clean with her either, if Maya's account was true. So, Billie had chosen to follow her conscience. The decision was proving more painful because Boo was being so understanding.

'But there's no reason for you and Ellis to break up. He was as horrified as I was and honestly, *nothing* happened.' *Except that Ellis appeared to have not been as comatose with drink as he had claimed, in truth.* Billie's inner devil jabbed her with his three-pronged trident.

'That's not the reason that he's toast,' Boo answered. 'This other guy, that you've already deduced I'm seeing, I knew him even before Ellis came back on the scene.' She took a swig of her coffee. 'It's getting serious, so I'm clearing the decks.'

'Really? You never mentioned.' Billie couldn't help cheering up at the news, despite the repercussions for Ellis. 'Is he hot?'

'Yeah.' Boo grinned. 'Give your handsome Max Strong a run for his money. He's coming here any day now. Been abroad for a bit. So, you'll get to meet him for yourself.'

'Sounds intriguing,' Billie teased. 'But poor old Ellis will be heartbroken,' she pointed out.

'So poor old Ellis shouldn't have cocked it all up first time around.' Boo referred to the time, nineteen years earlier, when she and Ellis had almost become romantically engaged. 'And seems he's still hopping into bed with other women at the drop of a hat now,' she added. Billie felt a rush of shame wash over her again.

'Like I said *nothing* happened.' Billie reached for Boo's hand, but she was busy spreading jam on her toast, seemingly relaxed about the situation.

'Still... look, don't get me wrong. I'm glad Ellis is back on the scene, and I hope we'll continue to be great mates, but someone once said that you should never go back. The truth is we are different people than we were then. Literally.' Boo bit into her toast, like she was eating for two. 'I once read somewhere that all of the cells in your body replace every seven years, so I'm essentially an entirely different person than I was then. I've been a different person more than once, so he can't expect me to feel the same.'

'Great idea, but I think that's just a myth,' Billie answered, 'otherwise why have I still got this scar here.' She held up her thumb. 'From where I fell off my horse aged eleven? And why haven't you got a completely new set of legs?' she continued. Boo wrinkled up her nose.

'Don't spoil my great excuse with your logic.' She pretended to be annoyed. 'I am in fact a totally different person than I was then and so is Ellis. He's got two kids, an ex-wife, and a barrel-load of responsibilities on his shoulders and I've got dreams of being free to swing from the chandeliers with a hot new hunk. Instead, I've been landed with a former work colleague, still so racked with guilt about my wheels, that he feels he has to be my carer twenty-four seven.' She stabbed her hash brown with her fork and took a bite. 'It's time to move on. But don't tell Max what you've just told me about your sleepover. I get the impression that he'll be unlikely to be quite so understanding.' Billie sighed.

'Fancy another cuppa?' she asked. Boo's face lit up.

'Yeah, oh, no it's okay. I've like, I've forgotten my purse... I'll pay you back for this, of course–' Billie cut Boo off mid-sentence.

'I told you I was paying. Christ, let me get you another coffee, make me feel better about taking your man to bed.' She still felt terrible no matter how easy Boo was trying to make this situation for her.

'Did he snore?' Boo chuckled, as she wiped around her plate with the last piece of toast.

'Oh yeah, and then some.' Billie finally giggled at the madness of the situation.

'Thank your lucky stars he didn't sleepwalk.' Boo laughed. 'He used to do that, years back, if he'd drank too much. Got us into one or two tight fixes when we were working undercover, I can tell you. Thought he was about to spill the beans on a couple of occasions. He even went walkabout and locked himself out of our digs one night. Got picked up by the local coppers, absolutely starkers, in the street.' She shook her head in amusement.

Billie's ears pricked up. Could Ellis's sleepwalking be the reason that he had left the pub in the dead of night, or had he been on some other nocturnal walkabout, the true nature of which he was determined to hide?

16

KILLING TIME

'Just killing time,' Fredi, the make-up artist, answered as Billie popped her head into the trailer and asked if she was busy. Billie stepped inside. 'Big set-up for the Queen of Hearts courtroom scene. Major special effects day, as Alice grows huge and knocks over the army of Playing Cards that come flying at her, when the Queen orders her beheading.' Fredi summarised the scene towards the end of *Alice in Wonderland* in a nutshell.

'Have you seen the size of the wind machine that they've brought in to create the effect of the draft from Alice's huge arm knocking the cards flat?' Fredi pointed out of the window towards the vast device, which looked to Billie like a giant fan, on the back of a trailer, being moved carefully into position behind a tree, as lighting and props crew rushed around setting everything in place to bring the story to life.

Billie recognised the dashing Knave of Hearts having some adjustments made to his costume, whilst the pack of Playing Card guards hung around eating biscuits and sipping drinks. It was a quite surreal sight as Billie picked out iconic figures from the *Alice* stories, following unlikely pursuits.

The White Rabbit sat on a fold-up black chair, flicking through his script, legs crossed, specs perched on his nose as he said his words out loud, to no one in particular. The King and the Lizard were perched on a mound of grass nearby, exchanging stories of film productions past, whilst they played a game of patience with a real pack of cards. The Mad Hatter, in full costume, was doing a yoga pose, as a tweenager dressed as Alice practised a handstand against a tree.

'All in a day's work.' Fredi chuckled. 'Everyone's as Mad as a Hatter around here.' Billie reached for the enlarged CCTV photo and handed it to Fredi.

'Seen anybody like this hanging around the film set? Could be one of the support cast, perhaps? You see them before they get disguised in make-up and costume.' Billie knew that it was a long shot, but she could be looking at the person in the photo right now and wouldn't recognise them, whereas Fredi just might. 'Someone who knew Maddie Taylor and maybe Pippa Sykes too,' she added as Fredi took the photo from her.

'Nope. But I can stick this up on the wall in here. One of the others might recognise them,' Fredi answered, reaching for some double-sided tape on her place. The beautiful actress who Billie recognised as Luna Da Costa, stood at the far make-up station, using eyelash curlers to accentuate her already stunning hazel eyes. She wasn't in costume today. In *Alice Through the Looking-Glass*, Billie remembered, Alice viewed the character of the Red Queen as the cause of all mischief. She wasn't looking at Billie in a particularly benevolent fashion right now.

Through the window Billie had a clear view of all of the preparations being made for the outdoor court scene. Characters had started taking their places in the jury box, not easy when dressed as animals and birds. One of the Guinea Pigs rehearsed his 'cheer' as the cast playing officers of the court flipped him over into a huge canvas bag and tied it with string. One of them sat on him.

It was all part of the original *Alice* story, which Billie had considered to be surreal when reading it, but the scene now appeared utterly bizarre as she watched actors bringing the story to life. It was a technically difficult move in the space provided, especially with the lighting director holding a light monitor to the Guinea Pig's face and a dresser trying to brush lint off the officer's jackets with a Velcro clothes brush in readiness for the scene. Fredi finished sticking the CCTV photo onto the wall and joined Billie.

'We've got loads of casual crew in today, this being such a huge scene. That's why so many people are wearing face masks. Everyone has to, in the vicinity of the actors, when they're on set. It just needs one of them to catch a bug and it would go around like wildfire. Our dear director would not be happy.' Fredi smiled mischievously at Billie.

'No one wants to lose a precious member of the cast to some unseen killer, that no-one can catch, after all.' Luna Da Costa joined the conversation, as she finished touching up her make-up and headed towards them, looking Billie up and down. She clearly appeared to find her somehow lacking. 'Don't you agree, officer?' Luna arched an eyebrow in question. 'Seems that instead of running faster and faster, you just seem to be staying in this same place. Not exactly winning *your* race against time, are you?' She referred theatrically to some of her speeches as the Red Queen.

'Difference is that I'm dealing with real life – and death,' Billie answered. 'Rather than make-believe.' Luna Da Costa smirked and squeezed past her, tossing her mane of dark curls as she headed out of the trailer and towards the edge of the set.

'I'll leave you to it. Thanks for doing that.' Billie nodded to the CCTV photo. She opened the door and headed down the steps. The make-up artist followed.

'Don't mind her,' Fredi whispered, taking a few steps out. 'She's okay. Just a jobbing actress with a couple of hits, hoping that this film will launch her onto the "A" list. I've seen them all come and go. My feeling is that she hasn't got that X factor, but she's certainly pulling out all the stops to make her name on this one.'

Billie wandered in the direction of the set as the actors assembled for a take, almost bumping into Ellis who was lifting a tea urn onto a trestle table. He was still looking worse for wear from the night before.

'Any news?' Billie badgered. He gave her a surly glance.

'I shouldn't even speak to you. I've just been given my marching orders from Beddy.' He gave his pet name for Boo. 'Been having a chinwag with her?'

'Let's just say that I've got a clear conscience. Can you say the same?' Billie folded her arms. Ellis didn't respond to her needling as he headed off to carry on with his undercover catering duties. Had he really been sleepwalking, or was he just a great actor?

'Oh, Billie, darling.' Lola rushed up and air-kissed Billie. 'So kind of you to come to see my big scene today.' Billie didn't correct her. Max's mother was a charmer, but it wouldn't for a moment have occurred to her that Billie would be here on the set for any other reason.

'I've just been doing an interview with darling Peggy here...'

'Perry,' the journalist corrected Lola as she joined them.

'Sorry, I really must fly. I have to take a moment to get into my character.' Lola headed for the set, desperate for her moment in the spotlight. Perry reached for a biscuit from the plate that Ellis had just left on the table.

'Talk about starving actors, the payment for this gig won't

cover my grocery bill, so I better stock up on the free grub while I'm here.' Perry poured herself a cup of coffee from the urn whilst she was at it. Billie decided that she would corner Ellis later about his reasons for being out and about in the early hours.

'You all right with *The Evening Post* spread last night?' Perry asked. 'I did warn you they would go to town on the story.' Billie poured her own cup of coffee.

'Yep. Job well done, thanks.' Billie nabbed a biscuit. 'Hopefully it drew enough attention to help move the investigation forward. We just need someone to spill a key bit of info.'

'Thanks. It was a nice little earner for me too,' Perry answered, looking around in admiration at the location. 'Don't you just love this spot? It's pure *Alice Through the Looking-Glass* even before the film lot turned up.' Billie looked around her. They were standing outside of a real ruined castle, which must have been magnificent in its prime.

'Hylton Castle, built by Sir William Hylton in the fourteenth century. See the heraldic display on the wall?' Perry asked. Billie nodded. 'It features all of the local aristocracy and landowners of the area. All were related to Alice Liddell. Boldon church and rectory are just a mile away and in the other direction, close by, lies Southwick Rectory, where Carroll's sister lived.

'It's believed locally that the Hylton Castle heraldic display is the real basis for Alice's moves in *Through the Looking-Glass* when she is involved in the chess game. Every single move she makes in the story can be seen as a wordplay, a game of logical paradox, on the different shields you can see on this wall. It's the sort of puzzle that appealed to the author, being a mathematician. The tree referred to in the book being Alice Liddell's family tree, rather than a real one that she was sitting under in the story.

'I've never heard that before.' Billie looked at the worn displays on the ancient walls.

'The area we are standing on now was known at the time that the *Alice* books were written, as Bunny Hill. It was said that a tunnel ran down from somewhere around here to Spottie's Hole, a cave on Roker beach. Lewis Carroll once had a conversation with a ship's carpenter there.'

'You're not claiming that a Walrus was hanging around at the time, too, are you?' Billie joked.

'Actually, yes.' Perry chuckled at Billie's look of surprise. 'Lewis Carroll's uncle, as I mentioned before, was a Sunderland customs and tax collector. He shared premises with a great friend, Captain Joseph Wiggins, who brought back a walrus from one of his voyages. The head's still in Sunderland Museum today.'

'You didn't know Charles Carroll, did you?' Billie asked. 'We're looking for a local killer, who has inside knowledge on the links between the stories and the area after all.'

'Not me, officer,' Perry joked. 'But I'll have a look through my old notes. See if any prime suspects come up amongst the local Lewis Carroll fans I interviewed for my article.' Perry pointed to Penshaw Monument in the distance. 'Home of the Jabberwocky,' she announced. Billie felt momentarily queasy, as the memory of the Chief lying dead at the top seared through her mind once more. 'Based on our own local Lambton Worm myth,' Perry added. Billie's heart started racing as she pictured the horrific 'worm' discovered in the Chief's stomach during his autopsy.

'Are you sure about that?' Billie asked. She, like everyone else in the north-east of England, had been told the tale as a child of a giant worm that had terrorised the locals, wrapping itself seven times around Worm Hill, until it was slain by a brave knight coming home from the Crusades. Perry shrugged.

'It makes sense. It's a matter of recorded fact that Lewis

Carroll completed the poem when he was visiting relatives in the area and the famous song was launched at the pantomime at the local Tyne Theatre when Carroll was here. He loved going to the theatre.'

'The Geordie dialect it's sung in, is certainly as hard to decipher as the poem,' Billie agreed.

'And it's a similar story. A terrifying monster slain, leading a father to outstretch his arms to his victorious son. The beamish boy referred to in the Jabberwocky, is believed by locals, to be Lord Lambton's son John, Knight of Rhodes, who killed the Lambton Worm. Beamish lies two miles from the Lambton estate. It was once owned by the Liddell family.'

'Curiouser and curiouser,' Billie joked, although the additional link to the Chief's death was in truth no laughing matter.

Their conversation was drowned out by the noise of the huge wind machine, as it started blowing and the cast got into their first positions.

'Quiet, everyone. Going for a take!' the first assistant, standing next to Arden Roy shouted loudly.

It was at that moment that the paper cups and plates that Ellis had just arranged on the table started flying away. Billie and Perry rushed to grab the items before they flew into shot. Even Billie could have some sympathy for Arden Roy, if this complicated scene was ruined by high-flying detritus. Having almost rugby-tackled the final cup, Billie turned, arms full, just as Lola stepped on a podium and shouted, 'Off with her head!' in character, pointing at the actress playing Alice.

The movement of the wind machine toppling was so quick from its position behind the tree, that Billie had no idea if it had been pushed forward, or simply fell. But one thing was for sure. The safety guard was missing as the huge machine plunged onto Lola. The effect was horrific and deadly.

It had been a harrowing afternoon, not least because Josta had needed to be forcibly prevented from accessing the scene, where her queen of nearly forty years lay slain and Billie could hear Perry, always the crack journalist, focused on a gripping story, ringing in the news, to some outlet.

'The spotlight went out on actress Lola Strong's life today, when she made a chilling prophesy,' she dictated. 'On the words "off with her head", the massive wind machine, lacking a safety guard, crashed down onto the film set, separating her skull from her torso.'

Though Billie now accepted that Perry had a job to do as a journalist, she was curious how she found it possible to switch off her emotions immediately to summarise the horrific death of a woman that she had been cheerfully interviewing about her life only moments before. 'If it doesn't bleed, it doesn't lead,' Perry had told Billie once. There would be no doubt that this story would lead the news via an international media, hungry for grizzly stories and Perry had no doubt negotiated a nice little fee for it. But Billie desperately hoped that it wouldn't be the way Max would come to learn of his mother's death.

She had tried his mobile endless times, but the line had sounded dead. Billie guessed he wouldn't be using his own handset for safety reasons wherever he was working, and she had absolutely no idea when he would return. Luckily, Josta's dear friend, Isabelle, a former nun, had arrived brimful of sympathy and red wine to help her through the initial shock and grief.

A locum forensic pathologist had been called to the scene in Josta's place, but there was no great mystery as to the manner of death. Everyone present, cast and crew, had witnessed it and Billie had seen it with her own eyes. The only question was as to why the safety guard had been taken off the machine. Billie remembered it having been on when Fredi had pointed the device out, only a few minutes earlier.

The normal operative had raced to the location when everyone had been careering around in shock, claiming that he'd just taken a quick bathroom break and the fan guard, now lying in the grass next to the tree, had been firmly clipped in place when he had left. He was also adamant that he hadn't switched the machine on. The first assistant reported that the starting of the appliance was the agreed cue for the scene to begin, hence his call to action. No one owned up to having been near the device.

Billie racked her brains. It wasn't often that a murder detective was likely to find themselves called as an actual witness to a suspicious death. She feared that she would be less use than a bag of frogs. There had been loads of cast and crew milling around by the machine, including Luna Da Costa, on leaving the make-up trailer. The actress had walked towards GG Mills and had stood beside the tree watching the rehearsals. Ellis had also headed that way, after making it clear that he was less than pleased with Billie about her having shared their bedtime story.

Billie actually noticed her hand shaking as she turned the handle to open the door to the murder investigation suite. She kicked it and walked through instead. Most of her team were still out interviewing all of the witnesses. They were on first-name terms with some of them by now. Filming had well and truly stopped for the day. Even Arden Roy had called a halt, appearing to have been genuinely upset by the horror show.

'You have got to be joking!' Billie heard Boo's angry voice as she loomed into view. She was shouting into the telephone receiver before slamming it down. 'Bloody banks!' She swore as Billie raised her eyebrows in question. 'They're refusing to release *my* money!'

'Is it anything I can help with?' Billie asked, an argument with a bank suddenly seeming like a session of light relief after the day she'd been through so far.

'No... it's okay. It's just that my guy, Frankie, he was due to be coming over this weekend and he's had temporary issues accessing his own accounts. He's been overseas in Ukraine on an engineering job, so I sent him some money. There's been some stupid new law since Covid and now he's got to pay a visitor tax before he can leave the country.' Alarm bells started to ring in Billie's head.

'You do know this guy, I mean personally?' Billie asked.

'Of course I do. We've been talking about getting married,' Boo answered, like she wasn't some kind of idiot. 'The tax office sent him a letter demanding money. Look, here's a copy of it!' Boo clicked on her PC and brought up a copy of a letter.

'And you paid this?' Billie looked at the bill for 50,000 US dollars.

'I *had* to,' Boo answered. 'They were threatening to sling him in jail otherwise. He's already sold his car and cashed in his pension to pay the rest. Now they're saying he can't have his passport back until he pays another 20,000 dollars in interest.' Billie's heart sank like a lead balloon.

'Which you aren't going to do,' she prompted.

'No. The bank's saying they've frozen my account, after I sent over 10,000 pounds to help with that.' Boo sounded completely agitated as she clicked on her keyboard and brought a picture up onto the screen. It was of a dark-haired, handsome man looking forlornly into the screen. 'But look at him. He's normally smiling, happy...' Boo trailed off as Billie clasped her hand.

'Boo. Have you ever met this guy, I mean, in the flesh?' Billie tried to keep her voice calm, even. But it was clear the penny had dropped already. Tears started to roll down Boo's face, as she shook her head.

'No. Just online. I've got mortgage arrears... I've even sold my other wheelchair,' she started explaining, as the photo of a man living somewhere in the world who probably had no idea at all that his likeness was being used in a romance scam, stared back. Billie reached for the internal phone and punched in some numbers.

'Is that the fraud department?' she asked as Boo started to wail in distress. Billie's mobile rang as she ended the call, wondering how someone as savvy as Boo could have fallen for an online scammer – probably a gang in fact, the fraud department had advised – promising to send someone straight over.

'Hello. DSI Billie Wilde,' Billie answered, her mind spinning with the various issues of the day.

'Billie, it's Max.' The voice made Billie's heart leap for more than just one reason. 'Have you been trying to get me? Are you okay?' His voice sounded full of concern. Billie took a deep breath in.

'I'm okay,' she started. Max seemed to exhale a sigh of relief.

'Thank goodness for that. With so many messages left on my phone, I was worried. Any news on how Lola's first day on set went?' Billie braced herself to deliver the news. If she had thought that the day couldn't get any worse, she was about to be proven wrong.

17

TALL STORIES

S he still felt like death, though it seemed like a lifetime ago
that she had woken up with a major hangover and Ellis
snoring in her ear.

'How's she doing?' Billie asked Isabelle as the older woman
opened the door. Billie stepped into the hallway of the home
that had always been Josta and Lola's, but would be known from
here on in simply as 'Josta's place'.

'Not too bad. I've been administering regular medicinal
remedies.' She waved the glass of red wine that she was holding.
'Can I get you one?' Billie shook her head.

Right now, her feeling was that if she never set eyes on
another glass of red wine in her life, it would still be way too
early. Josta looked up as Billie entered. Her face was blotched,
her eyes red-rimmed, puffed, and teary.

'No need for you to have come here so late, my dear.' She
sniffled quietly. 'Not after the day you've had.' She reached for a
hanky down the side of her chair and blew her nose. It seemed to
Billie that the usually big and bold woman had shrunk in the past
few hours, her round cheeks now looking sunken and hollow.

'I wanted to let you know that I've spoken to Max. It was only a quick call,' Billie advised, 'I think he was working.' Her stomach tightened at the recollection of Max's shock. Her own worry was that the news would cause him to lose concentration in whatever dangerous situation he had found himself in. She had heard tears in his voice, before a sudden whispered 'Got to go,' followed by his phone going dead. She wasn't going to share that detail with Josta. 'He's going to get back just as soon as he can,' Billie instead offered. Josta nodded, a wan smile on her face.

'Thank you for saving me that burden, dear. Max was always close to the mum who actually gave birth to him.' She wiped a tear rolling down her face and reached for a photo, amongst others in a big box perched on the coffee table next to her chair. It was of baby Max, wrapped in a shawl and being cradled by a very young and beautiful Lola.

'I'm sure it'll be only a few days before he arrives,' Billie reassured Josta as well as herself. The speed at which Max had suddenly curtailed their call had made her mind race as to the reason why. She couldn't bear the thought of him being so vulnerable. Right now, she was willing to forgive him his questionable behaviour the other night. In fact, right now she would be willing to forgive him absolutely *anything*, she mused, if only he would turn up safe. Her nervous system was in danger of becoming trigger-happy after all of the recent horrific deaths. She wasn't sure she could take more bad news.

'Here's something I think we should keep from him for a little while.' Josta lifted a pile of papers stapled together from inside the box. 'Typical Lola.' She smiled sadly. 'Always left her audience wanting more.' She handed Billie the bundle of papers. 'Her memoirs. She still had so much to tell, it seems. The funny thing is, had this film been a success, someone rather than those of us closest to her, may have actually wanted to read it.'

Billie took the bundle. The pages were all handwritten. The title '*Lola Strong. A Life in the Spotlight*' scrawled across the front page.

'It's the last page she had written that you might be interested in.' Josta took a sip of her wine as Billie flicked through. The final page was titled, '*A Question of Relationships*'. She glanced at Josta as she read the introduction to Max's conception. Billie remembered that both Josta and Lola herself, had told her that his father had been an American businessman whom Lola had met whilst appearing on stage in a Broadway play. He'd never accepted that he *had* been Max's father, resulting in a disgruntled Max heading off to Columbia as a teenager, to go to university and cause as much disruption as possible to his father's multinational company based there.

Billie quickly skimmed through Lola's words, scrawled in dramatically looped writing. She reread one sentence again as it simply wouldn't sink in. She finally looked up at Josta, in disbelief.

'Max's father *wasn't* an American businessman?' Billie was aware of her mouth hanging open like a guppy fish, as the ramifications of such a confession, an announcement from the dead, sank in.

'Oh what a tangled web we weave, when first we practice to deceive,' Josta quoted from Walter Scott's epic poem, *Marmion*. 'And alas, my dear lovely Lola expired before she had a chance to finish her story.' Billie thought that Josta was being unduly charitable. The way she saw it, Max's birth mother had her entire life up until now to have come clean on the subject. But the identity of Max's father hadn't been revealed.

'It doesn't matter,' Billie said instead. 'You and Lola were his true parents. The ones who love him more than anyone else could do.' She wasn't completely certain of her argument, but now wasn't the time to get into a debate about the issue. Having recently discovered her own genuine parentage, she figured that Max would have something to say when he finally got a chance to absorb the truth of his beginnings in life. 'Do you have any idea at all who his father might be then?' Billie asked. Josta shook her head.

'We were both in a mildly open relationship back then. If I remember, I had something of a crush on my boss at the mortuary and I never cared unduly if Lola played away from home from time to time. She always came back. I loved her precisely because she was a free spirit after all. Why would I want to change that? I imagine she told Max and indeed me, the fairy tale of the father on the other side of the world, to stop the boy from trying to make contact...' She chuckled sadly. 'That didn't work. Now we know why the hotshot businessman rejected Max when he tried to meet with him all those years ago.' Josta shuffled through the photographs on her knee.

'I do remember her showing me this photo though, after the party the other evening. She said that she had done a theatre tour, for over a year, in the mid-eighties with someone involved in the *Alice* film.' Josta handed a large photo to Billie.

A collection of people stood in front of a theatre looking very fashionable for the time, in a startling mix of jeans with rips at the knee, shell-suit jackets and New Romantic ruffled white tops. Lola, young and beautiful, her long legs encased in fuchsia-pink leggings, slouchy velvet boots on her feet, white puffed-sleeve shirt, open almost to the waist, was wrapped around a man suggestively as she smouldered into the lens. Of course, he had hair then, it was long and seemingly permed into a curled mullet. His clothes seemed to indicate that he was rocking his inner Adam Ant, but Billie still couldn't fail to recognise the man.

'When she landed the part of the Queen of Hearts, she said that it was because a friend from the past had influence and owed her a big favour.' Josta knocked back the rest of her wine in one gulp. 'And she always was very ambitious. Lola. As you've probably already realised, Billie, with your interviews, many actresses would sleep with the Devil himself in order to get a leading role.' *Or even the odious Arden Roy*, Billie silently answered.

The terrible development on set certainly hadn't done any harm to GG Mills's status as a leading actor, Billie reflected, as she drove homewards passing news-stands, with Ash's amour emblazoned across the cover of the evening newspapers. It was his name that blasted from the radio news when she switched that on, too, with discussions on Luna Da Costa's fast-rising career as an actress also featuring heavily within the broadcasts. Lola once again had been relegated to little more than a walk-on part in her own dramatic death. Billie felt sorry for the woman despite her tall stories.

As she approached a road leading off to the Chief's house, something made her turn the steering wheel in that direction. Perhaps, she considered, she just wanted to feel near to her godfather. Relive the memories of visiting him here since childhood, more recently popping in on occasion, to mull over a difficult case. She desperately wished he was here to do exactly that right now.

Billie drew up outside of the house, damning herself once more for having stashed the black box belonging to the Chief in her basement. Tiredness suddenly engulfed her. She leaned her forehead on the steering wheel for a moment, trying to think straight. Who on earth would want the recent stomach-churning deaths to have taken place? She had to wind this thing up soon, not only to prevent further murders, but to save her team. Miriam Nelson might have had a temporary thaw in her icy disposition, but Billie had no doubts she would follow through on her threats to freeze Billie and her crew out if she didn't come up with a watertight conviction.

Billie clambered out of her car, suddenly desperate to be inside the Chief's house just one more time, not only to feel his presence all around her, but to see if the investigation team that Miriam Nelson had sent in had left any vital clues behind, that might point Billie to his killer. She looked around and then skirted along the side of the large building. For as long as she could remember, the upper bathroom window had remained unlocked due to a faulty latch. It sometimes made the window bang when it was windy, but the Chief had been too busy at work to do anything about it and then after a year or two the quirky window had just become part of the furniture.

Billie clambered onto the top of a dustbin below the window and then began to pull herself up the drainpipe in movements worthy of a cat burglar. She hauled herself up onto the windowsill within moments, wrenching the frame back, sliding her fingers inside to lift the latch, before swinging back onto the drainpipe and pulling the window open as much as possible. Twisting her body, she somehow managed to slither inside without hurtling down to the gutter below. She landed on a fluffy bathmat. For a second, old memories almost engulfed her with emotion.

Billie took a moment to breathe out. It had been a long day, but she was determined to make use of every minute in order to find out the truth about the murders. They all hurt. But the Chief's unexpected demise was particularly personal to her. Billie had thought herself to be the golden child, closest to her godfather. But if the truth was that he *had* fathered a child, then she wanted to meet that person. Make certain that a former stranger or so it appeared, hadn't had a reason to prematurely bite off the hand that would eventually feed it.

As Billie opened the door from the bathroom and stepped out onto the upper landing, she could have sworn that she heard a noise. She stopped dead, peering over the banister into the lower hallway, attempting to acclimatise her eyes to the darkness. All she could hear was her heart beating. As she peered into the murky corners below, she was aware of the faint familiar smell of a once happy place, which now seemed to have sadly lost its soul.

Brushing her fingers through her hair, she stayed close to the wall as she moved down the stairs, pretty sure that her mind was just playing tricks. She pushed away the urge to call out to the Chief, knowing that part of the grief process was the refusal to accept that someone had really gone.

She heard another noise and stopped dead. Was her mind *really* making something out of nothing? Maybe the heating system had been left on, or a similar device? She heard it again. It seemed to be coming from the Chief's office on the ground floor. Her own planned first port of call. It sounded like the scrape of drawers being carefully pulled out. Was she imagining things?

Billie crept down the last few stairs and then quickly across the hall, her back against the wall next to the door. She held her breath as a dim light suddenly shone from under it. The golden glow was moving, as though someone holding a torch was searching for something. Billie edged slowly sideways, her fingertips stretching out to touch the door handle, being grateful that the layout of the room was familiar to her. The element of surprise being essential in such circumstances.

Then she swung in fast, kicking the door wide, almost knocking the dark-clad figure off their feet. The torch skittered away under the desk as Billie tried to grab an arm, taking advantage of the moment, the body having bounced heavily against the printing machine. Her other hand reached around for her handcuffs, just as her feet were kicked away from under her. Billie kept a grip of the intruder's wrist as she grappled for her restraints, but the struggling body swiftly broke free, spinning her over with amazing speed and strength.

Billie hooked her knee up fast and heard a groan of pain. That sorted out the identification of sex, Billie registered somewhere at the edge of her brain, as she slithered quickly to one side, rolling onto her knees. In the dim beam from the torch in the vicinity of the intruder's head, Billie spotted a dark balaclava and yanked it off, just as her other hand was pulled away from under her and clipped into a device. She toppled onto the floor.

'It's me, you numpty.' Billie felt her arm being pulled upwards as the intruder reached semi-upright. She heard the click of the light switch before the room was bathed in brightness from the spotlights embedded in the ceiling. Ellis Darque looked down at her. He was breathing heavily. 'That's just kyboshed any idea of expanding the family.' He clutched his crotch in pain.

'What the hell are you doing here?' Billie shook her cuffed arm. Ellis relented and unlocked the handcuffs.

'Same as you. Breaking and entering,' Ellis answered, sitting back on his haunches, still slightly breathless as Billie pulled herself upright.

'What are you looking for?' Billie eyed up the door. There was no doubt that Ellis could be a formidable foe if he chose to be.

'Anything that can point to the Chief's murder because you are clearly not going to share any real intel. You kept schtum even after two bottles of wine the other night.' He blew out a sigh. 'Nothing here, mind you. Nelson's search squad did a good job of wiping everything out.' He scratched his head in irritation.

'What's it to you anyway? Did you have some *special* relationship with him?' Billie folded her arms, the thought of heading out of the door now not as strong as her determination to get answers.

'Like I said, the Chief did me a big favour by bringing me in on the last investigation. I owe him, and I don't like to see one of our own knocked off. I only left the force a month ago...' Ellis started.

'But that's not the full story,' Billie persisted. 'I'm desperate for links between the Chief and the other people who've keeled over, so do me a favour' – Billie tapped his knee with her boot – 'and spill the damn beans.' Ellis hauled himself upright.

'Okay. But I'm not messing either. It's a different world outside of the force, mate, and I've got mouths to feed. The client wants complete confidentiality, so it's got to be give and take this time.'

Billie thought it over for a second. If she was caught sharing full details of a murder enquiry with someone not officially involved in the investigation and Miriam Nelson found out, a custodial sentence beckoned. End of her brilliant career. But if she didn't move forward on the investigation, her entire team would be out of a job, and it would still be the end of her career. Billie was well aware that Ellis knew the serious risk she was taking.

'If I tell you what I know, you better not stitch me up,' Billie said warily. She bit her lip. 'You go first.' She nodded. Ellis sighed.

'The Chief hinted he was being blackmailed, when he first took me on and then again, just recently, when he rang up asking to hire me, on the day I started my PI agency.'

'So why wouldn't he have told me to investigate?' Billie asked indignantly.

'Because he wanted to keep you out of it.' Ellis sighed. 'He didn't spill specific details, but let's just say that he was engaged in something to do with work in the past that he wasn't proud of. Sounds like someone was on to it and he'd been giving them sweeteners to keep their mouth shut. But they were ramping up the ante, wanting much more. Threatening to spill.'

'You are joking?' Billie's heart sank. *Maybe Miriam Nelson had found incriminating evidence on the Chief after all*, she thought. 'I would have sorted it. Kept quiet...' Billie finally accepted the truth that it wouldn't have been the first time she had covered up incriminating secrets about historical crimes involving those close to her. Maybe she wasn't the crack cop she claimed to be.

'Yeah, well I said I would take it on, just as soon as I had sorted the Arden Roy business out. Mr Director is paying top dollar for an exclusive contract. And as you can see he's a bit of a full-time handful. I'm only employing me at the moment, so... I let the Chief down. I feel really shit about it.'

'The Chief's murderer left clear links to the *Alice* stories and Arden Roy is working on a film version of the story... it's too much of a coincidence to think it might be two different blackmailers...' Billie started thinking fast.

'So I'm on the right track. I did pause to wonder when I was shinning up the drainpipe, rather than taking my kids out for a burger, whether I was losing the damn plot. But I was hoping to find the odd threatening note I could use to match the writing and you've just confirmed that I was thinking straight. If I can pinpoint Arden Roy's blackmailer–'

'Then chances are I've got my killer,' Billie answered. Rifling her pocket, she pulled out her mobile phone. Scrolling through, she found the photo she had taken, with shaky hand, of the 'Drink Me' label that had been attached to the bottle discovered with his body. 'This writing look familiar?' Ellis grabbed the phone.

'Bingo. We're onto something.' He rifled through his own mobile and held up a photo of a short threatening note with identical handwriting. 'Dead ringer. You've just saved my bacon.'

Billie hoped that this was the breakthrough she had been banking on, though she still hadn't worked out what Ellis had been up to on the night she had stayed at the pub. Could he really have been innocently sleepwalking in the street, as Boo had mentioned he was prone to do? She hoped so, rather than the other possibility, that he had been out rifling her house for the box she had taken from the Chief for safekeeping, having ensured that Billie was flat out at his place. He was clearly an adept cat burglar.

As they left the house together as stealthily as each had arrived, Billie's mind was racing. Could she finally be a big step nearer to bringing a murderer to justice, or was Ellis trying to send her on a wild goose chase? There was always the terrifying possibility that *he* was the blackmailer, who had been attempting to remove any incriminating evidence remaining in the Chief's house. But could he be a killer too? His training certainly made him capable. As Ellis turned the corner, whipping off his dark beanie hat and stuffing it into his pocket, before starting to whistle a cheery tune, like an honest Joe, Billie stared after him. Had she just been taken for a fool and given away evidence that could put an end to her?

'Mad About the Boy' was playing softly in the background as Billie finally arrived back home after midnight. She immediately spotted Boo, wrapped up in a fluffy sofa blanket, slumbering against piles of plumped-up cushions. The choice of music was either a faux pas, bearing in mind Boo's current situation, or simply a sign of the first flush of love, being experienced by the two leading men in her kitchen, quietly washing and drying dishes as though they had been happily married for an age. Either way, Billie could see that Boo had been well looked after by Ash and his new love, superstar or not, after Billie and her wingman had finally persuaded Boo to stay with them in Alnmouth for the night rather than go home to an empty house after the shocking day she had just experienced.

The fraud squad had explained that romance fraud was one of the most frequently reported crimes worldwide and that Boo's beloved long-distance boyfriend had, in actual fact, probably been a gang of people, swapping shifts, who had gleaned information from her various social media accounts.

The usual modus operandi was to befriend females online, grooming them carefully using a fake identity and by affiliating themselves to the target's various likes, dislikes, hobbies and so forth; the very useful information innocently volunteered by most people to friends via social media, like gold dust to persons with evil intent. The picture of the handsome man had probably been stolen from an innocent guy's account, with a new name and link created to lead Boo and her money straight to the fraudsters.

The revelation had been utterly humiliating for Boo, especially with her background as a crack undercover investigating officer and no matter how much the fraud officers, Billie and Ash had assured her that the gangs were astonishingly clever at their game, she was absolutely devastated at her gullibility, complete loss of savings and, Billie guessed, utter heartbreak for the death of her ghost lover.

'I'll have to sell my house,' Boo had whispered, burying her head in her hands. As far as Billie was concerned, hell would freeze over before she allowed that to happen. Boo had used the compensation received for having been injured in the line of duty to purchase the modest home, made accessible with lift, lowered kitchen, and ramps.

So far, offers of monetary help from Billie had fallen on deaf ears. Boo was fiercely independent and mortified to find herself in such a vulnerable position. When Ash had mentioned calling Ellis, she had nearly bitten his head off at the idea. Billie recalled that Max had once explained that anger was really fear in disguise. Ash appeared to have known that instinctively, because when the fraud officers had left, he made the call to Boo's bank manager, hoping to put an end to Boo's distress.

The appeal for understanding had fallen on deaf ears. The manager insisted there would be no refunds, pointing out that the bank had tried to dissuade Boo twice from transferring money, yet she had insisted on going ahead. Ash, having slammed the phone down, had then taken her into his arms in a huge bear hug and let her cry her heart out, whilst Billie had kept the door firmly locked.

'She's had a bit of chicken soup.' Ash nodded to the bowl placed on a little table next to Boo, as he handed a mugful to Billie.

Billie accepted the offer gratefully. 'Thanks for clearing up.' She looked around. Despite the red stains still visible on the sofas and walls, no one would otherwise have guessed that the house had been ransacked only that morning. Now it was a sea of calm.

'Frankly, I can't imagine how she couldn't have seen straight through the scam,' GG Mills whispered.

'Maybe they use out-of-work actors,' Billie countered, slightly spikily, though she secretly couldn't believe that she would be as gullible as Boo had been either. She kicked herself for not having seen the signs earlier.

'Time to turn in.' Ash kissed GG on the cheek. Billie

wondered when she was going to be in line for more fun. She sank down on the sofa opposite Boo and looked at her mobile, hoping that there would be news of a homecoming from Max soon. It was then she spotted the message and clicked it open.

'*Stay away from the father of my child,*' she read. A photo slowly opened up below. It was a picture of a child of about four years old, with captivating eyes, staring into the lens. Billie frowned. The delicate features and striking eyes reminded her of someone else. She glanced up, as Ash and GG headed for the door. The actor playfully ran his hand down Ash's back, turned to Billie, and winked. The beautiful child with dark curling hair could easily have been a miniature version of GG Mills.

18

IN THE CLOSET

'So, has GG always been gay?' Billie tried to ask Ash casually, as though the thought hadn't been playing on her mind all night long. Judging by the late-night message she had received, someone seemed to have gotten the wrong end of the stick, from seeing GG at her home. Ash looked up from his PC, where he was typing up a statement.

'Um... yeah,' he answered, his mind on other things.

'*Always?*' Billie persisted, looking down at the photo of the child again. She had tried to ring the number that the message had come from, but it was dead.

'What is this, an interrogation?' Ash grinned. 'You're starting to sound like my mother. I'm sorry to have to break a million female hearts, but he just ain't interested in girlie shenanigans. More luck me.'

Billie sighed, deciding to forget it. After Boo's bad news yesterday, she didn't want another key member of her team going into relationship meltdown, should they be having the wool pulled over their eyes. But there was a chance that the message had been sent to her totally in error.

'You okay?' Billie looked at Boo who was also hard at work.

'That's the fifth time you've asked me this morning,' Boo warned. She looked wrecked but was clearly in no mood to take to her bed with a fit of the vapours.

'Heard from Ellis?' Billie persisted. She had been thinking about him too, in the early hours. Hero or villain? She desperately hoped it was the former.

'No. Look, the fact that I've cocked up big time doesn't make any difference to my decision over that. He's a mate. Nothing else, so if you fancy bedding him again, don't let any misunderstanding about me stand in your way.' Boo began typing again.

'No. Don't be crazy,' Billie started, before Boo winked at her. She was one tough cookie, Billie reflected, mentally beating to death the monsters who had bled her dry. Billie suddenly had a thought. Had someone seen her with Ellis in the pub the other night and misunderstood the relationship?

'Does he have three children?' Billie asked, pretending to read through a report. Boo rolled her eyes in exasperation.

'You tell me. I only knew about Maya a few months ago and she's nearly nineteen! Like you, I know he's got another small daughter, from his marriage. But as you may have noticed in the last twenty-four hours, I'm not exactly the brain of Britain when it comes to men, so he could have more kids than Mia Farrow tucked away, and I'd be the last to know. Why do you ask?' She raised an eyebrow as Billie's phone rang.

'Saved by the bell,' Boo teased.

'Billie Wilde?' She recognised the voice immediately. It was Scott at the coffee shop and deli over the road, where Billie picked up her morning shot of caffeine before arrival at work. 'Yep. Is my order ready?' Billie asked. For as long as she could remember, at least once a week, she had ordered a tray of cakes and pastries for her team. By the look of them all this morning, beavering away, they were desperately in need of a sugar boost.

'Yes. Want me to bring them over when the rush calms down?'

'No thanks. Heading over now. I need a breath of fresh air.' Billie ended the call and headed out, still none the wiser from her enquiries about the owner of a child and irate partner. So much for being a crack detective, she teased herself.

Billie was just striding towards the counter of Scott's Deli, when she felt a touch on her arm. She spun around. In her job, she was well aware that anyone coming too close, out of the blue, could be foe rather than friend. For a split second, she didn't recognise the young woman, dressed in jumper, jeans and trainers.

'Hello. It's Steph from the film, you know, the Mad March Hare?' She wiggled her eyebrows and twirled invisible whiskers, bringing the character to life even without her costume. Billie smiled.

'Hey, that was good. Do you live around here?' Billie asked.

'Um, no. It's just that with filming having been stopped out of respect for the Queen of Hearts and police all over the place, I've got a day off.' She shook her head in disbelief, still clearly shocked by the horrific scene, which would no doubt be embedded in her mind's eye forever.

Billie was well aware that Lola's death had stopped play. So many people had been milling around, either in full make-up and costume, or wearing face masks at the time of the incident. The members of her team that she had sent out to take statements were having a bit of a job identifying who may have witnessed what. Someone clearly had tampered with the safety cover of the wind machine, but by accident or deadly intent hadn't been decided yet. Billie knew what she thought, but she wouldn't muddy the waters at the moment. Her detectives were searching for hard evidence.

'I was on the way to see you actually,' Steph added. Billie's ears pricked up.

'Really? Let's take a seat.' Billie took Steph's arm and led her to an empty table in the corner, deciding that there was no time like the present. 'Bit more relaxed here, than in the interview room,' Billie added, calling over to Scott, the deli owner, to bring two coffees. He delivered at the speed of light. Billie was obviously a valued customer.

'Well, it's not much really,' Steph started hesitantly. 'It's just that when I was taking all my make-up off yesterday after... I noticed the picture on Fredi's wall...'

'The CCTV still?' Billie stopped drinking her coffee mid-sip. Steph nodded.

'I'm sure I recognise the clothes the person was wearing...' She trailed off in recollection.

'Do you know who that is, Steph?' Billie gently coaxed. Steph shook her head.

'No. I mean I don't know, but it could have been almost anybody. You see, it looks exactly like the costume I wore for a college production of *Flashdance*. That's definitely the wig I wore, with the pink flash in it and the cowboy boots are the pair that I wore too. Middleton College is known for its fantastic drama department. We got rave reviews.' Billie's heart started beating faster.

'Did Maddie Taylor also go to Middleton?' Billie was aware that both she and Pippa Sykes attended the local college.

'Yeah, both of them did. That's how they got to be stand-ins. The extras were mostly shipped in from the local college by bus. It's cheaper to do that, I guess. Middleton is a twenty-mile journey. But it's worth it, great tutors, much more kudos if you want to be an actor. I left three years ago, and this is my second proper acting job–'

'So do you know what happened to the clothing in the photo?' Billie had her notebook out and was writing fast, words only she could decipher.

'I guess it's all still in the costume store in the college. Mind you, students would borrow stuff for auditions and they're pretty relaxed about it, so there's no guarantee it would all still be there.'

Billie looked up from her notes thoughtfully. The person in the CCTV footage had been tall and slim. Steph had just confirmed that they had been wearing a wig. So it could just as easily have been a man who had been approaching Maddie's flat, as a woman... Billie's musings were interrupted by a car horn and a screech of brakes. Someone had stepped out in front of a car onto a crossing at the last minute, it seemed, hence the angry driver reaction. Billie blinked, then blinked again as the scene came into focus. She wasn't imagining things. The man hastily striding out onto the crossing, looking distracted, was Max, carrying a large bouquet of flowers.

'Can you wait just a minute? There's someone outside that I need to have an urgent word with.' Billie had already risen from her seat.

'Em, well I don't know anything else, and my bus is due. I have to wait an age for another one–'

'Just sit there,' Billie called behind her as she weaved speedily through the tables to the door. As she raced out, Max was moving along the pavement across the road. Billie sprinted over, almost knocking over a cyclist in her haste to be reunited with her lover.

'Max?' Billie cut in front of him. He looked startled for a second, and tired, a growth of stubble over his chin making him appear even more attractive, despite his eyes having dark shadows beneath them.

'Billie.' The stressed look in his eyes softened. He looked like a little boy lost. 'They released me on compassionate grounds. I just got dropped off at home. I was taking these to Josta. I've wanted to ring you a thousand times since I touched down, but I wasn't sure you'd want to see me...' He trailed off. Billie glanced over to Steph who she could see through the window of the deli. She was standing up, slinging her bag over her shoulder. Billie turned back to Max.

'I'm so glad you're okay.' She ran her fingers through her hair. 'I'm working.' She looked back towards the deli again. Max followed her line of vision.

'Of course you are.' He shrugged like it was a given. 'Work comes first,' he added, smiling sadly.

'Not tonight!' Billie made the decision. 'Will you come around to my place tonight?' She touched his arm, wanted to offer him solace after the loss of his mother, she reasoned, before tossing the thought aside. Truth was she wanted to offer him much more than that. 'Just the two of us.' Ash had told her that he was staying with GG at his hotel that evening and now that Max was actually here in front of her, with that hint of lemony smell catching her senses in the light breeze, she felt the fury of their last confrontation dissolving.

'Please?' She heard the note of desperation in her voice. Max stared into her eyes, biting his lip for a moment before smiling that crooked smile of his.

'Tonight it is then,' he whispered, before bending forward and slowly kissing her. Then he pulled away and started walking, leaving Billie standing like a love-struck teenager on the pavement. She gathered her senses, remembering Steph. She couldn't see her now inside the café, as she sprinted back through the door and into the warm coffee-flavoured fug.

'Your friend had to leave. She saw her bus coming,' Scott called over as he served a customer. Billie rushed back out, too late to catch Steph, who turned and waved to her as she jumped on the bus. As it gathered speed and moved past, Steph winked and blew a kiss with a smile. She had obviously been watching Billie and Max. Not the most professional scene in front of a witness, Billie had to admit. But at least she and Max had got back on the right track, and she had gleaned some vital evidence. Time to get back to work and start investigating that useful nugget further.

'Got that tray of cakes, Scott?' Billie called over to him as he rushed around, serving a lengthening queue. She had spotted the tray waiting at the end of the counter when she had arrived.

'They were just at the end there.' Scott looked across as he took payment from a customer. 'Did you not pick it up?' He frowned at the empty space where the tray of cakes had been placed.

'A young lad and his mate just nipped in and took them, love,' an old woman at the back of the queue piped up. 'I thought it was theirs.' The news sank in with Billie that she had been robbed.

'The cop shop's just across the road, dear, if you want to report it,' the woman added helpfully. 'Though the way things are going these days, it would have to be murder before you would get them off their warm comfy arses to come out here on the streets.'

Billie sighed. She couldn't even hang on to a witness or catch a tray bake thief, let alone a killer right now and clearly public confidence was at an all-time low. Perhaps Max was right, it was time to seek out new adventures. Maybe she wasn't the right woman for this job anymore?

19
___

LIFE IS TOO SHORT

'I've got to run. I'm meeting some uni friends.' Maya smiled sweetly at Billie before swinging her rucksack onto her back and heading out.

'Hope you enjoyed your dress-up date.' Billie grinned at the young trainee. She had sent her out with Ash to Middleton College, only to find the place locked up and both students and staff on holiday. The caretaker had been left holding the fort during repairs. He resolutely claimed that he had no access to records other than the principal's landline number and at that moment he was somewhere in the middle of an unknown ocean sailing on an equally unmemorable cruise ship. Still, with a bit of arm-twisting by Ash, they had been able to access the costume store. Reports back were that it was like looking for a needle in a haystack, with several denim jackets and sets of leggings to choose from, but no sign of the vital wig and boots.

'Yes, ma'am, it was mint.' Maya giggled at the memory. 'Sorry we didn't find the stuff in the photo though.' It was an unfortunate outcome, but Billie was of the opinion that persistence would eventually pay off. In addition, regular photo messages throughout the day back to base from the investigating duo had lightened the load of the team, as either Ash or Maya had popped up on screen, posing in various pieces of costume, including a pirate hat and pantomime dame dress. Moments like those were few and far between during a murder investigation, Billie reflected, and in the case of her team it was invariably Ash who would deliver. She was thrilled that he was walking with a whole new spring in his step since he had nabbed his new Hollywood lover. Billie hoped her own spirits would be similarly uplifted that evening when she and Max were on target to put their recent estrangement well and truly to bed.

Boo logged out of her computer and started gathering her belongings. She looked tired and Billie was desperate to reach out to her with an offer to pay her mortgage – buy her flat even. Due to Billie's *annus horribilis* she had inherited a bob or two and she would be more than happy to send some of it Boo's way. But she knew that she would have to bide her time. Boo was far too proud to take handouts unless the situation turned absolutely desperate. Wheelchair warrior that she was, she didn't take kindly to anyone viewing her as a victim, whatever the situation. She had made it clear that she had been keen to keep conversations focused on work today and with so much on, Billie had been happy to agree, despite her ongoing concerns for her friend.

'I've had a word with Ellis, had to fess up about my idiocy. He's moving in as a lodger.' Boo finally broke the truce on the subject. 'Just to help pay the bills, until he gets the keys to the house his uncle has left him. A friend *without* benefits, by the way. That's definitely history. But he is coming over this evening to sort things out.'

Billie's stomach churned. She hoped that Boo wasn't jumping out of the frying pan into the fire. Ellis still hadn't spilled many beans about this uncle who seemed to have keeled over at the same time as the Chief. Her godfather's killing had always felt to Billie to be separate from the others. Unlike them, he had no interest in Lewis Carroll and the *Alice* stories, despite having similar-themed clues left alongside his body. It was possible that someone who wanted to kill him had knowledge of the other deaths, and would use the opportunity to make it look like he was targeted by the same killer. It would have to be someone extremely clever. Someone like Ellis Darque. She desperately hoped that her hunch was misguided.

'Oh and I meant to mention, I was just looking through the Charles Carroll files. One of the colleges that he lectured at was Middleton.' Billie was immediately alert.

'Boo, I could kiss you!' She leapt up, ran around her desk and gave Boo a kiss on her cheek. Boo good-naturedly fought her off.

'Urgh, get back before I take my footrest to you,' she joked. 'I might be a desperate case, but I'm not *that* desperate.'

As Boo left the room and headed for the lift taking the usual slice off the woodwork, a thought occurred to Billie. She headed out of the office, along the empty corridor towards Miriam Nelson's room. The woman was inside reading documents as Billie entered.

'Got no home to go to, Wilde?' She looked across at the clock. 'I know I'm asking for blood on this investigation, but a girl your age – must be way past your bedtime.' Billie thought that she was joking, but it wasn't always clear with the new chief. She was certainly a grafter herself, Billie had to admit.

'Just following a line of investigation, ma'am, with some new intel in. Can I ask something?'

Miriam Nelson blinked for a moment as though she felt that she would have been the last person that Billie would ask for advice.

'Fire away.' She nodded to the chair opposite her desk. Billie decided not to sit, feeling that she might need to make a quick getaway, depending on the reaction to her question.

'When your daughter passed away, ma'am,' Billie began, noticing a look, almost of panic, momentarily crossing the new chief's large, round face, 'you mentioned that a female was seen on CCTV entering her student accommodation. You mentioned that she attended Middleton College?'

'That's correct.' Miriam Nelson gathered herself and sat up straight, the hard shell that Billie sometimes recognised using herself, suddenly surrounding the woman's emotions like a shield. 'What of it?'

'Do you still have the CCTV footage?' Billie forged ahead despite the less than enthusiastic response to her opening question. Miriam Nelson looked down for a moment.

'I don't need the footage. I looked at it so many times when it happened, that it's embedded in my mind. I go to sleep thinking about it, wake up thinking about it and dream about it when I'm not working.' She nodded to the pile of paperwork on her desk. 'Hence the fact I'll be here at least until midnight. What's your excuse, Wilde?'

'Well, I was wondering if there was any chance that the girl you saw approaching your daughter's door on the night that she died, was actually a man?' The older woman looked startled for a moment.

'She was certainly tall...' She trailed off. 'Now you bring it up, that might have been something that wasn't investigated.' She looked crushed with guilt at the thought, as Billie ran through the intel that pointed to a killer wearing female clothing. 'I blame myself. She was a troubled girl and I thought she would sort herself out when she went to college. But I was flying up the career ladder and never put her top of my priorities.'

'The only one responsible was her killer, ma'am,' Billie answered gently. But despite having approached the conversation with trepidation, Billie had a creeping feeling inside that this serial killer, seemingly working with such sophistication, wasn't at the start of their career with the *Alice* murders. She had to ensure that no stone was left unturned and the new chief's daughter might just come back from her grave with a vital clue to solve the current cases.

'You have seen the enlarged CCTV photo of the person who we believe might be Maddie Taylor's killer?' Billie asked.

'Not yet, Wilde. At the rate I'm working through my pile, I reckon I might reach that at around two am with a bit of luck and a ton of black coffee.' Billie took a deep breath. She could save her a lot of trouble and might hit the jackpot. She had brought a copy with her. She turned it over and laid it on Miriam Nelson's desk, watching carefully for a reaction. It was immediate. The new chief gasped out loud.

'The hair and the boots. They're the same.' To Billie's alarm the woman suddenly burst into racking sobs, her veneer of cold hardness disintegrating within a split second. Billie was momentarily shocked by the severity of the reaction, though she had cried many similar floods of tears herself, in the darkness of her own home in recent months. She was even more surprised to find herself holding the big woman in her arms, having shot around to her side of the desk, smoothing her hair and reassuring the new chief of police that she would help heal her broken heart.

'I'm onto it, ma'am, I'm onto it. It's only a matter of time before I bring you their scalp. I promise,' Billie soothed in quiet tones. She owed it to both chiefs, let alone the other victims, to bring this case to a close and she felt in her blood that the time was drawing near. She was finally on the scent of this hideously evil killer.

∼

Billie drew up outside of the glossy new flats in the centre of town. The type that even had their own concierge on the smart reception desk. It was the sort of building that befitted a new chief of police. Secure, too, for a woman in a high-profile position, living by herself. Billie wondered if the Chief should have moved to similar accommodation. So many people these days with warped grudges against those trying to keep the peace, ready to take revenge at the drop of a hat, it seemed.

Miriam Nelson had calmed now somewhat, though her eyes were puffed and her breathing still ragged. She had pulled out an inhaler and used it on the drive back. Billie remembered reading somewhere that stress and anxiety could sometimes trigger an asthma attack. She was glad that she had been able to persuade her new boss to leave the office behind and head home. She was suddenly seeing the woman in a whole new light.

'Thank you, Wilde. I owe you an apology. It seems that I misjudged you,' Miriam Nelson said with sincerity.

'Ditto,' Billie answered through a small smile. Her boss gave a deep chuckle.

'I wish my daughter had lived to turn out like you. She certainly had your feistiness. Now get yourself home. I'm a miserable old bat with only success in my job left to give me purpose in my sorry life. I don't take many prisoners or make many friends. But take some advice from an old dog. Hang on to those who are precious. A high-flying career won't fill the space left when a person that you should have loved better is snatched away. You don't want to end up like me with an empty home you're in no rush to run back to and a barrel-load of old case files for company. Love it or lose it, just like I did.'

'Thanks. I'll take that advice on board, ma'am,' she

answered, as Miriam Nelson left the car. Billie watched her heading towards her glamorous yet empty flat. The only person welcoming her as she went through the doors to reception being someone paid to do it. As Billie pulled out into the traffic and headed off, she was no longer ambivalent about whether she wanted her relationship with Max to continue. Just as Miriam had pointed out, if she didn't love him she was definitely going to lose him.

'I'm really sorry about this.' Ash popped his head around the door of Billie's bedroom. 'If I'd known you were heading for a serious date night, I would never have agreed to have Indie and Happi stay. Jas is struggling a bit with the baby teething, and as GG called off our get-together tonight, I just thought...'

'I told you it's no problem.' Billie ran her fingers through her hair. She'd found a bottle of conditioner that someone must have given her for a Christmas present and it seemed to have done wonders for her normally wayward curls. 'Everything still hunky-dory with the Hollywood hunk?' she enquired as she wandered around in a pretty silk chemise, decorated with lace. She'd been given it to wear for her honeymoon a year earlier, so consequently hadn't taken it out of the box until now.

'Yeah. It's just that the film's big chiefs are flying in, and he has to be around to press the flesh. Apart from all the questionable publicity over Lola and fending off a possible charge of corporate manslaughter, they're thinking of recasting the Red Queen. Luna Da Costa's acting is not exactly floating their boat when they've been viewing the "rushes". He's already sent a text to say he's missing me,' Ash added through a wide grin.

'Next thing you'll be telling me I have to buy a hat,' Billie replied, grabbing a dress off a hanger in her wardrobe. *Ghost*, the label said. Her former fiancé, David, had bought it for her. Billie wasn't exactly up to date on fashion, but even she recognised the iconic status of the simple but stunning vintage white georgette slip dress.

'Can you help me with this?' she asked Ash, as she started to get into it.

'Yeah, I've got kids. I've had plenty of practice dressing girls.'

'And undressing men,' Billie teased as Ash carefully lifted the delicate dress over Billie's head and her outstretched arms. It seemed to fall in all of the right places. Tiny white embroidered forget-me-nots were scattered over the fitted sleeveless bodice, a single ribbon tie left to hang loose at her cleavage. The skirt skimmed her ankles and lifted in the breeze drifting in from the sea through her open bedroom windows.

'Max is in for a treat tonight. You look absolutely beautiful,' Ash said with sincerity.

As she caught her reflection in the full-length mirror, Billie had to admit that she had scrubbed up well. It wasn't the sort of thought that would ever normally enter her head, but tonight, she had tried to make a special effort for Max, as he came to terms with the shocking loss of Lola. She hoped that he would arrive before the sun went down and that they could walk along the beach on this beautiful evening, with the last warm rays of sunshine helping to finally heal their bruised relationship.

'Thanks for reading the bedtime story to the girls,' Ash added. 'They're asleep now and I'll keep well out of the way. Max gets a bit scary when he's angry.' Billie laughed, wrapping her arms around Ash and giving him a huge bear hug. The two weren't usually physically demonstrative, preferring to use jokes and banter to bond, but Miriam Nelson, of all people, had brought home to Billie just how precious those closest to her were.

'Don't be silly. You don't have to skulk away, and I've told you a thousand times, I *love* having your girls around.' It was true. Much as she was desperate to be reunited with Max, she would never relinquish the close relationships she enjoyed with friends such as Ash and Boo, who were so precious to her.

'Truth is, I'm tired out after last night.' Ash winked mischievously. 'I'm off to bed with my cocoa and a good book. Have a lovely evening with Magnificent Max.' He blew Billie a kiss and headed upstairs to his current bedroom on the top floor of her huge house.

The doorbell rang at that moment. Billie felt a sudden flutter of excitement in her stomach as she raced downstairs and flung the door open.

'Wow,' came the reaction. But it wasn't Max Strong standing on the doorstep looking Billie up and down. It was Ellis Darque.

'What the hell...?' Billie ran her fingers through her hair.

'Great to see you too,' Ellis said with irony. 'Sorry if I'm interrupting something,' he added, stepping inside the hall and nodding to Billie's dress. 'I'm used to seeing you in pit boots and scabby jeans... well, apart from your birthday suit yesterday morning, of course.' He smiled mischievously.

'You're supposed to be at Boo's,' Billie answered, thinking that she absolutely couldn't drop into conversation that Ellis had been with her on three nights running. Even allowing for Boo's claims that their relationship was all done and dusted. Billie herself would have thought it sounded suspicious, and Boo needed to be certain that all of her friends were supporting her right now.

'I'm on my way there. See if I can rifle her PC, shed some light on her phantom lover,' he answered. 'Shows what a bad option she thought I was, when she chose to plump for the Invisible Man. Anyway, I just thought I'd pass on some news, sharpish. Arden Roy decided this morning that the only way to stop his blackmail situation is to come clean about the cross-dressing thing. He's already been in touch with some reporter on a top international newspaper and the story started hitting the online news sites around teatime.'

He flicked on his phone and showed Billie the headlines flying around the world electronically, alongside a big photo of Arden Roy looking defiant in the very neat wig and outfit he had been wearing the other night at the Aunt Fanny's club.

'He thinks this will be the end of all the aggro and he can get this film completed on schedule, despite all the upset,' Ellis added. 'Though personally, I doubt it, with the world's media stampeding down to the film set in response. Either way, I've just been given my marching orders.' Ellis sighed. 'I can't say it's been a pleasure with Mr Roy, but the fee was worth the aggro. He's decided to dispense with my services now he's outed himself. He's convinced that will be the end of the matter.'

'Did you have your suspicions?' Billie enquired. She still had questions about his relationship with the Chief. The blackmail story hadn't been corroborated by anyone else and Ellis seemed to be aware of something the Chief had been keeping secret from his past. Perhaps it took a blackmailer to know one. Ellis shrugged.

'My money was on Luna Da Costa. He hinted he had a little flirtation with her when she was just starting out... possibly underage. Not that he would own up to that, so I couldn't get a proper handle on it. You really need the client's full co-operation with these jobs. I'm guessing she had somebody pulling her strings, sending the demands. Threat of coercing a minor into sex, along with the cross-dressing thing would be enough to finish him off. Same tack I would use if I was trying to squeeze out a regular income. But I don't think she had the brainpower to pull the scam off all by herself.'

'Well, I hear she's getting the push now, so let's see how the sex claim side of things pans out,' Billie answered. Ellis looked impressed.

'That's one bit of info I didn't know. You and I would make a great team, you know, if you ever decide to give up the cop shop.'

'Don't phone me, I'll phone you,' Billie replied. She hoped he was still one of the good guys. Until this case, she had felt that they'd been totally on the same wavelength, and he'd literally been a lifesaver to her in the past. It was hard to forget that. It would completely wreck her faith in human nature if it turned out that Ellis was in reality, dark in character as well as name.

'Hi. Am I too early?' Max was suddenly there in the doorway, looking from Ellis to Billie. By the look of his slightly crumpled cream linen suit, which looked stunning, he'd made an effort too.

'No. Ellis was just dropping in on his way to Boo's.' Billie felt her face flush and she wasn't sure why.

'Don't let me keep you.' Max looked at Ellis. Billie guessed that grief and stress over work was the cause of his less than polite greeting. A picture of her leaping out of Ellis's bed naked the night before momentarily flashed through her mind. She pushed it away forcefully.

'No chance. Got a whole PC hard drive to rummage through. Have fun, lovebirds,' Ellis called over his shoulder, as he left and headed for his car. Max shut the door firmly behind him, turning to Billie.

'You look beautiful tonight.' He sighed, before bending forward and kissing her softly on the lips. He pulled back, gently cupping her face in his hands. 'I've been dreaming of taking you down to the beach again...' A hint of a smile played on his lips. 'I've even organised the venue.' He took Billie's hand and kissed her fingers, before leading her to the full-length windows.

The breeze caught her hair and delicate dress as she gazed

out into her garden. A string of pure white fairy lights led down either side of her pathway, following the tiers of her garden, through the blue gate at the bottom and then seemed to turn left onto the beach where the sandy, perfumed, flower-strewn trail wove between dunes. They were shadowy dark shapes right now, under the star-spangled sky. Billie turned to Max, intrigued.

'What venue?' she asked.

'Our wedding venue,' he answered softly. 'Right now, you couldn't look like a more perfect bride.' Max leaned forward and kissed her on the tip of her nose. 'What do you say, Billie? Will you marry me?' Max asked.

'Now?' Billie answered, slightly startled. 'But it's nearly midnight and don't we need a licence and–' she started to say, whilst simultaneously wondering why she always needed to take control of situations. Max lightly touched her lips with his finger.

'I have it. A special licence. Special forces can get such things.' Max delved in his pocket and took the paper out. 'Perk of the job.' He smiled.

'You sound like James Bond.' Billie was still recovering from the shock.

'There have to be some perks,' Max replied reflectively, whilst Billie's mind started speeding. Should she call Ash and the kids? She had no bridesmaid dresses for them. Also, there was another thing still picking at her emotions. The elephant in the room.

'But, what about Natalie? You said–' Billie felt the pain of Max's words yet again, on the night that he had stormed out. She couldn't forget his comparisons between her and his first wife, in which Billie had been found sadly lacking.

'I was just talking nonsense, a crazy reaction, terrified that I would lose you.' Max frowned. 'I've learned that what makes someone right for another person is commitment. God knows Josta and Lola had their moments, just as we did the other day, but in the end, they were totally committed to each other, rubbing together until the rough edges smoothed away and they simply fitted. I want to do that with you, Billie. Life is too short, and I may have to go away again at any minute. Please let me make this special commitment to you tonight, so that you can be in no doubt about my feelings.'

Max looked into Billie's eyes as though he was looking into her soul. She swallowed hard. Wasn't this what she really wanted, to be with Max? She'd always hated the idea of a big wedding anyway.

'Where do we do it, at this late hour?' Billie smiled, pulling Max close.

'Follow me,' he answered, tugging gently on her hand as he led her out into the garden, following the fairy-light strewn pathway to her future. As they made their way down and out of the gate onto the beach, Billie was aware of the intoxicating lemony smell of his cologne as she allowed herself to lose control for a change, thinking that maybe she could get used to the feeling.

As they rounded the path, weaving between upturned boats, Billie realised that they were heading for the tiny disused ferryman's hut, strewn with more fairy lights around the door and inside the single window. Max led Billie inside, where two paint-peeled driftwood chairs, bedecked with ribbon ties, sat in the middle.

'Ah, the beautiful bride has arrived.' A woman in a dark suit and court shoes smiled kindly at Billie. 'I am the superintendent registrar, and this is the registrar, as required at ceremonies such as this.'

Billie nodded hello, thinking that the situation was even

more bizarre than a visit to the *Alice* film set to question the Mad March Hare or Humpty Dumpty.

'Are you ready, dear?' the registrar, decked in navy blue with a discreet brooch on her lapel, asked, smiling gently. Billie wanted to say that to be honest her head was spinning a bit. Five minutes ago, she had been discussing murder with Ellis Darque. Now she had just found herself at the start of her own unexpected marriage ceremony on a starlit beach. It was like some wonderfully mad dream that she felt she might suddenly awaken from. Max gently stroked her head, looking at her lovingly. The women exchanged glances, like starry-eyed grannies.

'This won't take too long, dear,' the first woman continued, in a soothing voice, before starting the first line of the marriage service. Billie swallowed hard. This was *really* happening.

Suddenly, Billie's mobile, incongruously stuffed into her dress pocket, started to ring.

'Sorry,' Billie whispered, cutting the call. The registrar started again. The phone rang.

'Turn it off.' Max sighed as Billie fumbled to get the device out of the tiny pocket on her dress, which must have been created for a fairy tooth or suchlike, rather than Billie's mobile which was wedged in tightly. Billie finally yanked it out and in doing so knocked the answer button on.

'Sorry,' she repeated, whilst the registrars exchanged disbelieving glances. 'Hello?' Billie could hear Maya's voice sounding panic-stricken. 'Maya?' She could also detect noise in the background, voices, squeals of horror. 'Are you all right?' Maya's tearful breathing told her that it was a pointless question. 'It's horrible. He's dead!' she sobbed.

'Who's dead?' Billie answered firmly.

'It's Arden Roy. At the churchyard in Boldon–' Maya had

hardly finished before Billie was on high alert, listening as the young trainee detective filled in essential details.

'Sorry. I've got to run.' Billie looked at Max hoping to God he would understand.

'You *are* joking?' Max replied, stony-faced.

'Please understand, Max,' Billie pleaded, torn for a second.

'This is *most* unusual.' The superintendent registrar had now dropped the sugar-sweet voice.

'You are right there. Man in female clothing impaled on a giant sword in a graveyard. Not the sort of thing I can expect a young rookie copper to manage herself,' Billie answered as she sped out of the door, hurtling away from the bright new future Max had promised.

20

A GRAVE ERROR OF JUDGEMENT?

'The vorpal sword,' Billie confirmed to Maya as the special police constable, who had been the first on-duty officer on the scene, was still stumbling around in panic mode. She wasn't playing the ace detective, as the words were spelled out on the hilt of the huge medieval falchion which had impaled Arden Roy against a tombstone in a half-standing position, having gone straight through the centre of his body, down into the earth below, leaving his pretty gold chain belt intact on the way. His resting place was only a few feet away from the grave in which Charles Carroll had breathed his last. 'In the poem *Jabberwocky*, the vorpal sword is the weapon used to kill the giant serpent.'

Billie had shone her torch over the entire body, thankful that she left some police kit permanently in the car. Arden Roy's fine denier tights were laddered, and he had lost a shoe, but otherwise, in her opinion, it had been a swift kill. The murderer clearly wasn't a novice. Billie thought of Miriam Nelson's daughter and Maddie Taylor. Would a female be seen on CCTV approaching the church? Billie was pretty sure that this was the work of a male, nevertheless. A tall and strong one, who had been able to manhandle the massive vorpal sword with such skill and precision.

'I'm doubting Luna Da Costa managed that by herself, if she was on the warpath about getting the push,' a voice whispered in Billie's ear. She spun around to face Ellis Darque. 'Just saying,' he added, stepping back to pull Maya into a hug.

'You again? Ever been done for stalking?' Billie answered. Ellis Darque suddenly seemed to be everywhere she went. 'I thought you were meant to be getting down and dirty with Boo's hard drive,' she added.

'Got a phone call from the young 'un here, in tears. She might be training to be a copper, but I was worried about her coming across this shocker by herself.' Ellis gave his daughter a kiss on the top of her head. 'Looks like this has put the kybosh on your romantic night in,' he added.

Billie didn't even want to go there. Whoever was responsible for Arden Roy's demise had probably also delivered the kiss of death to her happy ever after with Max.

'Ma'am.' Maya beckoned Billie over, as one of her uni friends whispered in Maya's ear. 'I was a bit late tonight meeting my mates, so they were waiting in the pub and Lily here spotted GG Mills getting out of his car over the road.'

'Are you sure it was him?' Billie asked the pretty teenager with long hair in various colours of the rainbow.

'Are you kidding me?' she answered. 'He's on the cover of every mag at the moment as well as millions of websites. He was also driving a bright-red Porsche and you don't see those around here every day.'

'What time was this?' Billie asked.

'Lily posted it on her social media account so the time will be embedded on it,' Maya helpfully added, as Lily rummaged through her bag looking for her mobile. She finally found it and held the upload for Billie to see.

'Seven thirty. We'd only just arrived,' Lily answered. 'I couldn't wait to show all my friends online.'

Billie frowned. It definitely showed GG Mills getting out of his car and heading towards a small cottage. Ash had mentioned that GG Mills had the use of a property here in Boldon, but hadn't he claimed that he was meeting TV executives at his hotel, tonight?

'He was with a young guy. I hadn't guessed that he swings both ways,' Lily added as she flicked through more photos. 'These weren't good enough to upload,' she said. But Billie could see that they were clear enough to tell a story. A younger man leaving the car behind the actor and then following him to the door of the house. They looked close. So intimate, in fact, that the Hollywood star had his hand cupping his friend's backside.

Billie immediately recognised GG's friend as Tom, the runner from the film set. Billie sighed. She was at least relieved that Ash was at home fast asleep, still blissfully dreaming, like she had, of a happy ever after. She wondered how she would break this news to him. Sadly, it looked like his relationship, like hers, had just been dealt a potential death blow, similarly on target to bleed right out.

It was already starting to get light when Billie eventually made her way home, with some hope that Max would be there waiting for her, though she had already known in her heart of hearts that it wasn't going to happen. She hadn't felt able to sleep. Instead, she had followed the still fairy-light strewn pathways to the tiny hut on the beach that had almost been her perfect wedding venue. It was empty now, except for the marriage licence crumpled into a ball in the corner of the floor, as though it had been kicked there. She guessed that said it all. She picked it up and smoothed it out.

Max's messaging service wasn't even allowing her to leave an apology anymore, simply announcing that the number could no longer be reached. Billie sighed, running her fingers through her hair as she stood on the sand outside of the tiny wooden building, still in the now weary-looking white dress, smudged with grass stains and a splash of Arden Roy's blood, watching the tide go out. It looked like her boat to happiness had sailed, perhaps for good this time. Could she really blame Max?

Billie's thoughts turned back to Arden Roy's death scene. Josta's temporary replacement had estimated that time of death had probably been around three hours earlier, which possibly put GG Mills in the vicinity. But without a strong motive and right now nothing more to go on than a relationship with the victim and a proven tendency to tell porkies, she couldn't arrest him on any charge. However, she did intend to aggressively question him on his movements, last night, along with Tom. It had been the young runner who had found Pippa Sykes after all. An officer had been sent to try and rouse them from the cottage that they had been seen entering, but no one was at home.

Billie turned back to the house, trying to calm the myriad of thoughts ricocheting around her head, like why did Ellis Darque seem to pop up everywhere and how much information had she shared with him that she should have kept confidential? As she dropped her crumpled marriage certificate onto the driftwood coffee table, Billie decided to try and get a couple of hours' sleep. She would need all of her faculties at full strength in a couple of hours when news of the latest showcase murder went global.

21

BREAKFAST IN BED

'Surprise!' Billie felt the full glare of the sun searing through her sore eyes and aching brain. She was aware of the long curtains covering the full-length windows of her bedroom being tugged open and little bodies jumping onto the bedspread. She opened one eye. Six-year-old Indie and four-year-old Happi, were certainly in wide-awake mode this morning. Billie checked the clock. She had been asleep for exactly ninety minutes.

'Morning.' She hoped her greeting sounded more upbeat than the cry of distress her head was making at her body having been being brought back to life so soon.

'We've made you breakfast!' Indie trilled, before both girls scampered back out of the room. Ash popped his head around the door.

'Sorry.' He grinned. 'I told them to wait a few more minutes, but they were excited about bringing you breakfast in bed. Has Max left already?' he asked, as Billie pulled herself slowly up, desperately attempting to regain full consciousness.

'Long story,' she whispered hoarsely, working out which bits to edit out, at least when she recounted the tale for the first time to him. 'Arden Roy's dead.' Billie finally managed to fling her second pillow behind her head and sit upright.

'You are joking,' Ash exclaimed, unable to question Billie further, as his daughters re-entered the room together carefully holding a tray which they slowly carried across to Billie and laid across her knees. The tray was covered in a tea towel, with what seemed to be a piece of paper with crayoned writing on top.

'That's the menu,' Happi announced proudly, as Billie kissed each child in turn on the forehead and took a grateful swig of the glass of orange juice which had been peeping out from the blue-checked tray cover. Indie ran across the room and dragged the curtain fully open, filling the room with even brighter light, which dazzled Billie for a moment, despite the smile fixed on her face for the children. She took an inner breath and opened her eyes wide. Then blinked. The children had wobbly written the word 'Menu' and then beneath it 'Cupcakes' in different coloured crayons on her marriage certificate.

The paper with the words *Registrar General's Licence* printed on top, suddenly brought home to Billie what she had just lost. She had heard of such licences, but thought they were only issued to people not expected to live long. Her heart felt like it was plummeting through her body. Maybe that's why people in Max's position were able to use them? She hoped to God that he hadn't leaped straight on a plane back to a place that he could reasonably be expected by the authorities not to survive.

'Take the cover off,' Indie directed, snapping Billie out of the terror scenario shooting through her mind. She did as she was bid, gasping in shock at what awaited her. Ash, who had come to join the girls by Billie's bed was similarly stunned silent. It was certainly one hell of a surprise breakfast. Two cupcakes sat on a plate. They had the words 'Eat me' spelled out in raisins. It was all Billie could do not to fling the tray away from her in astonishment.

'Where did you get these?' Billie asked, trying to keep her voice light, rather than sounding like a detective about to make an arrest. The girls weren't fooled. They took a step back, exchanging glances. 'Were they in the kitchen?' Billie tried again. Happi wrapped her arms around Ash's legs, snuggling against them for safety. She shook her head.

'Indie. Where did you get the cakes from?' Ash had the voice he usually used for bedtime. The one that the girls knew brooked no argument. Indie headed towards Billie who lifted her up onto the bed, hugging her close.

'Daddy's room,' Indie whispered into Billie's ear.

'Daddy's room?' Billie echoed the child's words, raising her eyebrows at Ash, who looked suitably staggered.

'Yes. In the cupboard on the other side of the bed to where daddy sleeps,' Happi advised. 'In the bag with the zip. Both of them were in there.' Billie watched the colour drain from Ash's face.

'GG left his washbag there. I thought he was giving me a sign that he would be coming back. That maybe it's getting serious.'

'You can say that again,' Billie answered. 'Serious isn't the word, if the kids had eaten them.' She flung back the duvet, suddenly wide awake. It was time to take some prisoners.

Despite the receptionist's attempts to insist that Mr Mills had directed that he did not want to be disturbed, Billie and Ash had catapulted themselves up the grand staircase and along corridors to the top of the hotel, where the carpet became golden and deeper and expensive scent was piped through the air. Billie had tried to convince Ash to stay in reception, but her efforts to verbally restrain him had fallen on deaf ears. He reached the door to GG Mills's room ahead of her and hammered on it.

'Police. Open the door!' Billie shouted, slightly breathless, giving a knock so hard that it hurt her knuckles.

'Open the door now!' Ash bellowed, then, 'Oh bugger this,' he said, before he gave a hard kick at the lock and then barged it open. The door banged loudly against the wall.

'What's going on?' Billie heard GG Mills's voice coming from the direction of a door in the corner of the room that they had entered. It was impressive, with two deeply upholstered sofas, an exquisitely inlaid coffee table holding a bowl full of exotic fruit, vases of fragrant white lilies positioned seemingly everywhere, a wide-screen TV and a smart, well-stocked bar in the corner. Clearly the joys of a motel with scratchy towels and bedbugs on tap weren't on the menu here, for the local boy made good.

Ash was first through the door into GG Mills's bedroom and stopped so suddenly that Billie nearly careered into the back of him. As she swerved, she saw the reason why. It wasn't Tom, the young runner, whose head popped up from the pillow next to the Hollywood star's, it was another man. He leapt out of the bed reaching for a gown to wrap around his naked body. Billie held up her identification. Ash was still looking like a rabbit trapped in the headlights.

'Mr Mills, we are taking you in for questioning with regards to these items, found in your bag, similar to a type which have been used in connection with the death of Pippa Sykes.' Billie held up the evidence bag containing the small cakes.

'This is outrageous!' GG Mills gasped, looking from Billie to Ash. She hoped to God that he wasn't going to claim that they had been planted.

'Not as outrageous as leaving killer cakes where my girls could innocently pick them up!' Billie caught Ash's arm. She thought he might use it to punch GG otherwise.

'I'm going to call our lawyer.' GG's bedmate announced with an American accent. Billie blocked his path. 'And you are?' she asked.

'Benjamin Fox,' he answered, 'GG's husband and publicist. The first fact is confidential by the way. His branding is curated. Targeted towards the Millennial Woman demographic.'

'Get dressed.' Ash spat the words out towards the actor. 'We're taking you to the station.' GG looked shamefaced and disgruntled as he climbed out of bed, showing his fit body. A memory of him coming out of her bathroom momentarily flashed through Billie's mind.

'As far as I was aware, the extra died after tripping over and smashing her head on a tree stump and I think you will find that I have a watertight alibi for when it happened. I was in the make-up trailer. Indeed, you found me there,' he said to Billie, sounding piqued.

'Our bad timing,' Ash muttered. 'She had a cake in her pocket when she died, identical to those you left in my *bedroom*.' Ash emphasised the last word, though Billie wished that he hadn't. It clearly hadn't gone unnoticed by hubby Benjamin. Billie took over.

'That cake contained traces of Death Cap mushroom, as did other food within her residence.'

'Is that the truth? No way. Nobody else has died from eating the things,' GG huffed as he pulled on trousers and top. 'If they were spiked with those then most of the crew and actors would be dead.'

Benjamin looked alarmed. 'You didn't eat any, did you, GG?' he asked.

'No, of course not. You know I'm on pure keto when I'm working. I just put them in my bag and forgot about them. *Politely* accepting a gift.' He skirted past Ash, as he headed for the bathroom to clean his teeth.

'Leave the door open,' Ash directed firmly, arms folded. Adjusting his position so that GG remained in his sights.

'So who gave you the cakes if you are claiming to be absolutely innocent?' Billie persisted as he emerged, in a temper.

'Fredi, in make-up,' he answered. 'Someone had gotten hold of some magic mushrooms and she just baked up a few cakes for the first day's filming. A tiny bit of mushroom in each, just to give a little buzz. A bit of fun to celebrate the new project. The whole story is so trippy anyway. I don't get that it's any big deal.'

'It is for you,' Ash answered. 'In the UK, just like most of America, magic mushrooms are illegal, and you knowingly had them in your possession. Now let's walk...'

'You can't do this!' Benjamin tried to chase after them. Billie held up her hand, unwilling to brook any interference. 'Class A drugs possession carries a sentence of up to seven years in prison. In addition, Mr Mills, you were seen in the vicinity of the church in the village of Boldon last night, around the time that Arden Roy was murdered there. We need to find out your movements in detail–'

'You are joking!' Billie noted that he did genuinely look shocked. 'Arden's dead... and you're trying to tie me in with it? You can't do this to me.' He looked all puppy-dog eyes at Ash.

'But I can,' Billie answered. 'You can either come with us quietly, out through the staff entrance, or if you prefer to play crybaby, we'll head out the front. I'm happy to rustle up a quick verbal press release, for the paparazzi hanging around out there, announcing that you are helping us with enquiries over multiple murders and the possession of class A drugs. Give your big publicity guru here a good reason to have jumped out of bed this morning.'

~

'That's crazy. Death Cap?' Fredi dissolved into sobs as Billie and Ash faced her over the table in the interview room. 'I would never have agreed to bake the cakes if I knew that they could kill someone.'

'But you were happy to use magic mushrooms, a class A drug as an ingredient.' Ash clearly still hadn't got over the shock of seeing his two young daughters carrying the drug-infused cakes on a tray with a glass of orange juice on the side. Billie was having some trouble wiping that memory herself.

'Only a weeny bit in each. I mean, it's not like the actors and crew are drug virgins. There's a supplier on every set. A little bit of coke to keep everyone awake, we work such long hours. A little bit of dope to calm the actors' nerves. Clen...' Fredi trailed off to blow her nose, her carefully applied mascara rocking a decidedly Alice Cooper vibe, as tears streamed down her face.

'Clen? Is that the name of your supplier?' Ash barked, scribbling on his pad. Fredi looked startled.

'No! Clen, Clenbuterol, the drug that makes you drop weight quickly.' Fredi sniffed. Billie kicked Ash's leg under the table, not able to stop herself having an inner smile at his mistake.

'Clenbuterol is used for treating asthma in horses.' Billie remembered her pony being treated for the condition many years ago, when she had lived in a very different world.

'Maybe, but ask any of the female actors, when they are called up by the film's doctor for their pre-shoot medical. They're always told to lose fifteen pounds. Even the girls who are already anorexic. Clen's the quickest way to do it. Same as all those exercise videos that they release with famous names. It's Clenbuterol that really builds muscles and makes them drop the fat.'

'So who's the supplier on the *Alice* set?' Billie looked Fredi in the eye. She appeared conflicted.

'I don't want to get anyone into trouble...'

'I imagine you don't want to be landed with a murder charge either.' Billie had tired of the soft-soaping. 'If anyone else picks up one of those rogue cakes you baked–'

'But I'm telling you, I didn't *know* that any had real killer mushrooms inside! No one else has died eating them.' Billie shrugged, unmoved by Fredi's pleas.

'They still might yet, unless you give us more information. We need to apprehend the film unit's drug supplier,' Billie said more firmly. 'Class A drugs hidden in cakes can also easily kill, so don't think that the lack of Death Cap gets you off the hook here.'

'Okay.' Fredi was hiccupping sobs, as the full realisation of the seriousness of her position seemed to hit her. 'Tom gave it to me, in a tiny packet, dried. He just takes the orders and delivers. He's not a big criminal or anything...'

Billie sighed. It was true that the people who got caught handling drugs rarely were. Tom seemed to be the eternal gopher, so set on a career in the bright lights, that he would agree to anything to follow his dream. She turned over a photo showing the fairy cakes found in GG's washbag.

'Can you confirm that these cakes are the items that you baked?' Fredi nodded tearfully. Billie confirmed her reaction for the purposes of the tape recording of the interview. She turned over another photo showing the cake that Josta had discovered tucked in Pippa Sykes's costume pocket.

'And this fairy cake too?' Billie asked. Fredi leaned over, rubbing her red eyes in order to have a better view, before shaking her head. She looked up, panic showing on her face.

'No. No, that's not one of mine. I know you won't believe me, but honestly, it's true! Look, all the ones I baked are in the same cases, just like these ones.' She pointed to the photos of the cakes that Billie had been offered for her breakfast in bed. 'This one's not mine.'

'Sounds like a proper little *Bake Off* set. How many people are likely to be cooking up *Alice in Wonderland*-inspired cupcakes?' Ash remained unconvinced, perhaps blinded by fury and fear for the welfare of his girls. But Billie could see what Fredi meant. The cases that she was claiming to be hers were plain white, but the one holding Pippa's version had the famous *Alice in Wonderland* hookah-smoking caterpillar printed on it. It was also bigger. Perhaps someone with evil intent had jumped on the cake bandwagon and slipped a deathly treat into Pippa Sykes's pocket, just in case the mushroom risotto wasn't doing the trick?

'So, clearly whoever spiked this one' – Billie held up the photo of the cake with the killer ingredient – 'didn't care that you might wind up here possibly facing a murder charge. So, if you know who the person is who supplies the drugs to the film set, then now is the time to spill, because they're seriously not doing you any favours.' Fredi swallowed hard, the blood draining from her face.

'I honestly haven't got a clue,' she whispered. 'No one ever broadcasts that. No one wants to know. After all, one word in the wrong ear and you could end up dead.'

22

LOVE LIES BLEEDING

'Word just back from forensics,' Boo called over to Billie, who was having a quick coffee break whilst reviewing the mound of information coming in from all directions.

'The two cakes belonging to GG have come back clean for Death Cap mushroom and contain only insignificant amounts of the magic sort.' Ash, sitting next to Boo, gave a huge sigh of relief, dropping his head into his hands. 'Custody officer is requesting release without bail for GG Mills,' Boo added, looking at a message popping up on her PC.

'No chance of bail, condition not to leave the country?' Billie knew that there was little hope. Try as she might, she couldn't control the whole legal system and the actor hadn't actually been caught in possession of the cakes. Indeed, they had been on Billie's premises.

As far as Arden Roy's demise was concerned, they had proof of GG Mills being in the vicinity at the still roughly estimated time of death, but no motive or evidence at all to connect him otherwise to the crime. It wasn't enough to hold him. Hubby Benjamin would also be sending in a top lawyer, to mitigate the fallout, without any doubt whatsoever. Boo had been typing as Billie spoke. She stopped to read the answer on the screen. The reply had clearly been immediate. She shook her head. 'Okay, confirmed,' Billie agreed through gritted teeth.

'Let him go. Good riddance to bad rubbish.' Ash threw the words out. Boo glanced across at him.

'Look at us two. Bitter losers in love,' she said through a chuckle. 'Billie's the only one of us that has her head screwed on, as far as romance is concerned.'

'Tweedledee and tweedledum.' Ash made a funny voice and pulled a silly face as he nudged Boo in jest. Billie wanted to say that they had no idea about the truth, that she'd been a runaway bride only the night before. Instead, she smiled, glad that at least her two colleagues were able to laugh, even for a moment, about their own disastrous love lives. She hoped that she might also be able to retell her own wedding horror story, with the odd giggle thrown in, at some time, much further down the line. Her thoughts were interrupted as Maya approached.

'Ma'am, I've just been looking through the details of the email threats sent to Charles Carroll before his death, as requested,' she said as Billie turned to her. She was impressed by the trainee's progress in such a short time working in the department.

'Good. Anything juicy crop up?' Billie asked.

'Well, most of the messages appear to have come from an encrypted device as you are aware. But on closer scrutiny one seems to have come from a server based at Middleton College...'

'Which both Pippa Sykes and Maddie Taylor attended,' Ash reminded Billie, not that she was likely to forget.

'And Charles Carroll worked there as a freelance lecturer,' Boo added.

'Miriam Nelson's daughter attended Middleton too.' Billie's mind was working fast. Now four different murder victims had a shared connection and Maddie's probable killer, as well as Olivia Nelson's, had been caught on CCTV wearing clothes that seemed to have originated from Middleton College's drama costume department. The telephone on Ash's workstation rang.

'Tom has been taken into interview room two,' he advised, reaching for his jacket. The young runner had been in the process of being lifted at his mum's home, even as Fredi's interview was underway. Billie had already been keen to question him about his movements the night before. He had been photographed at a location only a few hundred yards away from the crime scene and had now been confirmed as a drug runner. Billie felt they were only one step away from their big breakthrough.

'It's okay, I'll take Maya with me on this one. She needs the experience. You check up on the girls.' Billie gathered her paperwork. The children had been hurriedly dropped off at the school breakfast club on the way to lift GG Mills, and Jas would be on her high horse wanting to know why Ash had veered off the agreed plan. The joys of a less than genial divorce.

But more than that, Billie wanted to get the most honest account possible out of Tom and if he was aware of Ash's affair with the actor, he might be less than forthcoming. Ash hadn't seen the mobile phone footage taken by Maya's friend Lily yet, showing that the young lad was clearly having an intimate relationship with the actor. She could tell that Ash was quietly nursing a broken heart and she would always have his back. Now wasn't the time to go sticking the knife in.

'You were involved in an intimate relationship with GG Mills?' Billie had launched into questioning as soon as she had finished the required formalities. Tom nodded happily, seemingly glad to have come out of the shadows.

'He's not in any trouble, is he?' he suddenly asked. Shame that GG Mills hadn't given the young runner a second thought during his own interview, Billie recollected. He had simply shrugged when shown the photo of them together, mentioned that they had parted ways an hour after arrival and that he had no idea what Tom might have got up to after that.

'Can you tell us what your movements were last night?' Billie replied.

'Well, we got to GG's place in Boldon. It's a little cottage he likes to use as a hideaway. The time was, I think, around seven thirty,' Tom answered. 'I had to hide under a blanket in the back as usual, until we got right outside. If we're seen together GG says that it would break a million female hearts.' He sighed. 'We hate the subterfuge, but it goes with the territory.'

'Did you see Arden Roy when you were there?' Billie asked.

'No, it's kind of our special place. I've never seen anyone else from the film set there. You know what it's like. Sometimes we just like to shut the whole damn world out. Our time together is so precious after all.' Billie blew out a sigh. She couldn't help feeling a little sorry for the young man, who like Ash, had fallen so easily for the actor's charms.

'Okay. What time did you both leave?' Billie continued. Tom looked up as though deep in thought.

'It was about an hour later. Yes. Eight thirty pm. GG dropped me off at the bus stop about a mile down the road, on the country lane. It's quiet there, so no one would see us together. He had to rush off to the hotel. All the film bigwigs were flying in after the accident yesterday.'

Billie made a note to check CCTV from the buses on that route. He'd be caught out very quickly if he wasn't telling the truth.

'So he didn't drive you home?' Billie checked again. Talk about being taken for a ride.

'No. I'm still living with my mum, on a council estate. Imagine the attention the Porsche would get there?' Tom smiled for a moment, looking even younger than his tender years. 'But GG has promised that one day our time will come. I got home about eleven pm,' he added.

'So what were you doing during the two and a half hours between being dropped off and arriving back home?' Billie enquired. Tom was quick to answer.

'Either sitting on a bus or waiting for one. I have to change twice from the spot where GG has to drop me.'

'You are kidding?' Maya couldn't seem to help stop the words spilling from her mouth. 'Sorry, ma'am,' she corrected herself, but Billie had to agree with her sentiments.

'Well, I hope he is worth it, Tom, that's all I can say.' Billie made a note to check the whole route he had claimed to have taken and also have the movements of his mobile phone checked to corroborate his story.

'Definitely.' Tom smiled.

'Right. We have information that you deliver drugs from a supplier to persons involved in the film production. These include but are not confined to certain hallucinogenic mushrooms and other class A and class C substances. Is that correct?' Tom blinked, his love-struck smile dropping like a lead balloon.

'I... don't know–' Tom started to say. Billie was growing impatient. She cut across him.

'Whether they included Death Cap mushrooms too? I can inform you that Pippa Sykes death was partly due to Death Cap poisoning. Was she one of the recipients of illegal drugs delivered by you? Or Maddie Taylor?' Tom rose from his chair in fright.

'I may have delivered some stuff, I'll admit. Just to get by. My student grant doesn't cover all of my outgoings and I pay my mum rent. But I didn't kill them... I mean, I had no idea...' He held his hand over his mouth. 'The rumours are that Maddie committed suicide?' Billie wasn't quite sure if he was simply shocked or was trying not to be sick, but she wasn't keen to curtail the interview right now.

'She was murdered.' Billie decided not to beat about the bush. 'Please sit down, Tom. You found Pippa Sykes's body and were in the vicinity of the crime scene where Arden Roy was brutally murdered last night, so you can see how important it is that you answer these questions honestly and as accurately as you can.' Billie wanted to keep up the pressure.

'I did do some deliveries to Pippa and Maddie, even before the film started. They were regulars. Especially Pippa. But I only delivered the packages and took the money... or not in the case of Pippa. She kind of owed, like a ton...' He trailed off for a moment as though worried what to say next. Billie waited. She found that total silence could often jog nervous interviewees to start gabbing to fill the space. 'She'd been warned... threatened...' He looked up nervously.

'Did you threaten her?' Billie asked. He shook his head. 'No way. Pippa was like pretty insane when she was high and she was usually high,' he added. 'It's the guy that runs the show that puts the pressure on. I'm aware that he issued threats to make her cough up the dosh.' Billie noted that at least he was confirming that they were dealing with a male, as they had guessed.

'Did he threaten to kill her?' Billie stared hard at Tom. He squirmed in his seat, his right leg juddering up and down nervously.

'He threatens to kill anyone, you know, loads of people...' He trailed off, swallowing hard. 'Pippa, Maddie, if she squeaked...'

'Has he threatened you?' Billie softened her voice. Tom hung his head down and finally answered quietly.

'Maybe.... My mobile's been taken. You might see a few on there...'

Billie scribbled down a note to get that checked as soon as they were done.

'So let us put an end to this. What is his name, Tom?' Billie finally asked the question that no doubt everyone in the next-door observation room was waiting with bated breath to hear.

'I can't say.' Tom was even more agitated now. 'He knows where my gran lives, he even knows about her allotment. He said he'll hit her over the head and bury her alive and no one will ever know. He said he's done it before...' The word *bingo* lit up in Billie's mind as though she had been waiting for the last number on the winning card.

'Just give us his name and we'll bring him straight in. Your gran will never have to worry again.' Tom was shaking his head from side to side now, in an almost demented seated dance. Maya caught Billie's eye before suddenly addressing Tom.

'Didn't you tell me on set that you attended Middleton College?' she asked. Tom flicked his eyes in her direction.

'I left this year,' he answered. Billie sensed a defensive tone to his voice suddenly.

'Is that where your drug dealer's based? Let's face it, most colleges have one.' Tom started to seriously freak out.

'I want a solicitor. You said at the beginning I could have one if I wanted. I didn't then, but I do now.' His face was twisted in an attempt not to cry, but tears had started streaming down his cheeks. Billie sighed inwardly. She had been so close. She formally curtailed the interview and called the custody officer in to lead Tom away until the duty solicitor could be called in to do his thing.

'Sorry, ma'am. Did I speak out of turn?' Maya asked. Billie

had hoped that his concern for his gran had made him on the brink of spilling, but nothing was certain.

'No guarantee he was about to cough.' Billie hoped that she sounded convincing. 'And you did flag up yet another connection to Middleton College.' The killer piece of the jigsaw was at that location for sure. As soon as the interview finished Billie intended to get her team down there to rifle the records, holiday closure or not. She would apply for a special warrant if needed.

'But you do owe me a cup of tea. Go heavy on the sugar,' she added, as Miriam Nelson burst through the door which led from the observation room, in a state of high agitation.

'Where is the little bastard? If he hasn't killed my girl, he knows who did it!' Maya leapt back in shock as Billie sped forward, blocking Miriam Nelson's sprint towards the swing door, beyond which Billie could see Tom being led back to his holding cell.

'That wouldn't be wise, ma'am.' Billie grabbed Miriam's hand on the door handle, slamming it shut.

'Out of my way, Wilde.' The new chief struggled to push Billie out of the way, but she had now moved in front of her senior officer, firmly blocking her route. She grabbed both of the woman's arms, as Maya looked on in astonishment.

'We're nearly there, ma'am. I promise we're nearly there.' Billie felt the tension in the big woman's arms finally release. She ran her hand over her face. After a beat, she nodded.

'You're right, Wilde. I stand corrected. I need a drink...' She quickly turned and walked away, head down.

'You okay?' Maya asked, as Billie leant back against the wall, whilst mentally banging her head against it. She had been so close. 'Should I bring you a chair?'

'No, don't do that. If I sit down, I may never get up again,' Billie joked weakly, though the truth was that with stress and lack of sleep, she was dog-tired. 'Bring a handful of chocolate biscuits back with you instead.' She closed her eyes for a moment, determined to summon up all the reserves of energy that she had left. She would get the name out of Tom on the next attempt if it was the last thing she did. Brief or no brief.

'She was like a wild bison on heat, the way she shot out of here,' Ash quipped about Miriam Nelson's earlier race downstairs, as Billie sipped her second mug of sweet tea in the observation room and downed biscuits like they were about to become extinct. She should have guessed that he would have come along to watch, despite her attempts to soften the cold, hard truth of his relationship with GG Mills.

'Bit like you this morning,' Billie replied. 'Are the girls okay?'

'Yeah, they are great. I'm taking them out to the cinema tonight if we get done early enough. Jas has actually said that I can stay at hers. On the sofa.' Billie drained her mug, picking up crumbs of biscuit that had fallen onto her top and downing them.

'Hey, result. Thanks for doing this by the way, so sharpish.' She waved the printouts showing the threatening messages, some in photographic form, that Ash had found on Tom's mobile.

'No doubt, we're dealing with the same guy who killed Charles Carroll–' Ash was interrupted by an operative in the room, who had answered a ringing phone.

'Suspect and brief heading for interview room two now, ma'am.'

'Okay, we're on. I want you with me this time.' Billie caught Ash's arm. 'I've told Maya to trawl through all the other stuff that's been lifted from Tom's phone. Bring in all of those pretty printouts.'

Ash gathered his pile of papers. As Billie picked up her own hefty file, her mobile suddenly rang loudly. She made a grab for it, thanking God that she was being reminded to turn it back off now, rather than in mid-interview.

'DSI Wilde,' she answered hastily.

'Hi, it's me.' Billie immediately recognised the voice of Perry Gooch. Billie knew that the seasoned journalist would have guessed that something was kicking off when she and Ash had rushed through the entrance, where members of the local press had been huddled. She also guesstimated rightly, that Perry was long enough in the tooth to predict that any photo opportunity would present itself via the staff exit. Billie had caught sight of her, with her trusty camera at the ready, as she and Ash had led GG Mills out via the back kitchen of the hotel.

'Not a good time to call,' Billie warned.

'Relax. I'm not expecting any insider info. In fact, I'm handing some over. I've been going through all of my old Lewis Carroll research for that article I wrote about the *Alice* books being inspired by the local area. Loads of potential spin-offs with the latest developments. The guy who gave me most of the information was a bit eccentric, obsessive even, over his ownership of the facts. Said other clever clogs were claiming that they knew all the history, one had even cobbled together a film script about it...' – Billie's mind immediately turned to Charles Carroll – '...but he insisted that *he* was the real authority. To be fair, he knew his stuff. Might be one to add to your list of crazy suspects at least.'

'Spill,' Billie answered. She had stepped into the corridor now and Tom, flanked by the duty solicitor and custody sergeant, was being led towards the doors that Miriam Nelson had tried to break through.

'I want first dibs on the inside stuff, if this pans out, mind you.' Perry had never been one to miss a trick. She passed the name of the individual to Billie and her brain finally clicked on the connection. It took all of Billie's powers of restraint not to leap up and punch the air. They had their man.

'Perry, I want to marry you and have your babies,' Billie answered. She ended her call and headed into the interview room. She wanted to make this quick. Get final confirmation from Tom and shoot off to make the arrest.

'No comment,' Tom answered to Billie's first settling-in question, having switched on the recording equipment and gone through the required formalities. Ash glanced towards Billie. She guessed that those watching in the observation gallery were giving a communal groan of dismay. The 'no comment' reaction was a regular result of having engaged a legal representative, trotted out regularly by hardened criminals. But Tom was even now twitchily eyeing up his brief, wondering if he was doing the right thing.

'You have a right to remain silent, but I'm sure Mr Barnes has explained the important condition attached to any refusal to answer our questions. The court would be then at liberty to draw an adverse inference if a suspect does not mention, during a police interview, a fact which he relies upon in his defence.' Tom looked like a terrified rabbit trapped in the headlights.

'My client will be invoking his right to rely on the innocent explanation clause. Please refer to the evidence on my client's mobile phone on which death threats have been made to him, as well as vulnerable members of his immediate family.' *Blimey, Nigel Barnes is in a perky mood today*, Billie noted. Billie and he enjoyed a jovial relationship outside of the police station and courtroom, so his comments were like water off a duck's back. In any case, she was holding the ace card today.

'Tom, did you deliver drugs to Olivia Nelson, a fellow Middleton student, three years ago?' Billie hoped that her mother, the chief, wasn't going to burst through the door, intent on murder, at any second. Hopefully she's gone back to her golden cage upstairs, Billie thought. Tom reacted with wide-eyed terror at the question.

'No comment,' he answered breathlessly, beads of sweat starting to form on his smooth pink forehead. Billie lifted out a sheet of A4 paper from her file and turned it face up on the countertop. It was a still of the CCTV footage of the bewigged and booted killer approaching the student digs of Olivia Nelson.

'Is this you in the picture?' she asked carefully.

'No!' Tom cried out in shock, forgetting his plan to stay silent.

'We believe this to be Olivia's killer, who went on to strangle her to death immediately after this image was captured.' Tom was shaking his head. His body had started shaking too. Billie lifted out the second photo and turned it over, so that it lay next to the first. The similarities were plain to see.

'This image was taken by a CCTV camera just before the time it is estimated that Maddie Taylor had her throat cut. You knew both girls. Is this you in the second picture?'

'No, no. You've got to believe me...' Nigel Barnes put his hand out to calm the young man, but he swiped it away. 'I haven't killed anybody!' Billie paused for a moment before lifting out a crime-scene photo of Pippa Sykes, in costume, lying dead on the banks of the River Wear, a pool of blood under her head.

'Pippa Sykes may have hit her head on the tree stump that you can see in the photo or been attacked with a rock. Either way, she was at the time suffering irreversible poisoning by a deadly mushroom. A witness has confirmed that you supplied class A drugs in the form of dried mushrooms as well as other illegal substances to cast and crew involved in the film production. You also claim to have found her body. Did you kill Pippa Sykes, Tom?' Tom banged his hand on the table causing Ash to tense next to Billie. She touched her colleague's arm. She guessed the young man in front of her was as harmless as a mouse.

'No!' Tom cried. 'Never, I told you before...' He trailed off, sobbing.

'Then tell us who did. Because right now, you are shielding a killer, who may well have murdered three other people, including the chief of police, director Arden Roy and actress Lola–' Tom finally cut Billie off in mid-sentence, having clearly reached breaking point.

'Dougie,' he whispered. Billie glanced at the recording equipment. Had it picked the name up?

'Can you repeat the name again, Tom, for the purposes of the recording?'

'Dougie Meeks.' He said the name loudly now, his voice tinged with fear. 'You know him. He's one of the actors, and he's the drama teacher at Middleton...'

'And the supplier of drugs with menaces thrown in?' Ash was joining the dots for the first time.

'As well as local Lewis Carroll expert, who couldn't help showing off his superior knowledge by weaving it into his crimes,' Billie added. Tom nodded as he tried to calm his panic attack.

'Our nickname for him at college was The Mad Hatter. You've got to protect my gran. I'll tell you *everything*, if you promise.' He was spilling like a burst pipe now. 'I know what he's capable of, what he did to Mr Carroll, our English lecturer, when he found out about the drugs and threatened to spill the beans. They were always arguing anyway, over the Alice in

Sunderland thing, when we did our end-of-term play. Both claiming they knew the true story.' Billie suddenly understood the slaughtered pig dressed as a baby photo, along with the threat that Charles Carroll had received. Dougie Meeks had carried it through. Tom continued talking, as though desperate now to flush the dark secrets that he had been keeping, completely out of his system.

'I saw him put that cake into Pippa's pocket on the day she died. He said he'd tried to shut her up, but she was still threatening to open her big mouth about him, now that she'd met some stars and thought she was suddenly somebody.' Billie guessed that went for Maddie Taylor too.

'He followed her down to the river, muttering that he was at the end of his tether, as he walked past me. I followed him for a few steps. He was arguing with her, and she pushed him away. Then he picked up a big rock, hit her with it, and then threw it in the water right by the tree stump...' Tom stopped speaking for a moment, his pained expression showing that he was reliving that moment. Then he spoke again, quietly, his words full of sorrow. 'Maddie felt she was the one to blame. He'd spun her some stupid tale about aphrodisiac mushrooms. Went around to their flat himself with a free sample and she'd fallen for it. She said that she couldn't live with the truth of what she had done. I know she wanted to tell...' Now that Tom was finally talking, he seemed unable to stop.

Billie blew out a sigh as she finally wound up the interview and watched Tom being walked forlornly back to his cell.

'Let's crack on. We've got a killer to lift.' Billie touched heads with Ash.

They were out of the room and on the move at a pace

towards the exit, not even stopping to bask in the congratulations of the officers now spilling out of the observation room. Billie spotted Miriam Nelson heading down the corridor in their direction, blowing her nose on her handkerchief. Billie nudged Ash. They swerved left to a side door to the car park. Now wasn't the time for high fives and tearful thanks. The job still wasn't finished yet.

23

TWO FAT LADIES

'Two fat ladies, eighty-eight.' Billie and Ash could hear a bingo session in full swing. Clearly the political correctness police hadn't raided this particular cross-dressing venue yet.

'Legs eleven.' The room erupted with wolf whistles, as Ash and Billie stood, with their heads close to the door. Billie reflected that it would be the first time that she had raided an afternoon tea dance.

'Ready?' Ash asked. Billie gave him the nod and he swung the door open. The two quickly made their way up the side of the room onto the stage, to where Dougie Meeks was manning the bingo ball machine.

'Douglas Meeks, I'm arresting you in connection with the murders of Charles Carroll, Phillipa Sykes and Madeline Taylor.' Billie continued through the legal formalities, as Ash deftly handcuffed Dougie Meeks. She was sorry that she couldn't charge him for poor Will Cox's suicide as well. Billie was suddenly aware that the room had gone silent and that the microphone was turned on directly in front of her.

'What are you talking about?' Dougie played the shocked

innocent, today's beehive Ivor Fullcrotch wig wobbling on his head, heavily painted lipstick gashed across his mouth as he ranted his indignation. Billie wasn't convinced by the act for a moment.

'You could have waited five minutes, pet,' a man with a long grey hairpiece with a yellow flower clipped into it shouted out, in a slightly broken mezzo-soprano voice. 'I was knocking here. Waiting for one more number for a full house.' He looked suitably non-plussed as he hurled down his thick felt-tip pen, clearly more concerned about his lost winnings than the fact that a murderer was in their midst.

'This is all bollocks!' Dougie struggled with the cuffs, rocking his inner bolshie Ivor Fullcrotch role, as more members of Billie's team appeared through the door. Billie reckoned that there might be a goldmine of incriminating evidence stashed backstage in the props and costume room, set to one side. She switched off the microphone as the room erupted into shocked chatter.

'We will also be talking to you about the deaths of the former chief of police, Lola Strong and Arden Roy,' Billie informed Dougie. He obviously wasn't in the mood to go quietly.

'Arden Roy popped his clogs last night, didn't he? Well I was here for the whole evening. Arrived at seven and left at one am. We had a late licence. Most of this lot can vouch for me.' He turned to the room, shouting for quiet, even now not willing to relinquish control. 'How many of you lovely ladies can verify to the flatfoots here, that I wasn't out killing last night, I was killing it in here. Mavis's sixtieth birthday party. It was one hell of a do.' A pile of cheers erupted in confirmation.

'And the Queen of Hearts losing her head?' Dougie continued. 'You'll have trouble planting that one on me as well. Look at that there.' He pointed to a big poster on the wall in which he was wearing a purple top hat, promoting his *Mad*

Hatter Saturday Afternoon sports avoidance disco. 'It's a Mad Hatter once a month special and I was here regular as clockwork yesterday afternoon. I wasn't required for the courtroom scene on the film.'

'Well, don't worry, you'll definitely be required for a few coming up. Starting with the magistrates' court first thing in the morning.' Billie took one of his arms and Ash the other as they bundled him out of his spotlight, exiting stage left.

'Not staying for the party?' Ash nodded towards The Cop-Out pub next to their headquarters where those officers not directly involved in the arrest of Dougie Meeks had retired to celebrate the big breakthrough. Billie shook her head. She was certain that they had the right man for the murder charges she had initially read out and hopefully they would eventually nail him for Olivia Nelson's death too, but she was in no mood for celebration. Not least because strong drink and a bag of pork scratchings wasn't going to bring her godfather back.

All the glamour and glitz of the showbiz world didn't alter the fact that in truth, the deaths seemed to have started with exactly the same issues she regularly dealt with on the hardest of housing estates. Drug abuse, coercion of vulnerable people and crazy little arguments that escalate out of all proportion ending in heartbreak and death. It was beginning to take its toll.

'Nope. I'm all done in. I've left some money behind the bar to buy a few thank you rounds. The team deserve to chill-out a bit, having worked non-stop around the clock. But we still can't pin the last three charges on Dougie Meeks. As he said, his alibi is watertight for Arden Roy's death and Lola's still hasn't been classified as murder rather than an accident due to an unsafe working environment.' Billie couldn't help thinking that if Josta had been on the case then it would already have been confirmed as the former, family member or not.

'You are right,' Ash answered as he unlocked his car door. 'Boo said that Ellis was talking to her on the phone after he heard of the arrest and confirmed that he definitely saw Dougie in Arden Roy's trailer, from four am onwards on the morning that you found the Chief.' Billie's thoughts turned to Ellis and his claims to have been the one person that the Chief seemed to have been able to confide in.

'I still don't get why Ellis was there so early.' Billie leaned against Ash's car. She didn't need to remind herself that the Chief's mobile, with his last message to her, had still not been found yet, despite the last dying signal being pinpointed at the film-set base. Enquiries with Sid hadn't brought up anything special. Apparently he regularly walked around the base at night checking on odd sounds, in case opportunist thieves had come knocking.

'Seems the catering lot have to start peeling spuds before dawn to feed the marauding hoards throughout the day. He also had to get there extra early, because there was a pick-up shot of Tweedledum and Tweedledee first thing, so he had to suffer the make-up graveyard shift,' Ash explained. 'Do you think Dougie Meeks was working with someone else?' he asked.

Billie rubbed her face. She was so tired that she didn't know what to think anymore. She could see the motive for killing the three victims that he was facing charges on. It had been simply to stop them squealing about his drug-dealing set-up. The nods to *Alice in Wonderland* with each murder had turned out to be his Achilles heel. In the end his own ego had caught him out, but the Chief, Lola and Arden Roy? She was determined to find out eventually, but right now she needed to sleep on it.

'Get yourself off to the cinema with your girls,' Billie directed. 'And treat them to some popcorn from me.' She stuffed a fiver into Ash's pocket. 'I'm off to have a long soak in the bath and then bed.' She headed off towards her car.

'Thanks, boss. See you tomorrow. Oh, I'll shift that old battered black metal box that I dumped in the kitchen this morning when I get back. I was in such a panic over the cakes that I forgot to return it to the cellar.' Billie was instantly alert.

'What black metal box?' She spun around.

'The one that was in your cellar. Indie was staying for tea, you remember, the night before your break-in? She wanted me to fix up the bunk beds in their room and I was looking for a screwdriver. I thought it was a toolbox, but I couldn't get into it. We gave up and went out for a burger instead, but I must have left it under her bed amongst the toys. I remembered it this morning when I was checking that there were no more killer fairy cakes stashed there. Sorry.' Billie blinked as the information sank in. The Chief's black box of hidden secrets was sitting in the middle of her kitchen right now?

'No problem. It's probably just a load of old junk.' Billie didn't know why she wasn't telling the truth. Maybe it was because the box was such a personal item, so seemingly precious to the Chief that he had wanted only Billie to look after it. Not even his new best buddy, Ellis Darque. 'Have a great evening,' Billie shouted, breaking into a jog to reach her car.

She sped home, lucky not to have been pulled over by a traffic cop, so eager was she to complete the journey. As she entered the kitchen, she stopped for a moment and took a deep breath. The box was still there. Was she about to find the key she so desperately needed to end, once and for all, the recent vortex of death and destruction? Or was this a version of Pandora's box, ominously waiting to let loose even more murderous truths?

24

MAD AS A HATTER

My darling Billie, if you are reading this, then it is because I am no longer around in this world to hold your hand whilst I tell you my story.

Billie had only read the first sentence of the letter that had lain on top of other items in the box, before tears had started streaming down her face. It seemed as though the Chief had momentarily come back to life, but in the same instant, had confirmed once and for all that he'd gone, no matter how much Billie had tried to push that fact to the back of her mind in order to get her job done.

I always intended to explain the facts that I am about to impart to you now, once I had started my retirement from the force. I have dark secrets, Billie, that I am not proud of and that might have reflected badly on you, when I was still in my chief of police post, hence keeping the contents under lock and key.

Not that there had been a key, Billie noted. And the steel was reinforced. So it had been a real struggle to open the metal box.

Indeed, Billie had to ransack her actual toolbox, reverting to the advanced jemmy skills taught to her by an old burglar informant and his gift of a cutting wheel, in thanks for her getting him off on a charge, in return for vital information. He had assured her the tool would make short work of opening even a high-security safe. As unexpected gifts went, it had certainly come in handy.

The times were different when I started in the force. We were young men who felt supremely powerful, with the world at our feet. Everything was there for our taking. The chief of police in those days gave us that confidence. He did the same for you, being your beloved dad.

Billie swallowed hard. She'd had personal experience of how that situation had panned out and she had a horrible feeling that she was going to find out that history might have somehow repeated itself.

There were girls – very many lovely ladies willing to offer favours to the police, for those of us who turned a blind eye to their nocturnal money-making efforts...

Billie stopped reading for a moment, anger rising in her chest. Did those 'lovely ladies' in truth, have any choice in the matter?

Believe me, they were willing partners in the unofficial agreement, though nowadays such things aren't considered to be infra dig. Some females have come out of the woodwork recently, claiming that we abused our position.

'Damn right you did!' Billie said the words out loud,

suddenly seeing her sweet suave godfather with an undeniable eye for the ladies, in a different light.

> *Just over a year ago, I was approached by a past amour from those times, let's say a good-time girl, who finally did make good. She informed me that a child had been produced from our long-ago liaisons. I was shocked, but also intrigued, never having fathered a child of my own. You were and always will be the closest to a child of mine, Billie, my sweet.*

Billie suddenly had a sour taste in her mouth, as her tears dried on her cheeks.

> *I had no reason to disbelieve her. We had enjoyed our discreet liaisons over a long period, and she had never previously approached me on the subject to ask for support. But now the child is an adult and had asked her to make an introduction. I was open to the idea, relieved to discover that the man is a crack professional with experience of policing. Maybe I was blinded by the thought that my seed would live on as I approach my autumn years? We met and I was impressed, ready on retirement to come clean about the past. I put him on the payroll. There was no reason to doubt his credentials. But then there is no fool like an old fool...*

Billie's mind was racing. Had she met this guy? A picture of Ellis Darque spun through her mind. The Chief himself had invited him in to help with Billie's last investigation and he was a crack police professional.

> *I paid him well, but he wanted more. I was perplexed, but he was delivering results, so I paid him a bonus from a special community fund...*

Billie had already run out of sympathy somewhat. But the words made her sit up straight. She could sense a reason now for the Chief to feel vulnerable. Demands for money usually involved threats. Clearly there had been serious misdemeanours committed by her godfather in his career. Her eyes scanned the page. Here it was.

> *He turned out to be a fraudster. I discovered that he had used many aliases on numerous scams. He brought up the subject of my will, threatening to report my past, wreck my career unless I changed it in his favour. I reluctantly did as I was bid, knowing that you were already financially secure, from your own recent inheritances, Billie my love.*

Billie sighed. She'd hardly had any sleep in the past two days and this final letter from the grave was nearly more than her mind could take. Why on earth hadn't the Chief told her what was going on?

> *But Miriam Nelson was already on my case, it turned out. Taking on the sob stories of the old streetwalkers and now she wants answers about the missing money from the community fund. She has also been questioning my relationships with various staff members – including you, Billie. That's why it was safer for you that I've kept silent on this matter.*
>
> *When I got the opportunity, I managed to get material from my blackmailer, enough for a DNA test. It came back negative this afternoon. I have just informed him that I've drafted a replacement will back in your favour. You will find it here in the box. Billie, I know that my time is up on the force and that I might get a custodial sentence for this, or worse. The threat I have just received makes it clear that I have been duped by a highly dangerous individual. Show this to Miriam Nelson if I'm no longer here to tell the tale. He has to*

be stopped. Stay safe my darling god-daughter. You will remain in my heart forever. X

Billie sat still for a while, watching the sky. The bright blue of the day, giving way to the first streaks of saffron reflected in the water down on the Alnmouth estuary. How could the world keep turning without the Chief, her greatest supporter, still in it?

The Chief had clearly written the note just before she had come to see him and received the box. His life had come to an end only a few hours later. Billie's thoughts were conflicted. Horrified by the crimes committed by him in the past, yet she remained full of grief for the man that she had thought she had known and loved.

Billie finally made a decision and reached for her phone. She punched in Miriam Nelson's number at headquarters and waited. The call went to answerphone. Billie hoped that the new chief wasn't at this moment down in the cells trying to tear Dougie Meeks limb from limb.

She doubted that the bereaved mother would have joined in celebrations at The Cop-Out. Just as Billie had not responded to the numerous congratulatory text messages pinging on her phone, Miriam Nelson would be all too aware that the life sentence that Dougie Meeks was sure to get would be nothing compared to the one that she would be forced to live with for the rest of her life. Those forever-missing family moments, weddings, babies, christenings, even funerals. All of life's rich tapestries torn to shreds by the evil acts of a cold uncaring, individual.

Billie picked up the newly adjusted will, now back in her own favour, that had finally signed the Chief's death warrant. Underneath she suddenly spotted the old Toby jug from her godfather's mantelpiece that Billie had thought lost for good. She hugged it in her arms, unable to shake off her sorrow, no matter the unsavoury truths unveiled about its previous owner. There were other papers, too, that Billie had been left. Within them were details that left no doubt in her mind as to the person responsible for the Chief's demise.

After a short time reflecting on the truth, Billie slammed the box shut. The time had come to bring the killer down. In her mind it was fortunate that Miriam Nelson had not taken her call. This was personal and Billie had no wish to bring in the whole damn cavalry to watch her final reckoning with the killer. She took a deep breath and made another call, the biggest emotion now rising in her heart was fury towards the Chief's murderer, who clearly felt that he had a God-given right to hand out such a chilling death sentence.

'Ellis. It's Billie. I'd like to talk. Can you come over to my place?' she asked, detecting only the slightest of wavering in her voice.

'Celebrating, are you? Think you've got your man?' he asked.

'No. I'm all alone. I'll be here waiting for you,' Billie answered, ending the call.

The sky looked like it had been spray-painted by a graffiti artist by the time that Billie made her way down the winding pathway through her terraced garden and out through the blue gate at the bottom. Or perhaps the crazy streaks of orange, red and violet were scribbled across the sky by a celestial child let loose with crayons? After the truths that Billie had just unearthed, she felt that anything was possible.

Ellis wouldn't arrive for a while yet and she wanted a few moments alone to breathe in the salty sea air and listen to the soft crash of the waves as they rushed into the shore. The scene always cleared her mind and she needed to be focused for what was about to happen next.

Billie paused for a moment at the tiny disused ferryman's hut. She felt a wave of emotion as she recalled the enchanting scene only the night before, in which she had been led to her fairy-light-strewn wedding venue. A sudden gust of cold air made her shiver, just as she noticed a movement to her right, in front of the hut. She stepped forward.

'Hello, Billie.' Max smiled that soft crooked smile of his, his unique lemony signature scent kissing Billie's senses as the breeze caught her hair.

'Max.' Billie's stomach fluttered. He was wearing the same crumpled linen wedding suit, looking even more handsome now, with a shadow of dark stubble on his chin and hair tousled in the wind, despite the dark shadows under his eyes. 'I thought you wouldn't come back...' She trailed off. It was the truth. Max held his hand out to her.

'One last walk together, Billie. It's a beautiful night for it. Not a single soul around.' Max's voice was soft and inviting. Billie could see that it was true. But Ellis would be arriving soon. She needed to concentrate on that. 'I know now that we'll never be man and wife. You are wedded to your work, and I will be gone in the morning, but let's just spend these last few minutes together,' Max invited.

Despite her better intentions, Billie caught Max's fingers. He tugged her close as he moved along the seashore, the waves catching at their feet as the tide swept in and out.

'We could never be man and wife, Max.' Billie's voice was equally soft. 'You are already married after all. Luna Da Costa ring any bells? And what about your son?' Billie remembered the child crying in the background when she had thought that Max was boarding a plane to some far-off location, the exotic bird sounds, probably from his pet shop located in a dull

London suburb and the photo of the little boy, sent by his actress wife. She had been such a fool. But it wasn't her style to run away from the fact, despite Max's softly laced fingers now hardening to a vice-like clench. He smiled.

'Oh so clever, DSI Billie Wilde.' He moved in from the beach to an area of golden sand, clear except for a discarded sandcastle, decorated with shells. Billie had already absorbed the fact that Max's interest in marrying her was probably based on her recent inheritances and ownership of a large house. 'Let's sit and talk awhile.' He pulled Billie down beside him onto the soft sand. 'After all, you couldn't get enough of the beach the other night...' Billie felt sick at the thought now.

'I guess there's no need to call you Doctor Max Strong now,' Billie answered. The documents in the Chief's black box had told the whole sordid tale. 'The new chief is well aware of the forgery. Fake credentials two a dirham in the Middle East apparently.' Max smiled again. Billie could feel his strength through his grasp, but she was ready to fight.

'Seems that you haven't been in the army for ages. Never in any special forces. All that leaping on planes to dangerous places...you were here all the time. Did Natalie actually exist?' Billie asked sadly. She suddenly remembered having met one of the female army paramedic's grieving relatives. Natalie, Max's former wife, had been real. But what was the truth of her terrible demise?

Billie glanced back in the direction of her house. Ellis should be here by now. She hoped to God that he wasn't sitting politely by the front door. 'Why Lola?' Billie pressed on her mobile in her pocket. She hoped that she'd hit the 'record' button. 'Why kill your own mother?' Max softly chuckled.

'Because she was a fucking whore, Billie. First making me believe that my father was some big-shot businessman, leading me to chase him around South America for my formative years, then having me truly believing that the chief of police was the real culprit. She lived in la-la-land. Turns out she did shag him in the past, anything for money. She married Josta, after all, just as soon as she had inherited her parents' pile. But then your dear god-daddy proved to be a dud as well, threatening to turn me in. Truth is that she opened her legs to more actors than Equity too...' He shook his head as if amused by the knowledge. 'Imagine how I felt when I found out that runt of a film director Arden Roy was my real dad. Got the damn test confirmed on paper. Can you believe it, Billie? I was so easily taken in by her act.'

Billie wanted to retort that she knew the feeling, but she also knew that Max posed a formidable threat, hence asking Ellis over for a chat, to work out a plan. She had never suspected that Max would be mad enough to come back to her home. Her thoughts turned to Zelda Meads and her deduction that Billie had a process-focused serial killer on her hands. Someone who wanted to prolong the pain and suffering of his victims.

'Hence the *Alice* links to the murders.' Billie hoped that this was all being recorded.

'She would have loved that.' Max shrugged. 'She was obsessed with the fucking stories when I was a kid, and let's face it, she went out in the spotlight. Josta was banging on about the recent murders, so it felt like a good idea to get in on the act. Trust you to get it.' He nudged Billie like she was a mate who'd just sussed the culprit who'd carried out a silly prank. To her relief, she spotted Ellis winding his way down her garden terrace obviously on the lookout for her. Billie reached her free hand into her pocket and grabbed her handcuffs, clipping them quickly around Max's wrist. He glanced at them and then chuckled softly.

'Max, I'm taking you in,' she announced, trying to retain at least some air of control. Ellis had spotted her. He gave a wave. She breathed a mental sigh of relief.

'I'm not going anywhere, Billie and neither are you.' Max leant over and planted a kiss on Billie's cheek, now that the handcuffs had drawn them even closer. He waved his free hand in the air. 'See this area all around us, just here? I've planted landmines in it. Everyone thinks they're huge but anti-personnel mines, they are teeny, little plastic things, just under the surface. See them?' he asked. Billie looked all around. Was he lying? 'No, you don't.' He shook his head in a relaxed fashion.

'You won't feel a thing. Nats didn't when I finished her off. She found out about Luna and was going to blab to the army top brass. Bigamy. Big deal. She had family money and I have major outgoings. Marriage, it's just a signature on a piece of paper after all.' Billie's heart rate shot up. This wasn't some demented joke. He was deadly serious.

'First person to come along here and we'll go out together, with a bang. Believe it or not, I really do love you, Billie, but I just can't go on like this anymore. All the lies...' Max trailed off. To Billie's alarm Ellis emerged from behind the ferryman's hut, only a few metres away.

'Stay back,' she called. 'He's mined the beach.' Ellis stopped stock-still.

'You're having a laugh,' he said. But he wasn't smiling now. Maybe he had seen enough maniacs in his time to realise that Max was the real deal.

Suddenly Billie heard a loud bark as a large dog came bounding through the dunes towards them.

'Here we go,' Max said as though preparing for a fairground ride. Billie looked from the dog to Ellis, trying desperately to recall the safe route that they had taken along the seashore. It looked different now that the tide was rapidly coming in. She thought she could make out some footprints, faint marks in the sand. The dog was galloping nearer, she had to do something.

Billie unclipped the handcuffs and took off at speed, her heart pounding, concentrating hard on hitting the footprint marks in the sand as lightly as possible as she moved flat out in the direction of Ellis. As she reached him and turned back towards Max, he stood up and took a step forward towards her. The effect was immediate, a meteor shower of sand and rocks and noise as Billie's dream lover, whom in truth she had simply imagined existed, departed the world instantly. When the sandstorm settled, it seemed as though he had never been there at all, that she had just escaped from a nightmare.

25

WILDE AND DARQUE

Billie fiddled with her starched white collar, black suit and wayward curls which seemed determined to spring out from her tightly pinned-back hair. It was the nearest thing possible to a police uniform that a detective could wear to an award ceremony; one which Billie had been summoned to attend despite her vociferous protests. The chief, Miriam Nelson, was absolutely determined to hand out a public bravery award to the detective who had finally tracked down her daughter's killer, and got justice, arguably, in one form or another for all of the other victims caught up in the *Alice* murders.

Billie took a deep breath and pulled down her skirt, already riding way too high on her long legs. Of course, she agreed that her team deserved recognition for the work that they had done on the case, but Billie alone was being singled out and she hated being a target. She looked across to Ash and Boo sitting in the audience. They gave a little wave of encouragement.

Waiting at the side of the stage in the grand old hall, next to an impressive marble fireplace as speeches were being made, Billie caught sight of herself in the huge ornate mirror over the mantelpiece. Her mind started to wander back through time. Sadly she couldn't turn it back, because she felt tormented by a harrowing truth. That by not speaking out a year ago when she had discovered her own birth secret, she had been complicit in the deaths of many other innocents. The effect on Max of his own birth story, riddled with lies, was still almost too horrific to dwell upon.

She recalled him insisting that truth was simply the version of a story that the majority chose to believe, be it social media stars curating photos to portray a perfect life when they might really be dying inside, her own now deceased father's place in history as an outstanding and upstanding police chief or Max as a dream man rather than a romance fraudster – and then some. None of it was actually based on fact. Who knew the truth of *anything* that was happening anymore? It had to stop.

The huge door into the room creaked open, catching her attention as Ellis Darque slipped inside. Giving her a cheeky wink, he took a seat at the back, in between dozing press reporters; rookies who had been landed the boring job of recording local awards. The only person there with a video camera was Perry Gooch, just as Billie had planned. She owed her an exclusive story.

Billie heard her name being called. She nodded to Perry, who moved forward to the stage, camera on her shoulder and recording via a live feed to the local TV news. Billie stepped up into the spotlight and started to tell her story.

'My name is Billie Wilde. Thirty years ago, my father was the chief of police. He presided for many years over a force then rife with corruption. The truth has remained hidden, yet the devastating consequences continue to wreck lives even today. It is for that reason that I am now ready to tell my story, call for a full enquiry into the shameful past and also hand in my own resignation.'

Billie handed her letter confirming the fact, to Miriam Nelson, caught like a haddock on a fishing line, wide-eyed, mouth flapping in horror. The truth, after all, was sometimes hard to swallow, but Perry had it all on camera. Her own exclusive.

All hell broke loose as Billie left the stage pulling the clips from her hair, free to follow the truth at last, rather than live a lie, that of the perfect, high-flying offspring of the perfect police chief. Ellis Darque gave her a round of applause.

'Present for you.' He nodded at the mysterious bundle of brown paper and sticky tape. 'Just say yes.' Billie ripped the paper off. A business sign was revealed, already engraved in bold letters. It read *Wilde and Darque, Private Investigators.* Billie smiled. He already knew her well.

'Now it's in print, how can I possibly refuse?' Billie answered, immediately recognising the truth that Ellis was offering the perfect get-out route. As she left to celebrate new beginnings, she vowed to shed no more tears about the past. After all, she was a different person then. Now she was looking forward to a rebirth as Billie Wilde, Private Investigator. The path ahead was sure to be dark in places as well as wild, but from now on the only time she would be looking back, was to see just how far she had come.

THE END

ACKNOWLEDGEMENTS

I first became aware of the vast number of links between Lewis Carroll's Alice stories and North East England, after interviewing novelist Bryan Talbot. Bryan is known as the godfather of the British graphic novel and the interview took place as part of a TV series on art and hidden history that I was producing with my husband Bob Whittaker, for our TV production company, Orion TV.

As a local lass, born in the village of Boldon, I had been aware that Alice Liddell's grandfather had once held Boldon rectory, but that was where my knowledge on the matter ended. I can still remember the moment that Bryan Talbot showed me his latest graphic novel, *Alice in Sunderland*. I immediately fell in love with the package of entertainment, almost a theatrical production, wrapped up between the stunning covers of the work. It offered up a feast of history and also presented the stories of how Lewis Carroll could well have been inspired by his experiences with the people and places so familiar to him in North East England, when creating *Alice's Adventures in Wonderland* and *Through the Looking-Glass*.

Bryan in turn, gave credit for almost all of his research into the Carroll and Liddell family links to the area, to the late scholar Michael Bute, a Sunderland man who wrote *A Town Like Alice's*. Big thanks to both brilliant authors for inspiring me to weave this background information into my own work Huge thanks, as always to the Bloodhound Books team, led by Betsy Freeman Reavley and Fred Freeman – the dynamic duo. They have led me through my first baby steps on becoming an author of three books in one year, making the journey a complete dream. Special mentions too, to Tara Lyons, Hannah Deuce, my amazing editor, Ian Skewis, and proofreaders Shirley and Maria.

Last and as always, not least, to my amazing husband Bob Whittaker. He's simply the best.

A NOTE FROM THE PUBLISHER

Thank you for reading this book. If you enjoyed it please do consider leaving a review on Amazon to help others find it too.

We hate typos. All of our books have been rigorously edited and proofread, but sometimes mistakes do slip through. If you have spotted a typo, please do let us know and we can get it amended within hours.

info@bloodhoundbooks.com